MODEL BEHAVIOR

What Reviewers Say About MJ Williamz's Work

Shots Fired

"MJ Williamz, in her first romantic thriller, has done an impressive job of building the tension and suspense. Williamz has a firm grasp of keeping the reader guessing and quickly turning the pages to get to the bottom of the mystery. *Shots Fired* clearly shows the author's ability to spin an engaging tale and is sure to be just the beginning of great things to follow as the author matures."
—*Lambda Literary Review*

"Williamz tells her story in the voices of Kyla, Echo, and Detective Pat Silverton. She does a great job with the twists and turns of the story, along with the secondary plot. The police procedure is first rate, as are the scenes between Kyla and Echo, as they try to keep their relationship alive through the stress and mistrust."—*Just About Write*

Forbidden Passions

"*Forbidden Passions* is 192 pages of bodice ripping antebellum erotica not so gently wrapped in the moistest, muskiest pantalets of lesbian horn dog high jinks ever written. While the book is joyfully and unabashedly smut, the love story is well written and the characters are multi-dimensional. ...*Forbidden Passions* is the very model of modern major erotica, but hidden within the sweet swells and trembling clefts of that erotica is a beautiful May-September romance between two wonderful and memorable characters."—*The Rainbow Reader*

Sheltered Love

"The main pair in this story is astoundingly special, amazingly in sync nearly all the time, and perhaps the hottest twosome on a sexual front I have read to date. …This book has an intensity plus an atypical yet delightful original set of characters that drew me in and made me care for most of them. Tantalizingly tempting!"
—*Rainbow Book Reviews*

Speakeasy

"*Speakeasy* is a bit of a blast from the past. It takes place in Chicago when Prohibition was in full flower and Al Capone was a name to be feared. The really fascinating twist is a small speakeasy operation run by a woman. She was more than incredible. This was such great fun and I most assuredly recommend it. Even the bloody battling that went on fit with the times and certainly spiced things up!"—*Rainbow Book Reviews*

Heartscapes

"The development of the relationship was well told and believable. Now the sex actually means something and MJ Williamz certainly knows how to write a good sex scene. Just when you think life has finally become great again for Jesse, Odette has a stroke and can't remember her at all. It is heartbreaking. Odette was a lovely character and I thought she was well developed. She was just the right person at the right time for Jesse. It was an engaging book, a beautiful love story."—*Inked Rainbow Reads*

By the Author

Shots Fired

Forbidden Passions

Initiation by Desire

Speakeasy

Escapades

Sheltered Love

Summer Passion

Heartscapes

Love on Liberty

Love Down Under

Complications

Lessons In Desire

Hookin' Up

Score

Exposed

Broken Vows

Model Behavior

MODEL BEHAVIOR

by

MJ Williamz

2019

MODEL BEHAVIOR

ISBN 13: 978-1-63555-379-6

THIS TRADE PAPERBACK ORIGINAL IS PUBLISHED BY
BOLD STROKES BOOKS, INC.
P.O. BOX 249
VALLEY FALLS, NY 12185

FIRST EDITION: APRIL 2019

CREDITS
EDITOR: CINDY CRESAP
PRODUCTION DESIGN: SUSAN RAMUNDO
COVER DESIGN BY JEANINE HENNING

Acknowledgments

First and foremost, I need to thank my wife, Laydin Michaels, without whose love and inspiration I wouldn't be able to write a single word.

I'd also be remiss if I didn't thank Sarah and Karen for their help in keeping me focused and getting *Model Behavior* ready to submit.

A huge thanks to the team at Bold Strokes Books—Rad, Sandy, Cindy, Ruth, Stacia, and everyone else for their never ending support and belief in me and my work.

And finally, a heartfelt thank you to you, the readers, who make all of this worthwhile.

Dedication

As always and in everything, I dedicate this book to Laydin

Chapter One

The dinner party was not going as planned. There was little to no conversation. The only sound in the room was the clinking of silverware against dinnerware. Shit! How could this have gone so awry so fast?

Ronnie Mannis usually had no trouble seducing women. But Lana seemed different, like a class act. So Ronnie invited her friends and Lana over for an actual dinner party rather than just invite Lana to the bar with them. Her friends knew she was trying to impress Lana, but they sure weren't helping her.

She excused herself from the table and called for her best friend, Susan, to join her.

"Why aren't you talking?" Ronnie said in a loud whisper.

"I don't know. What do you want me to talk about?"

"I don't care. Your day in the office. The softball team. Anything. Just help me keep the conversation going. I'm afraid Lana's gonna fall asleep and not with me."

"I don't get it. What's so special about Lana?"

"I don't know. She's just different. Like the kind of woman I could settle down with. She has all the traits I value in a woman."

"Okay. I'll try to think of something to say."

"Thanks."

"Say, is it just me or does Lana remind you of someone?"

Ronnie thought about denying it, but decided against it.

"Yes. She reminds me of Constance. But I have high hopes that Lana won't destroy my heart like Constance did."

"She really did a number on you, didn't she?"

"Yep. And I've protected my heart long enough. I'm ready to give love another try. With Lana. But you're not helping the cause."

"Sorry."

Ronnie looked around the room at all the takeout containers.

"Now let's get back out there before she comes in here and realizes I cheated at making dinner."

They went back to the dining room and Ronnie took her seat at the head of the table. Lana was on her left and Susan was on her right. Susan's wife, Katie, sat next to Susan and Ronnie's other bachelor friend, Nancy, sat across from her.

"So, Susan," Ronnie said. "How's your team doing in softball this year?"

"We're killin'. Too bad you couldn't play this year."

"Yeah. I can't believe I sprained my ankle just before the season started."

"How did you work with a sprained ankle?" Lana said.

"I had to take some days off, obviously, but then I just grinned and bore it, you know?"

"That must have been so painful."

"Ibuprofen really helped. And I took lots of breaks to rest. But I got through it. I still get a little sore, but that's to be expected I think."

"I really don't know how you'd do it," Lana said. "I mean, you stand the whole time you're photographing any of us models. I can't imagine doing that with a sprained ankle."

Ronnie wondered if she should work the pity card to try to get Lana to stay the night. But no. She would let Lana take her time. She knew she'd come around. They usually did.

"Shall we move this into the living room?" Ronnie stood and started to walk that direction. Lana stood as well.

"I hate to eat and run," she said.

Ronnie groaned.

"Oh, please. Say you'll stay for a little while."

"I'm sorry. I really can't. We have an early shoot tomorrow, remember?"

"I'll be there," Ronnie said.

She walked Lana to the front door.

"Thank you for coming tonight," Ronnie said.

"Thanks for having me. I'll see you in the morning."

Ronnie closed the door and sank back against it. Damn. She'd blown that chance. She shook it off. Lana was just one woman. A woman she was clearly drawn to, but one woman nonetheless. There were many other fish in the sea. And she could bait her hook with the best of them.

"You guys want to go to the bar?" she said when she walked back into the living room.

"Dressed like this?" Susan motioned to her slacks and nice shirt.

"I know we're a little overdressed, but what's the harm?"

"Sure," Katie said. "Why not?"

"I'm up for it," Nancy said.

They all looked expectantly at Susan, who finally relented.

"Fine. I'll just feel like an idiot."

"You'll be among friends," Ronnie said.

"Great. So who's driving?" Susan said.

"I'll drive, honey," Katie said.

"And I'll drive," Ronnie said.

"I'll take my own car, too. I'd hate to get stranded there if loverboi here gets lucky."

"Okay, then that settles that," Ronnie said. "Let's get going."

They drove to the women's club closest to Ronnie's house. It was located smack in the middle of downtown, and was the one they frequented most often. They parked, paid their covers, then walked in to the feel of music vibrating through the floor.

"Get us a table," Ronnie called to Susan. "I'll get the first round."

She fought through the crowds and finally got to the bar. She ordered the drinks and turned to take them to the table, but Nancy was there offering to help.

"Thanks, man. I was wondering how I was gonna carry them to the table."

"No sweat."

They got back to the table and Ronnie surveyed the women dancing, wondering if any of them would be willing bedmates. She left her group and followed one woman off the floor. The woman was tall and willowy with long blond hair that fell past her shoulders. She looked like an angel.

"Excuse me," Ronnie said when she caught up with the woman. "Would you like to dance?"

"I just finished dancing and I'm parched."

"Can I buy you a drink?"

The woman looked Ronnie up and down before she smiled.

"Sure. That would be great."

"What are you drinking?"

"Gin and tonic."

"Coming right up."

Ronnie got to the bar and ordered herself another beer and a gin and tonic for her angel. She took them back to the table.

"Won't you sit down?" the angel said.

"Thanks. I'm Ronnie, by the way."

"Angelica."

Perfect.

"The name suits you."

Angelica laughed. It was a sweet tinkling sound that made Ronnie quiver.

"Thank you," she said. "So, what are you doing here? Watching women and waiting to swoop in on them?"

"Something like that."

"I see. Well, you're very easy on the eyes, Ronnie, so I don't mind one bit."

"Thank you. We have that in common then."

"Oh. Aren't you a sweetheart? And a smooth talker."

"I only speak the truth."

Angelica laughed again. This was going very well. If only Ronnie could get her on the floor for a few dances, she was certain she could take Angelica home with her.

"I'm tired," Angelica said.

Ronnie felt her heart sink.

"You are? But the night is still young."

"Why don't we get out of here? We could go back to my place for an after party."

"Are you sure?"

"Well...if you're not interested..."

"Oh no. I'm interested. Lead the way."

Ronnie followed Angelica out into the warm night air.

"This is my car," Angelica said.

"Mine's parked over there." Ronnie pointed to her truck. "I'll go get it and follow you."

Ronnie followed Angelica to her house in the suburbs. Angelica pulled up in front of a modern ranch-style house and Ronnie parked in the driveway next to her. She got out and followed Angelica to the front door.

"Nice neighborhood," Ronnie said.

"Thanks. I like it. I've only lived here for a few years, but it works for me."

Inside, Ronnie took a moment to look around. Angelica's house was filled with antiques. Ronnie didn't know much about antiques but knew Angelica had to have some money to have that many.

Angelica moved close to Ronnie. So close she could smell her heady perfume. It certainly wasn't the dime-store variety.

"So." Angelica's voice was low and seductive. "Did you want another drink?"

Ronnie swallowed hard. She could feel moisture pooling in her boxers.

"No, thanks. I think I'm okay."

"Good."

Angelica rested her palm on Ronnie's chest. Ronnie felt it burn through her shirt. She took Angelica's hand and kissed her palm.

"Hm. That's nice," Angelica said. She slid her arms around Ronnie's neck and pulled her close.

Ronnie kissed Angelica's neck, her cheek, and finally allowed her lips to hover over hers.

"Kiss me, Ronnie."

Ronnie closed the distance between them and claimed Angelica in a soul searing kiss. Her head spun, and she lost herself in the feelings of it. Angelica was a wonderful kisser. Her lips were soft and pliable, and when she ran her tongue along Ronnie's lips, Ronnie's knees buckled.

"Is there somewhere we can sit?" Ronnie said.

"I have a better idea."

Angelica took Ronnie's hand and led her to a large bedroom. Ronnie took in the antiques and the furniture but mostly focused on the king-size bed in the center of the room. That's where she needed to be with Angelica. And soon.

Angelica released Ronnie's hand and slowly began to undress. Ronnie stood in awe as she watched each item of clothing hit the ground. When Angelica was finally naked, she lay on the bed and spread her legs. She absently stroked herself, and it took Ronnie a moment to shake herself out of her trance and strip.

She joined Angelica on the bed and gently grabbed hold of her wrist, pulling her hand away from her pleasure zone. She brought her hand to her mouth and sucked each finger, reveling in the flavor of Angelica. She was delicious and Ronnie needed more.

Ronnie kissed Angelica again hard on the mouth while she dragged her hand the length of her. She brought her hand up to cup and tease one of Angelica's nipples. She pinched it between her fingers and smiled as it hardened into a pebble. She slid her hand lower and found her curls wet. She knew what was waiting for her just a little lower. She dragged her hand back up and cupped Angelica's jaw as they kissed.

Angelica broke the kiss and looked up at Ronnie with heavy lidded eyes.

"Please, Ronnie. Please touch me."

Ronnie didn't have to be asked twice. She skimmed her hand down Angelica's body again, and this time slipped past her wet curls and into the slick heat that awaited her. She buried her fingers inside, and Angelica moaned in pleasure. Ronnie moved them in and out, deeper and deeper while Angelica arched into her and met each thrust.

Ronnie took one of Angelica's nipples in her mouth and sucked playfully on it while she played her tongue over it. She heard Angelica's breathing become rapid and could feel her twitching inside. She knew she was close. She swiped over her clit with her thumb, and that was all it took for Angelica to clamp down hard on her as she came.

Ronnie waited until Angelica's spasms stopped, then slowly withdrew. She released her hold on her nipple and kissed her way back up to her mouth. She slid her tongue into Angelica's mouth and relished the moist warmth she found there. Each stroke of tongue against tongue fanned the fire burning inside her.

"My turn now." Angelica broke the kiss. She kissed down Ronnie's body, stopping to suckle first one and then the other nipple.

Ronnie's nipples were hardwired to her clit, and the sensations Angelica was causing were driving her wild.

Angelica released the nipple and kissed lower. Ronnie placed her hands on her shoulders, urging her on. When Angelica got comfortable between her legs, Ronnie thought she might self-combust.

"You're beautiful," Angelica said. Her warm breath brushed over Ronnie, causing her to twitch.

When she felt Angelica's mouth on her, she groaned in delight. Angelica knew her way around a woman. That was for sure. Her tongue was in Ronnie and on her. She sucked her lips and delved deep inside. And then she finally moved to Ronnie's rock hard clit.

She sucked it between her lips and flicked it with her tongue. In no time, Ronnie was clenching the sheets as one orgasm after another racked her body.

Angelica moved back up and cuddled against Ronnie. Ronnie hated this part. She knew she had to leave but didn't want to hurt Angelica. She rolled over and propped herself up on an elbow.

"Hey, Angelica. This has been a lot of fun, but I need to get going."

"Oh yeah. An early meeting?"

"Actually, an early shoot. I'm a photographer."

"That's okay. I mean, sure it would have been nice to have a sleepover and a repeat in the morning, but I understand. Thanks for the good time. Can you find your way out?"

"Sure."

Ronnie dressed quickly, kissed Angelica, and left the way she'd come in.

❖

Lana Ferguson woke early the morning after the dinner party. She lounged in bed for a few minutes replaying the party Ronnie Mannis had invited her to. It had been awkward and uncomfortable for everyone there. Or so she thought. The other guests had all been friends, and Lana felt like the odd woman out. She wondered again why Ronnie had invited her.

She'd heard rumors of Ronnie's womanizing ways, but had no intention of falling prey to her charms. Sure, she was attractive with her short, spiky dark hair and her piercing blue eyes. And her tall, lean body that seemed to move on its own when she snapped picture after picture of her models. Still. Lana wasn't interested. She enjoyed being a model, but had hopes of turning that into a career in acting someday.

She got out of bed and made some coffee, still puzzling over the dinner party. Had Ronnie thought that would get her into bed? Or was she just being nice because Lana was an up-and-coming model? It was hard to know with that one. At any rate, Lana was determined to keep a close eye on Ronnie Mannis.

She made herself some breakfast of toast and eggs. She was one of the lucky ones who didn't have to watch everything that went in her mouth. After breakfast, she took a nice long shower. If she was so determined to avoid Ronnie, why was she occupying her thoughts? Her whole shower she thought of nothing else.

She toweled off and wrapped a blue fluffy towel around herself. She went to her dressing table and carefully did her hair and makeup. She wasn't exactly sure what they would be shooting that morning, and they'd probably redo everything she was doing, but she'd be damned if she was going to out in public with no makeup on.

When Lana pulled into the studio, the first thing she noticed was that Ronnie's truck was already there. Whatever else they said about her, Ronnie was a professional. She was never late and was always spot-on in her photography. She knew just how to capture her models in such a way that was the most flattering and suited whatever the theme of the shoot. Speaking of shoots, she'd better get inside and find out what was on tap for the day.

Ronnie was sitting in the little kitchen area sipping coffee.

"Good morning," Lana said.

"Good morning. How are you today?"

"I'm great. So, what's this fun new shoot we're doing this morning?"

"We're doing a fundraiser for the Rainbow Women's Center this morning."

"What kind of fundraiser?"

"They want a calendar of our most beautiful models posing like pinup girls."

"And they're going to sell them? Seriously?"

"Yep. Is that a problem for you?"

"Not at all. I think it's a real fun idea. And how fun to do a shoot like that."

"Good. Now, we're gonna keep it clean. Just so you know."

"Oh, so no Bettie Page type photos?"

"Right. But if you're willing to show some skin, that's great."

"I have no problem showing skin. Not for a good cause."

"Great. I've put some outfits in the dressing room. Choose one and come on out. Your hair looks great for this shoot, by the way."

Lana was glad she'd spent extra time curling her hair that morning. Excited, she went into the dressing room and picked out a red polka dot outfit. It had a short skirt and a halter top. She put it on and it fit perfectly. She checked herself out in the mirror. She liked what she saw. She stepped out of the room and went to the kitchen area.

Ronnie raised her eyebrows.

"Dang. You look amazing."

Lana felt herself blush. What was up with that? She was used to being told she looked good. It went with being a model.

"Okay," Ronnie said. "Get to makeup. We've got to get this done. I've got a lot more pinups to photograph today. But tell them not to get near your hair."

Lana sat patiently while the makeup artist worked her magic. Lana looked like something out of the forties or fifties when she was through. She wasn't sure which, but she really liked her look. She walked back out to find Ronnie ready for the shoot.

The background was of a grassy knoll with trees. There was a large ice chest in front of it.

"Where do you want me?" Lana said.

"We'll start with you sitting on the ice chest. One leg bent, one sticking straight out."

Lana did as she was asked. Snap went the camera.

"Head back. Good."

Snap.

"Put your hand behind your head."

Snap.

"Okay now stand up and put your hands on the ice chest. Stick your ass out. Good."

Snap.

They did a few more poses, and Ronnie announced she had enough.

"Are you sure?" Lana said. She was a perfectionist and wanted to be sure Ronnie got some good pictures. "May I see them?"

"Sure. Come on over."

Lana crossed to where Ronnie stood. She stood on her tiptoes so she could see over her shoulder. Ronnie scrolled through the pictures. Satisfied, Lana moved away.

"Looks good. Thanks."

"Thank *you*," Ronnie said. "You were amazing. You're free to go now."

Lana went back to the dressing room and changed back to her street clothes. She went to say good-bye to Ronnie as she left, but Ronnie was talking to another model already, so Lana just left.

CHAPTER TWO

Ronnie pushed her creativity hard that day. She used interesting props and had the models in sexy, but not overly so, outfits. She felt like she was an old school photographer and could imagine taking pictures of the greats. She was bummed when the day ended and half the models had already been photographed. At least she had one more day of shooting for the project. She wanted it to be perfect.

Perfect. Like Lana Ferguson. With her curly blond hair and cherubic face. And lips that begged to be kissed. Not every shoot had gone as smoothly as hers had that morning. She was a professional in every sense of the word. And apparently, off limits. Not that Ronnie had given up. She was simply regrouping. Her time would come. She knew it. Sure, Lana might mean forsaking all her one-night stands but she would be worth it. Ronnie knew it.

She went to the kitchen area and popped open a beer. Whitney, the final model of the day, came out of the dressing room.

"You have any wine?"

"Sure. Have a seat."

Ronnie poured her a glass of wine.

They sat together in a comfortable silence.

"You're very good at what you do, you know?" Whitney said.

"Why thank you."

"Can I ask you a personal question?"

"Sure."

"You're surrounded by beautiful women all the time."

"That's a question?"

"No. My question is, why has nobody snatched you up yet?"

Ronnie threw her head back and laughed. She took a sip of beer.

"Maybe because no one's been interested."

"Oh, don't you feed me that bullshit, Ronnie Mannis. You're gorgeous, you're successful, you're available."

"I don't know about all that." She allowed her mind to drift back to the real reason she was single. She'd been dumped. Hard. She had no intention of experiencing that pain again. Unless Lana…

"Well, I do."

"I guess I'm married to my job. Though I suppose if truth be told, I'm about ready to settle down."

"Is that right?"

"And you? Why are you single?" Ronnie said.

"If I'm honest, I'd have to say because I enjoy playing the field too much."

Ronnie laughed again, this time almost spitting out a mouthful of beer.

"Well, there you go. I like your honesty," she said.

"So is this what you do after work? You sit here by yourself and drink beer?"

"I'm not by myself now, am I?"

"You know what I mean, smartass."

"I usually have a beer as I wind down. But I don't hang here too late, usually."

"So what are you doing after your beer tonight?" Whitney said.

"I have no idea. Look through the pictures, I guess."

"Why don't you do something fun?"

"Like what?"

"Like take me to dinner."

Ronnie was surprised at the offer but didn't want to turn it down. She wondered where it might lead.

"Okay. I suppose that can be arranged."

"Don't sound too excited."

Ronnie laughed. Whitney had spunk. She liked that.

"Where shall we go? I mean, being a model I'm guessing your choices of what to eat are limited."

"I have a great metabolism. I can eat anything."

She winked, and Ronnie felt the heat rising to her cheeks.

"Well, I'm in the mood for a steak," Ronnie said. "How does that sound?"

"It sounds good. And if I change my mind, I'll find something else on the menu."

"Right on. Well, let me just lock up and we can go."

She got everything from the last shoot put away and locked her camera in the safe. Then she walked over to the door.

"You ready?"

She watched Whitney gracefully stand and walk toward her. Ronnie's pulse quickened. Whitney was gorgeous with a bob of dark hair and dark eyes. She had high cheek bones and full lips. Ronnie really hoped she'd be up for dessert. Because Ronnie wanted her in a big way.

Once Ronnie had locked the door behind them, Whitney slipped her hand in hers.

"So, are we taking two cars or can I ride with you?"

"I think it would be best to take two cars."

Whitney pouted.

"Why? Are we not on the same page here?"

"Oh, yeah. I think we're on the same page. I just think having both cars is a good idea."

She sighed heavily.

"Okay. If you insist. I'll follow you to the restaurant."

"Great."

Ronnie pulled into the steakhouse with Whitney right behind her. They parked next to each other and Whitney looped her arm through Ronnie's elbow as they walked inside. It was a weeknight, so there was no wait for a table. They were seated and Ronnie ordered a bottle of wine for them.

"So, is the steak here really that good?" Whitney looked around. The booths were logs covered in red material and there were pictures of cowboys and cattle on the wall. It was small, though, with only enough seats for maybe thirty people. "I've never heard of it."

"It's the places you've never heard of that have the best food."

"Okay. I'm going to have to trust you. Because believe me, if I get food poisoning, you'll never hear the end of it."

Ronnie laughed.

"Fair enough."

They ordered their dinner, then chatted amicably while they waited for it to come.

"So, where are you from, Whitney? Are you from Houston?"

"No. I'm originally from Tallahassee."

"Wow. You don't have much of an accent."

"Neither do you."

"Touché."

"What brought you to Houston?"

"I'm going to the University of Houston. I'm studying to get my BFA in graphic arts with a minor in film study."

"Dang. You must be smart." Ronnie regretted the words as soon as they were out.

"Not all models are airheads, Ronnie."

"Yeah. I realized how that sounded as soon as I said it. I'm sorry."

"You're forgiven. Especially if you pour me another glass of that delicious wine."

"Fair enough."

"And what about you, Ronnie? How did you end up as a photographer?"

"I always knew I wanted to be a photographer. My degree is in digital photography."

"Where did you go to school?" Whitney said.

"TCU."

"Did you always know you wanted to photograph beautiful women?"

Ronnie laughed.

"No. I just kind of lucked into that. It was the first job I got when I moved back to Houston. I enjoyed it and found I was good at it, so as soon as I could, I opened my own studio."

"Very nice."

Their dinner was served and they ate in comfortable silence. When they were through, they finished the bottle of wine and chatted some more. Finally, the wine was gone and it was time for Ronnie to make her move.

"Tonight's been fun," she said.

"Yes, it has."

"I really don't want it to end."

"It really doesn't have to then."

"No?" Ronnie arched an eyebrow.

"Of course not. Why don't you follow me back to my place?"

Ronnie followed Whitney to an apartment not far from her own house downtown. She parked in a visitor's spot and crossed the parking lot to where Whitney was waiting for her. Hand in hand, they walked to Whitney's apartment. It was on the ground floor and nicely furnished for a college student's apartment.

"Nice place," Ronnie said.

"Thanks. I like it. Make yourself comfortable. I'll go get us some more wine."

Ronnie sat on the couch in the living room. She kicked her shoes off and rested her feet on the coffee table. She sat up straight when Whitney came back. She handed Ronnie her wine glass, and Ronnie felt like an electric current had shot through her. Their fingers touched for a minute longer than necessary.

Whitney sat next to Ronnie and looked at her over the top of her wine glass. Ronnie looked into her dark eyes and saw a desire there that matched her own. Why were they wasting time drinking wine? There was so much more Ronnie would rather be doing.

"Are you okay?" Whitney said.

"Yep. Are you?"

"I'm fine. You just seem kind of antsy."

"Well, if I'm honest, there are other things I'd rather be doing than drinking wine."

"Patience, my dear. All in good time."

Ronnie fought the urge to gulp her wine down and be done with it. She took a sip.

"This is really good."

"The agency pays me well."

"I'm happy to hear that. Because you're a natural in front of the camera."

"And you work miracles with that camera of yours."

"You make it easy."

Whitney laughed.

"So we're the mutual admiration society, huh?"

"I guess so."

Ronnie moved closer to Whitney.

"Patience. Remember?" Whitney said.

"I'm being patient." She took another sip of her wine. "As patient as I can be."

She pressed her leg into Whitney's, and the heat made her boxers wet. She knew she was in for a good time. But could she wait for it?

They sipped their wine, and Whitney seemed intent on keeping the conversation light.

"I really like that calendar idea we shot today," she said.

Ronnie leaned back against the couch and took another sip of wine.

"Yeah. It's for a great cause, and so far, I think it's going really well."

"How many models did you shoot today?"

"Six. I'll shoot the other six tomorrow."

"Sounds good."

They each had a swallow left of their wine. Ronnie finished hers and set her glass on the table. She looked at Whitney who swallowed hers and set her glass next to Ronnie's.

Ronnie placed her arm around Whitney and drew her close. Whitney smelled clean and fresh, and Ronnie buried her nose in her hair.

"You smell amazing."

"Thank you. So do you. Whatever you're wearing is subtle but woodsy. It suits you."

"Thank you."

Ronnie moved away and placed her finger under Whitney's chin. When she was looking directly at her, Ronnie dropped her gaze to Whitney's lips. Whitney parted them slightly, and Ronnie dipped her head to taste them. The kiss was brief, but it still made her heart race. She tried to pull back, but Whitney had her arms around her tight. She kissed Ronnie and ran her tongue along Ronnie's lower lip. The move was dizzying, and Ronnie opened her mouth and welcomed Whitney inside.

Their tongues tangoed in a dance of lust for what seemed an eternity. Ronnie was breathing heavily when the kiss ended. She needed Whitney and didn't want to wait another minute.

"Let's go to your room," Ronnie said.

"Yeah. Like, now." Whitney's voice was deep and husky. She stood and offered her hand to Ronnie. Ronnie took it and allowed herself to be led down the hall to the small bedroom with a queen-sized bed that occupied most of it.

Ronnie pulled Whitney to her and kissed her again. As they kissed, Ronnie untucked Whitney's shirt and ran her hands over the exposed skin. Whitney moaned into Ronnie's mouth, fueling her desire. Ronnie moved her hands higher and deftly unhooked Whitney's bra. She had to have more. She had to see her naked. She broke the kiss and backed up.

Whitney took her shirt off and shrugged out of her bra. Ronnie bent and took a nipple in her mouth. She straightened and ran her hands over Whitney again.

"You're beautiful," she whispered. "So perfect."

Whitney pulled her back in for another kiss. It caused Ronnie to melt. Her insides were flip-flopping and her toes curled. She needed to be naked with Whitney and soon. She unbuttoned Whitney's slacks, but Whitney backed away again.

"What?" Ronnie said.

"We need to get your shirt off, too."

Whitney unbuttoned Ronnie's shirt. It seemed to take forever. After she slid it off her shoulders, Ronnie lifted her undershirt over her head. She moved close to Whitney again and stood breast to breast. The feeling was electric. She kissed Whitney again, an intense, passionate kiss that had her boxers drenched.

She unzipped Whitney's slacks and admired the black lace thong that was left when they fell to the floor. That thong was all that was between Ronnie and paradise. She knelt down and peeled it off with her teeth. She inhaled the scent of Whitney. She was all woman. Ronnie's mouth watered. She kissed up one inner thigh but felt Whitney's hand on her arm, pulling her up.

"What now?" Ronnie said.

"You're still dressed from the waist down. I want to see all of you."

Ronnie made short work of stripping out of her jeans and boxers.

"Happy now?" She smiled.

"Very," Whitney purred.

Whitney ran her hands all over Ronnie's body. She brought them up to cup her breasts and tease her nipples. She ran them down to cup her ass and press their pelvises together.

"Let's lie down," Ronnie said. "My legs are like jelly. I can barely stand."

"I know what you're saying. Yeah. Let's get in bed."

Whitney lay down, and Ronnie climbed on top of her. She held her close, bringing their breasts together again. She kissed her with fiery abandon and brought her thigh up between her legs. Whitney ground into her thigh, and Ronnie felt her wetness and felt her own clit swell. She had to have Whitney. She couldn't wait any longer.

Ronnie released her claim on Whitney's lips and kissed down her neck to her shoulder. Whitney moaned her appreciation. She was arching her hips and gyrating by the time Ronnie kissed lower and took a nipple in her mouth. Whitney held her head in place as Ronnie sucked and flicked her tongue over it.

Whitney pressed her hands into Ronnie's shoulders, urging her downward. Ronnie kissed down her soft belly until she arrived where her legs met. She placed Whitney's knees over her shoulders and bent to taste her. She ran her tongue over the length of her before delving in as deep as she could go. She lapped at all the juices flowing there before sliding her tongue over Whitney's slick clit. She circled it several times.

"Please," Whitney said. "Please don't tease me. I need to come. Please get me off."

Ronnie ran her tongue over her clit and Whitney arched up off the bed, froze for a minute, then collapsed.

"Damn. I was so right about you," she said while catching her breath.

"What's that?" Ronnie nuzzled her neck again.

"You're damned good in bed."

Ronnie laughed.

"Why, thank you. And how long have you pondered that?"

"Since our first photo shoot together."

"Is that right?"

"Yep. One look at your long, lanky frame in those tight black jeans and black shirt you always wear and I was curious. Then I saw your blue eyes and knew I had to have you."

"Well, you succeeded in your goal."

"Hm. But I haven't had you yet. Lay back, sister, because the fun has just begun."

Ronnie lay on her back and opened her legs for Whitney. Whitney kissed her on her mouth, her neck, and the hollow just above her chest. She took first one and then the other nipple in her mouth. She sucked hard, almost to the point of pain. Rather than being turned off, Ronnie found it quite stimulating.

As she suckled, Whitney slid her hand down Ronnie's body.

"Your body is so tight," she said. "I love it."

She went back to sucking her nipples as she slipped her hand between Ronnie's legs.

"Hm. You're so wet."

"Imagine that."

Whitney laughed, a low seductive sound that made Ronnie cream even harder. Whitney thrust her fingers inside Ronnie, who bucked off the bed and met each thrust.

"More," Ronnie said. "Give me more."

Whitney complied. Ronnie had never felt so full.

"Oh, my God. You feel amazing," Ronnie said.

Whitney kept moving in and out, going deeper with each thrust. Ronnie arched her hips and gyrated, forcing Whitney deeper. Finally, when she didn't think she could wait much longer, Whitney moved her fingers to her clit which was swollen with need. She rubbed it hard and fast, and Ronnie felt her whole body tense. She held out as long as she could, but finally the tension released as wave after wave of orgasm washed over her.

She held tight to Whitney until her body quit convulsing.

"That was something else," Ronnie said.

"Yeah. We're pretty good together, aren't we?"

"That we are."

They lay in silence, and Ronnie finally mustered up the courage to do what she hated to do.

"So, listen, Whitney. This has been fun."

"But?"

"But I've got an early shoot in the morning."

"Of course you do."

"I do."

"I believe you. It was fun though. Maybe we can do this again?"

"Maybe."

"I'm not asking for a commitment, Ronnie. I'm asking for a good romp in the hay."

"Are you sure?"

"Even though you said you're ready to settle down. I'm not. So can I hope for a repeat?"

"Yeah. I don't see why we can't do it again."

"Great. So I'll see you at the studio, huh?"

"Yep," Ronnie said. "I'll see myself out."

She quickly dressed then let herself out.

CHAPTER THREE

Lana was feeling good after her shoot that morning. She knew she'd looked good and had done everything Ronnie had asked. She was glad things hadn't been awkward between them. Especially after that horrific dinner party. But Ronnie was nothing if not a professional. There'd been no mention of it, nor had there been any offers for another date. That was just as well. Lana sensed Ronnie was trouble in the personal department and planned to stay as far away from her as possible.

She went to the Galleria and shopped for new dresses and new shoes. Not that she needed them. She just felt like rewarding herself for a job well done. After she was through, she drove to her modeling agency to see what other jobs they had lined up for her. She relaxed in the waiting room while she waited for her agent. She flipped through magazines on the table there and saw several pictures of herself. It always surprised her to see herself there. Sure, she knew she was in magazines, but it was still surreal to see her face smiling back at her.

"Lana?" Madeline's voice cut through her reverie. "Did you want to see me?"

Lana stood.

"Yes, ma'am. If you have time."

"I always have time for my star."

Lana laughed and blushed. Madeline was the agent to many models, and she doubted seriously that she was her star. But she appreciated it, nonetheless.

"Actually," Madeline said. "Why don't we go to lunch? There's a new bistro around the corner I've been dying to try."

"That sounds great."

Madeline turned to her receptionist.

"I'll be out of the office for a couple of hours. Keep things going for me."

"Yes, ma'am," the young woman said.

Madeline and Lana walked around the corner to find the bistro empty. It was two o'clock and they were happy they'd missed the lunch rush.

Madeline ordered a Caesar salad and Lana ordered a turkey sandwich. They sat and waited for it to be delivered.

"So, you're one of those lucky ones who can eat carbs and stay thin, huh?" Madeline laughed.

"Yep. At least so far. I suppose as I get older my body will change. But for now, I do love my bread."

"So, how was the shoot this morning? Tell me everything."

Lana described the shoot down to the very last detail.

"It was so much fun," she said.

"Oh, good. And it's for such a good cause."

"I know. I'm really excited to see the whole calendar."

"I have to ask. And I know it's unprofessional, but come on, this is girl talk, right? What's it like to work with Ronnie Mannis?"

"What do you want to know?"

"Did she come on to you?"

"She did invite me to a dinner party at her house last night."

Madeline arched an eyebrow.

"Do tell."

"It was awkward and uncomfortable for all of us. I'm not even sure why she invited me."

"You know she has quite a reputation, don't you?"

"How so?" Lana feigned ignorance.

"She's reputed to be quite the womanizer."

"Well, if she's trying to womanize me, she's barking up the wrong tree."

"Why's that?"

"I have no desire to sleep with her."

"Well, she is drop-dead gorgeous. Have you looked at those blue eyes? I think I'd even be tempted at my age."

They laughed together.

"No," Lana said. "She's my photographer and that's it."

"Well, if she invited you to her house for a dinner party instead of just trying to take you at the studio, that's got to count for something."

"She wouldn't dare?"

"Again," Madeline said. "Just gossiping here. I probably shouldn't, but why not?"

"Well, she's got a whole stable of women who I'm sure she could get with. I doubt I'm even on her radar anymore."

"So, do you date at all, Lana?"

"Mm. Not much. My early shoots and overall mental health keep me from doing so."

"Well, I can always schedule your shoots for later on."

"No, I'm not complaining."

"But you're a beautiful young woman. You should get out and meet people."

"Like who?"

"I don't know. There are lots of eligible women in Houston. Unless you don't swing that way?"

"Oh, I do. I dated a man once and that was a disaster. I'm a lesbian, just not practicing." She laughed.

"Well, I for one, think it's a waste. You should get out there."

"And I'm telling you I wouldn't know where to meet a woman. I don't do clubs, so that's out. And I'm perfectly happy in my solitary lifestyle."

"What a waste," Madeline said again.

"Well, thank you, but I'm happy."

Their meals arrived, and they ate in companionable silence.

"So, what's next up for me?" Lana asked when she'd finished her sandwich.

"I have a new magazine that's just starting out. They're looking for models. I sent them your head shot and they want to use you in their inaugural edition."

"Really? Sounds good. What photo studio will you use?"

"Ronnie's. Like it or not, she's the best."

"I don't mind. She was nothing but professional this morning."

"Good. The shoot will be the day after tomorrow."

"I can handle that. That means I'm free all day tomorrow. Maybe I'll drive to Galveston."

"Or maybe you can meet some nice lady to spend the time with."

"Lord, Madeline. You sound like my mother."

"Can't blame us for trying."

They walked back to the agency and said their good-byes. Lana drove back to her house and packed a few things to take to Galveston with her. She loved it there so much she kept a beach house away from the crowded part of the island.

She drove to Galveston proper and stopped for dinner at her favorite restaurant. It was busy that afternoon so she sat at the bar and sipped a martini. A woman came up and sat next to her.

"Excuse me," the woman said. "You look familiar. Do you live on the island?"

Lana bristled against an obvious pickup line. She quickly softened when she turned to face a lovely young lady with auburn hair and a full figure. Her eyes held nothing but innocence.

"No, I'm not," Lana said. "I must have one of those familiar faces."

Sure, she could have said she was a model and the woman had probably seen her in a magazine, but why bother?

"Oh. Okay. I'm sorry to have bothered you. Do you mind if I sit here? It's the last stool available."

"Of course not. Have a seat."

Lana liked this woman. She was sincere and not pushy. All things Ronnie was not. Where had that thought come from? She quickly shook it out of her mind.

"I'm Danielle," the woman said.

"Lana."

"Nice to meet you."

"You, too."

Danielle had beautiful blue eyes and a warm smile. Lana found herself thinking of lunch with Madeline. Maybe it was time to broaden her horizons.

"So, Danielle, do you live on the island?"

"Part-time. From March to September."

"Oh. And what do you do?"

"I work for a rental property agency."

"Nice."

"Yeah. I like it. What do you do?"

Lana hesitated then decided there would be no harm in telling the truth.

"I'm a model."

"For real?" Danielle's eyes went wide.

"For real." Lana laughed.

"That is so cool."

"Thank you."

Lana was called to her table. She was sad to have to say good-bye to Danielle.

"Would you like to join me for dinner?" she said.

"I'd love to. If I'm not imposing."

"No imposition at all."

They shared a nice dinner and pleasant conversation. Lana was sad when it was over.

"So there's a women's club here on the island," Danielle said. "It shouldn't be very busy on a weeknight. Would you like to go have a drink?"

"I'd like that. I have no idea where it is so I'll have to follow you."

She followed Danielle to a building out on the pier. The music was low, as were the lights, but there were very few people there. They got their drinks and went to a small table on the edge of what Lana imagined must have been a dance floor.

They kept the conversation going until Danielle looked at her watch.

"Oh my. It's gotten so late. And I need to be at work early. I hate to end the evening, but I really should get going."

"Well, here," Lana said. "Hand me your phone."

She entered her number in Danielle's phone and Danielle did the same in hers.

"I'll be back through here tomorrow evening," Lana said. "Can we have dinner again?"

"That would be great."

They walked back to their cars, hugged each other tight, and promised to see each other the following evening.

❖

Ronnie was at the studio early the next morning. She was tired from her night with Whitney but felt good. Whitney had been a willing and able bedmate, but it was time to concentrate on the day's shoots.

She was drinking coffee when Whitney walked in bearing coffee.

"What are you doing here?" Ronnie said. She was decidedly uneasy at the early morning intrusion.

"I just thought you'd like some coffee after your late night." Whitney smiled.

"Well, it's not that I don't appreciate it, but I have coffee here." She raised her cup.

"But this coffee is better."

"I like my coffee, but thank you. I'm sure I'll enjoy this, too." She took the proffered cup."

"Do you mind if I join you?" Whitney said.

Yes, Ronnie wanted to scream, but didn't want to offend her.

"I'm really trying to get mentally prepared for my morning shoot."

"I understand. Say no more. I'll see you later."

She kissed Ronnie briefly before she left.

Ronnie sat pondering what she'd gotten herself into. Whitney had been fun, but was she seeing more than Ronnie wanted to offer? Maybe she never should have mentioned wanting to settle down. She was wondering if they'd get together again when her first model, Miranda, showed up.

"So what is this exciting shoot I've heard I'm doing today?" she said.

"We're doing a calendar as a fundraiser for the Rainbow Women's Center."

"What kind of a calendar?" Miranda looked suspicious.

"It's like the olden days pinups. Showing a little skin, but not too much."

"Ooh. How fun."

"It should be. The models who I've shot so far have really enjoyed it. Now go on into the dressing room. You'll find a sailor's outfit. I'd like you to put it on and come on out."

While Miranda was changing, Ronnie set up the scene. The background was the hull of a ship, and the prop was a huge anchor. She was sure Miranda would take this and run with it.

Miranda came out of the dressing room looking absolutely adorable in the white skirt and the matching halter top. She hugged the anchor in several different positions, and Ronnie caught them all. She was happy with the shoot and dismissed Miranda to get changed back into street clothes.

She checked her schedule. A newbie, Christine, was scheduled next. She sipped the coffee Whitney had brought while she waited for Christine to show up. She still had a few minutes.

A tall, willowy blonde walked in.

"You must be Christine?" Ronnie stood and offered her hand.

"And you must be Ms. Mannis."

"Please. Call me Ronnie."

"Okay, Ronnie. Are you ready to get started?"

"I like your attitude. Yes, I'm ready. The dressing room's right over there. In there, you'll find an old-style two-piece bathing suit. Go ahead and put it on and come on out."

Ronnie got out the ocean backdrop while she waited. This was going to be a simple shoot.

Christine listened to directions very well and the shoot went smoothly. Ronnie was impressed.

"You did great," she said. "Are you new to modeling or just to me?"

"I'm new to the whole thing. This is my third shoot ever."

"Well, you were wonderful."

"Thank you. That makes me feel good."

"Say, would you like to grab dinner this evening?"

"Are you serious?"

"Sure."

"Is that ethical?"

Ronnie laughed.

"Why wouldn't it be?"

"I don't know. Are you supposed to show preferential treatment to one model over the other?"

"Well, for one thing, I'm the photographer, not the agent. And for another, I just thought it would be nice. To welcome you to the fold, per se."

"Sure then. What time and where?"

"Are you familiar with Houston?"

"Not really."

"Okay. Why don't you give me your address and I'll pick you up at, say, seven?"

"Sounds good to me."

Christine wrote her address down for Ronnie and left the studio with a smile on her face. Ronnie couldn't help but smile either. Christine was quite a looker. She could only hope dinner led to a sleepover.

The rest of the day didn't go as smoothly. Some of the models protested at the idea of being a pinup girl. Some just couldn't quite do what Ronnie was telling them to do. How could she put this calendar together if her vision for it didn't play out in the models?

She finally finished at just after five. She ran through the pictures again and realized she could make them work. It had just been a long, grueling day. Some models were such prima donnas.

She sat at the table in the kitchen and opened a bottle of beer. She finished it and was about to open another one when she remembered her date with Christine.

"Shit," she said. She checked her watch. It was five thirty. She just barely had time to get home, shower, and dress for dinner.

Ronnie used some gel to put the finishing touches on her hair and she was ready. It was six forty-five. Time to go. She arrived at Christine's apartment at precisely seven o'clock. She knocked on the door and actually found herself nervous. She was never nervous for a date. She just knew she needed to be careful. She'd watch Christine's gestures carefully. She hoped the night would end back here at her apartment, but she couldn't risk alienating a new model.

Christine opened the door wearing a short skirt that showed off long, firm legs. The top, a matching green, made her eyes look like emeralds. She was a knockout. There was no doubt about it.

"You ready for dinner?" Ronnie finally found her voice.

"I sure am. I'm famished."

"Great. Do you like seafood?"

"I love it."

"I know just the place."

Ronnie drove them to one of Houston's famous seafood restaurants. There was no wait so they were seated immediately.

"Oh wow. Everything looks so good," Christine said as she perused her menu.

"Order whatever you like. This one's on me."

"Are you sure?"

"Positive."

Ronnie decided on what she wanted and set her menu down.

"I'll have the seafood salad," Christine said.

"Are you sure? That's all?"

"Gotta keep my girlish figure."

"Fair enough."

The waiter came and took their orders and they sat in awkward silence. Ronnie finally thought of something to say.

"So, you're new to Houston and modeling? How did you end up here?"

"My dad's company transferred him here. I didn't want to be too far from them, so I moved here, too."

"Ah. Where were you before?"

"Dallas."

"Oh. So not that far then."

"No."

Ronnie felt like she was pulling teeth.

"And how did you become a model?"

"People always said I should be. So I got some head shots made and dropped them off at several agencies. Someone called me in, and voila."

"Nice. Well, welcome to the business."

"Thanks. The three shoots I've done have been a lot of fun. I really enjoyed the one we did today. It was my favorite so far."

"Well, you're really easy to work with. I hope we get to work together some more."

Their dinner was served and they chatted as they ate. But as the evening wore on, it was clear to Ronnie that she was barking up the wrong tree. She wasn't getting any signal from Christine that she was interested in anything more than a nice meal.

After dinner, she dropped Christine at her door and headed home to an empty house. She liked her own company just fine, but some nights, she just really didn't want to be alone. This was one of those nights. She checked her phone and regretted not having gotten Whitney's number.

CHAPTER FOUR

Lana spent the day on the beach. She was careful not to get too much sun. She knew how important it was to keep her complexion the same. She waded out into the warm gulf water and sat, letting the waves rock her. She loved Galveston. And she loved her beach house right on the water.

She thought back to the previous evening and the time she'd spent with Danielle. She was such a sweetheart. Lana hoped they'd be able to spend more time together. Maybe she'd take a break from work and spend a week down there getting to know Danielle even better. She knew that wouldn't be the case, though. She loved her work too much. And she could stay in touch with Danielle and take an occasional day off to see her.

Whoa. She was getting way ahead of herself. She'd had a great time with her and she was looking forward to seeing her again, but she didn't need to be planning some long-distance relationship. It was just because she was so relaxed with nothing on her mind that let her thoughts wander in such a direction. And it kept her thoughts off Ronnie. Or not. There she was, invading her daydreams again. Why couldn't she keep Ronnie out of her mind? Lana wasn't interested in her. Even if Ronnie was interested in her. Although she knew that any interest on Ronnie's part was of the one-night kind.

And that's not who Lana was. She got out of the water and lay out in the sun for a few minutes until she was dry. She walked

MJ WILLIAMZ

back to her house and took a brief shower in the outside shower to rinse off all the salt and sand. Satisfied that she was clean enough, she walked up the stairs to her house where she took a real shower and dressed for her date that evening.

She texted Danielle to see what time she got off work.

"I'm off at five," Danielle texted back.

"Great. So, dinner at six?"

"Sounds great."

It was four o'clock, and with nothing to do, Lana picked up a new book and started reading it. She got into it and was surprised when she checked her watch and saw that it was five thirty. She had to get going. She grabbed her overnight bag and went downstairs to drive into town to meet Danielle.

Just before she got in the car, she checked her phone. There was a message from Danielle suggesting a restaurant. Lana sent a quick response that it sounded good and drove off into town. She arrived at the restaurant to find Danielle in the bar waiting for her.

"Hi." Lana kissed her cheek.

"Hi." Danielle got up from her seat and engulfed Lana in a bear hug.

Lana was happy to know this thing, whatever it was, wasn't one-sided.

"Have you been waiting long?" Lana said.

"No. Just long enough to order a drink. Would you like one?"

"Sure."

Lana ordered a martini and sat next to Danielle on the barstool.

"It's not crowded, as you can see," Danielle said. "So we can eat any time. I just thought a drink first would be nice."

"It is nice. No worries. And one won't hurt me since I have to drive to Houston tonight."

"When do you think you'll be back in Galveston?"

"That's hard to say. It'll have to be a day that I'm not scheduled to work. But I do love my work and try to have as many shoots as possible."

"I'm sure. That must be such an exciting life to have."

Lana laughed.

"It's a fun life. That's for sure. But it's not too exciting. Unless we do shoots in exotic locations, which hasn't happened to me yet."

"Maybe you'll do a shoot in Galveston someday."

"Wouldn't that be wonderful?" She smiled broadly. "I'd love that."

"And then I could see you again."

"True."

"I know you have to get home tonight, so we should probably get a table."

"Yeah, we should," Lana said.

They took their drinks and walked over to the hostess stand.

"Would you like to sit inside or outside?" the hostess said.

"Outside, please," Lana said. She turned to Danielle. "If that's okay with you?"

"That's fine by me." Danielle favored Lana with another warm and genuine smile. Lana felt something shift inside her.

They were shown to a table overlooking the bay, and they sipped their drinks and chatted amicably before picking up their menus to choose their meals. When they'd decided, they set their menus down and Lana gazed into Danielle's eyes. They looked like sapphires, and Lana thought they were the most beautiful eyes she'd ever seen. Except maybe Ronnie. Ronnie had the most piercing blue eyes Lana had ever seen. She shook her head to get her thoughts of Ronnie out of her head.

"Are you okay?" Danielle said.

"Hm? Yeah. I'm fine. Just unbidden thoughts sometimes work their way into my brain. I'm sorry. You have my undivided attention."

"You want to talk about it?"

"No, thanks. I'm fine."

The waitress came by and took their orders.

"I love the bay," Danielle said. She stared out over the open water. "Does your house overlook the bay?"

"No. It's right on the gulf."

"You're so lucky."

"Tell me. I love having a house I can just disappear to."

"I'd like to see it sometime. If that's not too bold of me."

"No. Of course it's not. We'll plan on grilling there the next time I'm in town."

"That'll be wonderful."

"And you should bring your suit and make a day out of it."

"It depends on what day it is. I have Mondays and Thursdays off."

"Fair enough. I'll try to make it down on one of those days."

"That would be great. Thank you. You know? I never imagined I'd ever meet a real live model. And I never dreamed one could be as nice as you are."

Lana laughed.

"Really? What did you expect?"

"I guess I figured you'd be conceited and all."

Lana laughed again. She wasn't lacking in the self-confidence department, that was for sure. But she didn't like to think she was conceited, either.

"Well, I'm glad you don't think I'm stuck up. That wouldn't sit well with me."

"Oh no. You're very approachable."

"Good."

Their dinners were served, and they kept up the pleasant conversation as they ate. When dinner was through, Lana paid and they walked out to their cars. The silence grew awkward, and Lana finally spoke.

"So, it's been fun getting to know you."

"Yeah. It really has. Will we keep in touch?"

"I hope so. Please don't be afraid to text me. I'll respond as soon as I'm able, okay?"

"Okay. Thanks."

"No problem. I've really enjoyed our dinners."

"Me, too."

"Okay. Well, Danielle, I need to get going."

"Okay. Drive carefully."

"I will."

She forced herself to turn away from Danielle and get in her car. She wanted to stay a little longer, but she needed to get home and in bed. She had another shoot the next day with Ronnie.

Lana put her car in reverse, waved to Danielle, and backed out of the parking lot. She thought a lot about Danielle as she drove home. She wondered if she was really ready for a relationship. She didn't think so, but then Danielle made her think she might be willing to try. It was an odd sensation she got whenever she thought of her. Oh well. Who knew when she'd be in Galveston next? She'd stay in touch with her and just see where things went.

She got home and climbed into bed with thoughts of Danielle and Ronnie running through her mind. She wished she could forget about Ronnie, but she had to see her the next morning at her shoot. She was sure that was the only reason she was on her mind as she drifted off to sleep.

Ronnie was up early the next morning. She had another long day of shoots, starting with Lana Ferguson. Her pulse raced at the thought of working with her again. Lana was gorgeous, stylish, and completely unattainable. But that wasn't why Ronnie was so intent on having her. She knew, if she were honest, that the reason she wanted Lana was because Lana looked almost exactly like Constance, who had unceremoniously dumped Ronnie after a six-year relationship. She'd found someone new, she'd announced, and said good-bye without even giving Ronnie a chance to fight.

Constance was the reason Ronnie had sworn off relationships. And she intended to stay that way. Unless she could have Lana. She had a feeling Lana wouldn't settle for a one-night thing. And that was okay with Ronnie. She truly believed she could settle down if Lana just gave her a chance.

Ronnie showered and dressed for her day. She drove to the studio, unlocked it, and got ready for the models. She made a pot of coffee and was sipping a cup when Lana walked in.

"You're early," Ronnie said.

"I'd rather be early than late."

"And I appreciate that. Have a seat. I'll get you a cup of coffee."

"Thanks. Cream, no sugar, please."

Ronnie fixed it as instructed and set the cup in front of Lana.

"I hope I didn't interrupt your private time or anything," Lana said.

"Oh no. You're fine." Ronnie was thrilled to have a few extra minutes with Lana. "Did you enjoy your day off yesterday?"

"I did. I went to Galveston."

"Oh man. I love it there. I even have a house there that I hardly ever get to use."

"Really? Where is it?"

"Jamaica Beach."

"Oh wow. Mine, too."

"Really? Now there's a coincidence."

"How is it we've never seen each other on the beach?" Lana said.

"I don't know. Like I said. I don't get there that often. Maybe this weekend I'll give myself a break and go down there."

But even as she said it, she knew it wasn't true. She'd be at the club seducing women. Then she thought, what harm would it do to take a break and go to the beach?

"You really should," Lana said. "I don't know about you, but I always come back so invigorated and inspired."

"I'll tell you what. I'll go to my beach house this weekend if you'll go to yours. We can hang out on the beach together and I can grill us dinner after."

"I'll think about it. I was just there yesterday, but I suppose it wouldn't hurt to go back in a couple of days."

"Great. You about finished with that coffee?"

"Hm? Oh, yeah. I'll go get changed."

"Yeah. I hear the makeup people in the dressing room now. They'll get you all hooked up."

"Thanks."

Ronnie thought again about Constance as she got the lights set up and the white backdrop down. Could she actually put her heart on the line again for Lana? She was getting tired of the string of meaningless sex she'd been having. She thought she could seriously settle down with Lana.

She was looking forward to this shoot. She couldn't wait to see how Lana looked in the red dress. She set the fans up for later in the shoot.

Lana came out of the dressing room looking stunning. Ronnie's heart caught in her throat. She looked so much like Constance it was almost painful. She shook the thought out of her head and focused on the shoot.

Lana was a perfectionist and insisted they do several shots over and over until she was happy with them. Ronnie didn't mind. She was a perfectionist, too and would have made them redo the shots as well.

It was after one in the afternoon when they finished.

"You want some lunch?" Ronnie said. "You've earned it."

"Oh, I don't know."

"Sure. I'll have my assistant go pick us up some sandwiches. Do you eat sandwiches?"

Lana still looked leery.

"I don't know, Ronnie. Don't you have other shoots lined up?"

"My next one isn't until three. Now, you go get changed and I'll have Devon pick up some lunch. What would you like?"

"Turkey and Swiss on wheat?"

"Sounds good."

Ronnie sent Devon out to pick up the sandwiches, and she set about taking down the lights and fans from Lana's shoot. Devon was back by the time she had everything broken down. Lana came out of the dressing room looking equally beautiful in her street clothes as she had in the red dress.

"Come on into the kitchen. Our sandwiches are here."

"Great. Thanks."

They sat at the table together and each unwrapped her sandwich.

"So, have you given any more thought to going to Galveston this weekend?" Ronnie said.

"I don't know."

"What's not to know? We'll just hang out on the beach and then grill some steaks. It'll be fun. No pressure. Just fun."

"Okay. I'll do it. I'll drive down tomorrow after work."

"Sounds great. So will I."

"Will you be bringing any of your friends?"

"No," Ronnie said. "It'll just be me. If that's okay?"

"Sure. Why don't we exchange phone numbers so we can let each other know when we arrive?"

"Ah. Good idea."

They put their numbers in each other's phones and finished their sandwiches.

"Thanks for lunch. I appreciate it."

"No problem. Thank you for being such a professional. It's a treat working with you."

"That's very kind of you. Okay. I should get going."

"Yeah, and I should set up for my next shoot."

"Okay. I'll see you Saturday?"

"Or maybe even tomorrow night?"

"We'll see."

"Fair enough."

"Good-bye, Ronnie."

"See ya later, Lana."

Ronnie watched Lana leave with a smile. She sort of had a date with her. And that made her very happy.

"Ronnie?"

Ronnie jumped at the sound of her name.

"I'm sorry. I didn't hear you come in," she said.

"It's okay. You looked like you were lost in space."

"I guess I was. Why don't you go on into the dressing room and I'll set up the shoot?"

"Okay."

Ronnie got everything set up and turned as she heard Whitney come out of the dressing room.

"Damn. Lookin' good, woman."

"Why, thank you."

Whitney was wearing a black curve-hugging dress. It showed off all her assets, and Ronnie knew it was going to be a fun shoot.

She took picture after picture of Whitney over the next two hours. When the shoot was over, she had many excellent photos.

"You did good, Whitney."

"Thanks."

"Why don't you go ahead and get into your street clothes?"

"I will on one condition."

"What's that?"

"You pour me a glass of wine. I feel I've earned it."

"Fair enough. One glass of wine coming up."

Ronnie popped the top off a beer and poured a glass of wine for Whitney. She sat at the table waiting for her. She didn't have to wait long. Whitney came out of the dressing room wearing shorts and a tight-fitting shirt. She looked amazing. Ronnie wondered if she had plans for the rest of the night.

"Can I ask you a question?" Whitney said.

"Sure."

"Why do you always wear black?"

Ronnie looked down at her long-sleeved button-down shirt and her black jeans. She laughed.

"Mostly because I don't want to distract the models by wearing anything bright or showy."

"That makes sense. I thought maybe it was to show off that bod and those killer blue eyes."

Ronnie laughed again.

"No. Nothing so nefarious."

They finished their drinks.

"So, dinner tonight?" Whitney said. "My treat this time."

Ronnie's pulse quickened. A night with Whitney would be just what she needed to take her mind off Lana. But was Whitney safe? Why not? And she didn't want to go home to an empty house again.

"Sure," she said. "Dinner would be great."

"Most excellent. You follow me this time. I know just the place I want to take you."

Chapter Five

Ronnie followed Whitney to a little hole in the wall that she'd never heard of. She parked her truck and got out. The scent of garlic and herbs assaulted her nose. Her stomach growled as she walked over to Whitney.

"How do you know about this place? I've never been here."

"If you must know, I worked here for a while before I got into modeling."

"Oh. And the food is good?"

"It's delicious. Come on. Let's get inside and eat."

They went into the tiny restaurant that smelled even better inside than it had in the parking lot.

"It smells amazing in here."

"Wait until you taste the food."

Whitney was greeted in a hug by the hostess.

"So good to see you, girl," she said.

"It's good to see you, too," Whitney said. "I have a special guest tonight, so please treat us right."

"You know I will."

They were seated at a back table and Ronnie ordered a bottle of wine. Then they looked over their menus and each decided on a delicious sounding Italian meal.

"So, after dinner," Whitney said. "Do you want to come home with me?"

"I'd love to," Ronnie said. "But, Whitney, I'm really not looking for a relationship."

Whitney laughed.

"Oh, I know. Neither am I, sugar."

They ate their dinner and after, Ronnie followed Whitney back to her apartment. She parked in the same spot she had the other time and crossed the parking lot to Whitney's door. Whitney looked so inviting there that Ronnie's mouth watered. Her palms itched to touch her. She pulled Whitney inside and closed the door behind her.

Ronnie pressed Whitney against the door and kissed her hard on her mouth. She leaned into her and her breath caught when she felt their breasts against each other.

"Let's get out of these clothes," Whitney said. She pushed Ronnie off her and took her hand. She led her down the hall to her bedroom.

Ronnie pulled Whitney's shirt over her head and unfastened her bra. She ran her hands up and down Whitney's back.

"You're so soft," Ronnie said.

"I'm glad you think so."

Ronnie brought her hands around to cup Whitney's breasts. She ran her thumbs over her nipples and smiled as they hardened for her. Whitney pulled away and unbuttoned Ronnie's shirt. She pushed it to the floor and took her undershirt off. She stepped into Ronnie's arms and moaned while their breasts rubbed together. They kissed again, a long, slow, languid meeting of tongues. Ronnie felt her clit swelling and knew she'd have to have Whitney soon.

"Let's get naked," Ronnie finally said.

She backed away and moved to unbutton her jeans.

"Oh, no," Whitney said. "That's my job."

She unbuttoned Ronnie's jeans and dragged the zipper down. She knelt and pulled them off, as well as her boxers. She rested her cheek on Ronnie's inner thigh.

"You're so beautiful," she said. She straightened up and licked her.

"Oh, no," Ronnie pulled away. "You first."

She finished undressing Whitney, then they lay together on the bed. Ronnie kissed her again, first on her mouth, then down her neck to her breast. She sucked first one nipple and then the other into her mouth, playing her tongue over each of them.

While she sucked, she slid her hand down Whitney's body and between her legs. She was wet and warm and ready for her.

"You feel so good," Ronnie said.

"So do you."

Ronnie slipped her fingers inside and thrust them as deep as she could get them. Whitney gyrated her hips and arched off the bed, meeting each thrust.

"Oh yeah," Whitney said. "That's right. Fuck me, baby."

Her words made Ronnie swell more. She thought she would explode on her own but forced herself to concentrate on Whitney. She kissed lower down her body and took her clit in her mouth. She ran her tongue over it once, twice, three times, and Whitney screamed as she clamped down around Ronnie and came.

Ronnie waited for the spasms to subside, then withdrew her fingers and kissed her way back up Whitney's body.

"That was awesome, baby," Whitney said. Ronnie had a weird feeling. That was the second time Whitney had called her baby. Was she thinking there was something between them? Surely she understood it was just fun?

She didn't have time to contemplate it, though. Whitney was kissing down her body, and Ronnie was in serious need of release. Whitney took her place between her legs. She kissed one inner thigh and then the other. Ronnie trembled in her need. Whitney licked her then, and Ronnie moaned at the contact. She licked all over her before dipping her tongue deep inside. Ronnie moved all over her face, loving the feelings Whitney was creating. Whitney moved her tongue to Ronnie's clit, and it only took a few licks before Ronnie's whole body tensed up, then released as she climaxed over and over.

"So can you stay the night tonight?" Whitney said when they were lying side by side again.

"No. I have another early shoot. Well, not too early, but still, I need to be fresh, and if I stay here we won't get much sleep."

Whitney pouted.

"I wish you'd reconsider."

"Sorry. Oh, and, um, do you remember when you said you weren't looking for anything serious? You said you enjoy playing the field?"

"Yeah. What about it?"

"Well, um, we're just having fun, right? You aren't seeing commitment here are you?"

"Of course not. It's all fun and games. Don't you worry."

"Great. Okay. I'll get going now."

"I'll bring you coffee in the morning."

"You don't have to."

"But I want to. You go on home now. I'll see you in the morning."

Ronnie dressed and left, still not convinced Whitney wasn't looking for a relationship. Which meant Ronnie would have to scratch her off her list of who to sleep with. It was a shame because Whitney was so much fun, but Ronnie couldn't or wouldn't risk her freedom by messing around with her again.

She got home and slept five hours before her alarm went off, signaling the start of yet another day of work. She yawned and stretched and smiled. She loved her job and was looking forward to another day of it. And then she remembered. After work, she'd be heading to Galveston. She got out of bed and took her shower. She paid extra attention to how she looked that day, as she knew she'd want to impress Lana that night. If she saw her that night. But she was sure she would. She had her number. She'd invite her over for dinner. Even if she didn't accept her invitation for that night, they were locked in to spending the following day and evening together. Ronnie couldn't wait.

Ronnie packed an overnight bag with changes of clothes and swimwear and tossed it in the backseat of her truck. She drove to work and opened the studio. She had just started the coffee when Whitney showed up with two cups of coffee.

"I told you that wasn't necessary," Ronnie said. "Besides, I make coffee here every morning."

"Yeah, but that stuff isn't as good as this. Here. Just have this cup."

Ronnie took the cup and took a sip. It was delicious, she had to admit.

"Why are you up this early?" she said. "Do you have a shoot somewhere?"

"No. I've already gone for my morning run. Hence this attractive outfit."

She motioned to her shorts and sweaty, short-sleeved T-shirt.

"Ah. I see. So that's how you keep your girlish figure, huh?"

"It is indeed. It's how I can eat pasta and drink this caramel flavored coffee."

"Now I understand."

The door to the studio opened and Christine walked in.

"You should go now, Whitney," Ronnie said. "I need to get to work. But thank you for the coffee."

"You're welcome. I'll see you soon."

Ronnie breathed a sigh of relief as Whitney walked out. Yes, she'd indeed have to cross her off her list of bedmates. She was just too clingy. She turned her attention to Christine.

"Would you like some coffee?"

"I'd love some."

"How do you take it?"

"Black."

Ronnie poured her cup and set it on the table.

"You're early," she said.

"Better early than late."

"That seems to be a motto with models. And I like it."

"Should I head to the dressing room?"

"You have a few minutes. Relax and enjoy your coffee."

"I wanted to thank you again for dinner the other night. That was very sweet of you."

Ronnie bristled at the comment. Her intentions had been anything but sweet, but Christine would never know that.

"I'm just glad you enjoyed it," she said.

Christine finished her coffee and went back to get changed and get her hair and makeup done. Ronnie finished her coffee and set up the shoot. By the time Christine came out of the dressing room, Ronnie was ready for her.

The shoot went very smoothly, though it took several hours due to clothing changes. When it was over, Ronnie waited patiently for Christine and the hair and makeup artist to leave, then she locked up and got in her truck. She was on her way to Galveston and she couldn't wait.

Lana was frustrated. Her shoots weren't going well. She didn't like the photographer Madeline had scheduled her with. He was a prima donna who had no real talent. She finished her first shoot and asked to see the pictures. He hemmed and hawed and finally agreed to let her see them. She wasn't happy with them and demanded a reshoot. He was not amused but finally gave in.

The rest of the day was more of the same. She was tired and in a foul mood when the day finally ended. She went home and took a long bath and drank a glass of wine. That helped. A little.

She got out and toweled off. It was then that she remembered her promise to Ronnie to drive to Galveston for the weekend. She almost called her and canceled. She really just wanted to be by herself. But she'd made plans and she'd keep them. She loaded an overnight bag and headed down the road.

Lana listened to the Indigo Girls on the drive, and her mood was much improved as she turned onto Seawall. She stopped in town for a bottle of red wine and one of white and wondered if she should pick up something for dinner. She remembered Ronnie saying they could get together for dinner, but Lana had been noncommittal. She called Ronnie.

"Hello?" Ronnie said.

"Ronnie? It's Lana. Lana Ferguson?"

"Sure. What's up?"

"I was just wondering if we were on for dinner tonight or if I was on my own."

"I picked up some trout, if you like that."

"I've never had it, but I like all kinds of fish."

"Great. Are you at your house now?"

"No. I'm still in town. I'll head that way now. I'll call you again when I get there."

"Sounds good. Drive carefully."

"I will. Good-bye."

Lana was in better spirits as she drove along the gulf toward her house. The water always lifted her spirits, and she was anxious to get to her little slice of paradise. The drive to her house was uneventful. She pulled into her house and saw that the house next door had Ronnie's truck parked under it. How coincidental was that that they had houses next door to each other? And how was it they'd never seen each other there?

She parked her car and carried her bag and the wine upstairs to her house. She set everything down and contemplated opening one of the bottles of wine but thought better of it. She would take the white wine to Ronnie's for dinner. She called Ronnie.

"Hello?"

"Hi, Ronnie. Me again. I'm here now. And I see that you're my neighbor? Can I come over now or are you in the middle of something?"

"I'm just working a puzzle. Come on over."

"Great. Be right there."

She hung up, grabbed the wine, and headed downstairs. She walked up the steps to Ronnie's and knocked on the door. She stood admiring the water while she waited for Ronnie to answer.

Ronnie opened the door.

"Lana. Come on in."

She stood back and let Lana walk in. Lana handed her the bottle of wine.

"Excellent," Ronnie said. "I have a bottle chilling, but I'll put this in the fridge to cool as well. Are you ready for a glass?"

"You have no idea."

"Uh-oh. Bad day?"

"Again, you have no idea."

Ronnie laughed.

"Okay. Well, make yourself comfortable and I'll pour us some wine."

Lana sat at the bar that separated the kitchen from the living room and stared out at the water through a large window.

Ronnie placed a glass of wine in front of Lana, then sat with her own glass next to her.

"I love your setup here," Lana said. "Mine is very similar, but I don't have a bar."

"Well, relax and enjoy it," Ronnie said.

"The water looks calm from up here."

"I walked along the beach earlier. It was pretty calm."

"Good. I'm looking forward to spending some time in the water tomorrow."

"Me, too. So, you want to talk about your day?"

Lana let out a heavy sigh.

"Where to start? Let's just say not every photographer is as professional or as talented as you."

"Well, thank you, but I'm sorry you had to deal with an untalented, unprofessional photographer. What did she do?"

"She was a he, for starters."

"Ah."

"Yeah," Lana said. "Male photographers are the worst. But they all think they're wonderful. This guy told me one shoot was over, but when I finally got him to show me the pictures, I made him reshoot. He just couldn't capture the essence of what we were going for, you know?"

"I'm sorry. And you're such a perfectionist. That had to be frustrating."

"So very frustrating. Ah, but let's not talk about it anymore. Let's relax and enjoy the evening."

"Sounds good. You ready for a top off?"

"Please. Now, what can I do to help with dinner?"

"You hungry already?"

"Actually, I am."

"Okay, well, I've had the trout marinating, so it should be ready to go on the grill. Let me just go fire it up."

"Do you mind if I sit on the deck while you do that?"

"No problem."

Lana was starting to relax. She took her wine out to the picnic table on the deck and sat enjoying the view while Ronnie started the grill. Ronnie came over and sat with her.

"It'll take a few minutes to warm up," she said.

"No problem. I'm not going to starve to death or anything."

Lana laughed and Ronnie laughed with her.

She realized Ronnie had a great laugh. It was deep and soulful, much like her voice. Lana warned herself to be careful. She knew Ronnie's reputation and wasn't going to fall victim to her. Though, Lord knew it would be easy to do.

Ronnie announced the grill was ready and went inside to get the trout and the wine. She came back out and topped off Lana's glass and left the bottle on the table. Lana sipped her wine while she alternated between watching the gulf and watching Ronnie. Ronnie was very handsome in her black shirt and black jeans. Lana had never seen her in anything else. She wondered what she would wear on the beach the next day.

"What are you thinking about?" Ronnie said.

"Well, I've never seen you in anything but black jeans and a black shirt. I was wondering if that's what you'll be wearing on the beach tomorrow."

Ronnie laughed.

"Oh no. I've got swim trunks for tomorrow."

"Oh, good."

"Dinner is ready, by the way. Would you like to eat out here or inside?"

"Out here, please."

"Great. Just sit tight. I'll get everything we need."

She went in and got the salad and silverware. She got them situated on the picnic table and sat next to Lana.

"I hope you don't mind. But I love looking at the water as well."

"I don't mind at all."

They ate their dinner in relative silence, broken occasionally by Lana praising Ronnie for her culinary skills.

"I'm glad you're enjoying it," Ronnie said. "It's pretty basic."

"But it's delicious. And it's just the right amount."

They cleared the table together and Lana started to do the dishes.

"Oh no," Ronnie said. "Leave those. I'll do them later."

"Are you sure? That doesn't seem fair."

"I'm sure. Now come on. Let's top off our wine glasses and we can go for a walk on the beach."

Lana kicked off her shoes and followed Ronnie downstairs and over a small dune to the beach.

"Are we supposed to have glass on the beach?" Lana said.

"I won't tell anyone if you don't."

They walked until it was dark, then turned around and walked back. When they got back to the house, Ronnie poured yet another glass of wine for Lana. She was definitely feeling the effects of it. She sat on the couch and Ronnie sat next to her.

"Thanks for a wonderful evening," she said.

"It doesn't have to end now," Ronnie said.

"Oh I think it should."

"Do you?"

She looked over to see Ronnie looking at her. Her eyes had deepened to a dark shade of blue.

"I don't know..." Suddenly, she wasn't so sure she did want it to end. Somewhere in the back of her mind were warnings about Ronnie, but all that mattered at that moment were the butterflies in her stomach as she looked at her.

Ronnie took her wine from her and set her glass on the coffee table. She set hers next to it. Ronnie moved over on the couch, never taking her gaze off Lana. Lana swallowed hard. Ronnie was going to kiss her. And she wasn't about to stop her.

CHAPTER SIX

Ronnie leaned into Lana, her gaze on her eyes the whole time, begging for permission but very aware that permission might be denied. When Lana didn't protest, Ronnie brushed her lips against hers softly, tentatively. Lana kissed her back, and Ronnie's whole body shook in pleasure. She applied more pressure, and Lana opened her mouth to allow Ronnie to slip her tongue inside. She tasted sweet, like wine, and Ronnie wanted more. So much more. But she didn't want to blow her chances. She didn't want a one-night roll in the hay. She wanted, needed more. But was she really ready to make a commitment? Constance's ghost reared her ugly head. No. Lana wasn't like Constance. Lana wouldn't hurt her. Would she?

She broke the kiss and sat back to catch her breath. Lana reached for her and pulled her back for another intense kiss. Ronnie returned the kiss before breaking it as well. Lana looked at her with heavily lidded eyes, and a flushed face and Ronnie knew she wanted her, too. It took every ounce of self-control not to take her down the hall to her master bedroom.

"Those were nice," she finally said.

"Yeah, they were. Thank you for stopping, though. I'd hate to do something we might regret."

"Oh, I'm sure I wouldn't regret a thing," Ronnie said. "I just really like you and respect you. And I want more than a one-night stand with you."

There. She'd said it. Her heart raced. She'd never felt so vulnerable.

"Are you serious?"

"Dead serious."

"Ronnie. That's a lot to take in."

"I know. But don't be scared, okay? We'll still spend tomorrow together and have a great time, okay?"

"But how can we be friends now that I know how you feel?"

"Well, judging from those kisses, you feel something for me, too. Let's just not worry about it right now. We can talk about it tomorrow, okay?"

Lana simply nodded as she looked at her hands. Ronnie reached out and took a hand in her own. It was soft and warm, and Ronnie knew the rest of her body would be as well. It took every ounce of self-control not to kiss her again.

"Come on." Ronnie stood. "Let me walk you home."

"I just live next door."

"Still. I'd feel better walking you home."

"So you're chivalrous, too? Why are you single, Ronnie Mannis?"

"I've been waiting for just the right woman."

"Hm."

Ronnie walked Lana to her house. She climbed the stairs that led to the house.

"Okay. I think I'm safe now," Lana said.

"Great. So I'll see you tomorrow?"

"I'll be over as soon as I'm awake."

"Sounds good. I'll make pancakes for breakfast."

"And coffee?"

"Lots and lots of coffee."

They laughed together, then Lana kissed Ronnie's cheek and let herself inside.

Ronnie tossed and turned that night. She kept playing over the evening in her mind. The kisses were wonderful, but had her declaration been too much? There was nothing she could do about it now. She'd already said it. And Lana was still coming over in the morning, which was a good thing. Ronnie finally fell asleep and slept fitfully until seven, when her internal alarm clock went off. She got up, started the coffee, and jumped in the shower. She knew that seemed stupid since she would be getting in the gulf later, but she wanted to look and smell good for Lana. She poured herself a cup of coffee and took it out to the picnic table where she tried to calm her nerves for the day.

She heard Lana's footsteps on her stairs and turned to say hello.

"Coffee," Lana said.

Ronnie laughed.

"That bad, huh?"

"You got me drunk last night, woman."

"I'm sorry. Here. Have a seat. I'll get you coffee."

She was back in a flash with coffee and cream for Lana.

"Do you feel that bad this morning?"

"Not really." Lana laughed. "I mean, I can tell I had too much wine, but it's okay. I'll survive."

"Good."

"And how are you this morning?"

"I'm okay."

"Just okay?"

"A little nervous," Ronnie said.

"Ah. Because of our talk last night?"

"Yeah. I'm a pretty private person. I don't usually discuss my feelings."

Lana reached over and placed a hand over Ronnie's.

"Well, you've got nothing to worry about with me, okay?"

Ronnie looked down at their hands. Was that a true statement? Did that mean what she thought it did? She could barely fight down the excitement.

"Good," Ronnie said.

"Now, I believe there was a mention of pancakes?"

"Coming right up. You gonna stay out here or come inside with me?"

"I'll come in and watch you."

"Sounds good."

Ronnie made thick, fluffy pancakes which they drowned in maple syrup and devoured. Ronnie was dumbfounded at the amount of food Lana could put away.

"I needed that to absorb the rest of the alcohol in my system," Lana said.

"Well, good. I'm happy to help."

"Can I help you clean up?"

"No. You go on out with another cup of coffee. I'll have this place cleaned in a jiffy."

Ronnie hurriedly rinsed the dishes and loaded the dishwasher. She couldn't wait to be back outside to Lana. She poured another cup of coffee and walked outside.

"It's a gorgeous day today," Lana said.

"It really is. And there's no one on the beach out here."

"I know. It's going to be great to have the place to ourselves."

"Are you ready to hit the water?"

"Let me go change into my suit. I'll be right back."

Ronnie watched her walk down the stairs, enjoying the sway of her hips as she went. Yep. Ronnie had it bad for her. And it sure seemed like she was interested as well. She shook herself out of her reverie and quickly changed into board shorts and a muscle shirt. She packed a cooler full of sandwiches, water, and beer and grabbed her towel. She opened the door to find Lana standing there.

"Wow. You're already ready?"

"I am. Are you?"

"I am now. Let's go."

Ronnie gave Lana the ice chest to carry so she could carry the chairs and towels. They got their spot set up and walked toward the water. As was the norm in the summer, the gulf was bathwater warm. There were very few waves. They walked out to the second sandbar where the water came up to just under their chests.

Lana dove under and Ronnie watched as she emerged, breasts first, then her head came up with her wet hair behind her. She looked like a goddess. Her suit clung to her curves and made Ronnie itch to touch them.

"Your turn." Lana pushed Ronnie hard enough that she stumbled and fell backward into the water. She got salt water up her nose, and when she emerged, she knew she was nowhere near as graceful as Lana.

Lana was laughing.

"Sorry. I suppose I should have asked if you could swim before I unceremoniously pushed you in."

"It's all good," Ronnie said. "I just got water up my nose from going in backwards."

"Oh. I'm sorry.'

"No. I'm fine. Really."

They spent a while diving in the water and swimming around. Ronnie hadn't felt that relaxed in a long time. She liked spending time with Lana, and she actually was looking forward to a Saturday not spent at the bar. She had her sights set on someone important for a change. And things were looking good.

After a good while in the water, Ronnie got hungry.

"You up for a sandwich?" she said.

"Sure."

They started the long walk back to shore. Once they were there, they dried off, and Ronnie got their sandwiches out.

"I packed water and beer. Which would you prefer?" she said.

"I'll have a beer. Why not?"

"Great."

They ate their lunch then went back out to the water. It was late afternoon when they finally decided they'd had enough. Ronnie was sad to see the day coming to an end.

"It's been such a great day," she said. "I want it to last forever."

"Me, too," Lana said. "But we still have tonight."

"That's true."

"And maybe part of tomorrow?"

"Are you sure?" Ronnie said hopefully. "You don't have to hurry and get back?"

"I can't think of any reason I'd have to. I don't have to be at work until Monday morning, do you?"

"No. I can't think of a reason we can't make a day of it tomorrow as well."

They packed up their things and walked back to Ronnie's house.

"I guess I should go shower and get ready for dinner, huh?" Lana said.

"Yep. I'll do the same."

They stood in awkward silence. Ronnie wasn't sure what to say. Lana was still standing there.

"Okay. I'm going."

Lana leaned in, kissed Ronnie briefly, and left.

Lana walked back to her house on shaky legs. She'd had so much fun with Ronnie and she hoped she hadn't blown it by kissing her. But, heck, Ronnie had kissed her the previous night, right? So it should have been fine. She replayed all the kisses they'd shared while she showered and dried. Her heart was racing, and parts of her felt more alive than they had in a long time. But she was feeling these things for *Ronnie*. How smart was that? Was Ronnie just setting her up for a one-night stand? She'd said she wanted more, but did she tell all the women that? Lana was confused. She really liked Ronnie. They'd had a great day that day and an enjoyable evening the night before. She vowed to be careful but could feel her heart already beating a special pace for Ronnie.

She finished drying her hair, dressed, grabbed the bottle of red wine she'd bought, and headed over to Ronnie's. Ronnie was outside with a glass of wine when Lana got there.

"Hey," Ronnie said.

"Hi. I brought a bottle of wine for tonight as well."

"Great. I've already got one open. Would you like a glass?"

"Yes, please."

Lana sat at the picnic table and waited for Ronnie, who was back in a minute with a glass of delicious red wine.

"This is really good."

"Thanks. It's from my private collection."

"You collect wine?"

"I do indeed."

"You're a woman of mysteries, Ms. Mannis."

"Really?" Ronnie cocked her head. "I think I'm pretty much an open book."

"No. You have secrets."

"Maybe because I've never met a woman to share my secrets with."

"And you think I could be that woman?"

Ronnie looked terrified. Lana could almost see the wheels spinning in her head.

"You already said as much last night," Lana said.

"I guess I did, didn't I?"

"Yes."

"So did you have a good time today?" Ronnie said.

"I had a blast. Thank you for that."

"Nothing to thank me for. I was enjoying myself as well."

"Good. I'm glad."

Lana held up her glass.

"Can I get a top off?"

"Sure. I should have brought the bottle out with me. Hold on a second."

Lana tried to compose herself while Ronnie was inside. Maybe she was misremembering Ronnie's words from the previous night. She'd certainly had enough wine to. But no. She was pretty certain she remembered how the conversation went.

Ronnie was back and filled her glass.

"Thank you."

"No problem. Are you hungry? Should I fire up the grill?"

"I'd rather you sit with me for a few minutes. That is, unless you're starving?"

"No. I'm fine."

Ronnie sat down and looked into Lana's eyes. Lana's heart raced again, and she wondered if Ronnie was going to kiss her again. Every ounce of her being prayed she would.

"So, you'd really be willing to give me a chance?" Ronnie said.

"I think so. I really like you."

"I really like you, too. I have for a while now, but today and last night pretty much sealed the deal for me."

"Good. So, can I ask you a favor?"

"Anything."

"Kiss me?"

Ronnie slowly closed the distance between them. Lana watched her gaze drop from her eyes to her lips. She watched Ronnie's lips part, and then Lana closed her eyes and just felt. She felt Ronnie's soft lips on hers, pressing into them. She felt Ronnie's tongue tracing her lower lip and she opened her mouth and welcomed her in. Their tongues danced a dance of lust for a while before Ronnie broke the kiss and sat up.

"That was nice," Lana said.

"Yeah it was."

"Thank you."

"My pleasure."

They sat there quietly. Ronnie took Lana's hand and held it in her own.

"I think we're going to be good together," Lana said.

"So do I."

"And now I think I'm ready to eat."

"Okay, let me fire up the grill."

Ronnie turned it on, then sat with Lana while it heated up. She poured them each another glass of wine, then took Lana's hand in hers. Lana liked the feeling. She felt like she was where she belonged when she was with Ronnie. As if she'd finally come home. It was a bit scary, but it was there nonetheless.

"Okay. Time to grill," Ronnie said.

Lana sipped her wine and watched Ronnie work the grill. Lana went in and grabbed two plates and brought them out for Ronnie to put the steaks on. Then she went in and got the salad out of the refrigerator and some utensils from the drawer. She took everything outside to find Ronnie topping off their wine again.

"You're going to get me drunk," Lana said.

"No. I'll make sure that doesn't happen."

"This steak is amazing. So tender and flavorful," Lana said.

"Good. I'm glad you're enjoying it."

After dinner, they did the dishes together, then filled their wine glasses with the wine Lana had brought and headed down to walk on the beach.

"I'm embarrassed," Lana said. "My wine is nowhere near as good as yours."

"Nonsense. It's delicious. Now, just relax and hold my hand."

Lana was happy to oblige. They walked until it was past dark again, then turned around and walked back. They sat on the couch sipping their wine until Lana set hers down.

"What are you doing?" Ronnie said.

"Getting ready to kiss you."

"Oh. Is that right?"

"Yes, it is."

Ronnie set her glass down as well. Lana leaned into her and kissed her firmly. Ronnie draped her arm over Lana's shoulders and pulled her closer. Lana opened her mouth and Ronnie's tongue was inside it, teasing her, urging her passion onward. Ronnie broke the kiss and pulled away.

"What's wrong?" Lana said.

"Nothing. I just don't want to get carried away."

"Why?"

"Lana, I'd hate to do something you're going to regret."

"Please, Ronnie. I'm a big girl. I won't regret anything."

"Are you sure? God, I hope you're sure."

"I'm positive. Now, kiss me again."

Ronnie kissed her, full on the mouth. As they continued to kiss, Lana eased back onto her back. Ronnie climbed on top of her. They continued to kiss and, once again, Ronnie broke it and sat up.

"What now?"

"Lana, I have far too much respect for you than to take you on a couch."

"Then take me to bed, Ronnie. Please."

"Are you sure?"

She searched Lana's eyes. Lana was nervous. That was true. But she knew what she wanted.

"I'm positive. But I have to warn you. I'm not very experienced, so I hope you won't be disappointed."

"There's no way you could disappoint me, baby. No way in hell."

Ronnie stood and offered her hand to Lana. They walked down the hall to Ronnie's bedroom. Ronnie pulled Lana to her and kissed her again, this time running her hands up and down her sides.

"You're driving me crazy," Lana said. "I need you so bad."

"Patience, my dear."

"I don't want to be patient. I want you to take me."

Ronnie pulled Lana's golf shirt up over her head. She admired her briefly before unhooking her bra. Lana gasped as Ronnie caught her breasts when they came loose. Ronnie massaged them before she took Lana's nipples between her fingers and twisted and tugged on them. Lana threw her head back and groaned. Ronnie leaned forward and kissed and sucked up Lana's neck before she claimed her mouth again.

Lana was breathing heavily. She was already so aroused. She couldn't imagine what else Ronnie could do to her. She was afraid she might come just from Ronnie's fingers on her nipples.

Ronnie finally let go of her nipples and unbuttoned and unzipped her shorts. Lana quickly stepped out of them and then her underwear. She was naked for Ronnie, and while she felt vulnerable, she couldn't imagine anyplace she'd rather be.

She climbed up onto the bed and watched Ronnie quickly undress. When Ronnie was on the bed with her, she opened her arms and welcomed her on top of her. Ronnie's skin was so soft as Lana ran her hands up and down her muscular back. She felt

Ronnie's thigh against her center and moaned. She ground into it, feeding her need.

Ronnie rolled off Lana and kissed her again while she skimmed her hand over Lana's curves. She slid her hand down to her hip and back to her breast where she continued to tease and please her nipples.

Then she kissed down Lana until she came to where her legs met. She rested a cheek on her inner thigh.

"My God, you're beautiful," she said.

"Please. Touch me."

"Gladly."

Ronnie slid her fingers inside, and Lana trembled at the touch. She moved her fingers in and out until Lana was writhing on the bed. Lana felt her mouth, her warm breath, on her throbbing clit. Ronnie sucked and licked it like a pro, and Lana felt her insides coalesce in a ball of energy. She focused on nothing but what Ronnie was doing, and she felt the energy release, sending white heat throughout her body as she rode climax after climax.

She was only barely aware of Ronnie moving up next to her. She opened her eyes and saw Ronnie propped up on an elbow looking at her.

"You okay?" Ronnie said.

"Never better."

It was her turn to love on Ronnie. She was nervous but excited. She wanted to make her feel all the things she'd made her feel. She kissed Ronnie and tasted herself on her tongue. It was a heady feeling. She kissed down Ronnie's chest and took a nipple in her mouth. She sucked on it and played her tongue over the hardened tip.

"Oh yeah. That feels so good," Ronnie said.

Lana smiled to herself, pleased that so far at least, she'd made Ronnie feel good. She played with the nipple a little while longer until Ronnie's breath was coming in gasps. Lana kissed lower on her until she was between Ronnie's legs. She took it all in, not even sure where to start. She licked all over before sucking her lips and dipping her tongue as far as it would go inside her.

Ronnie was gyrating on the bed, pressing herself into Lana's mouth. Lana sucked her way to Ronnie's hard clit and took it between her lips. She ran her tongue all over it. Ronnie's hand was on her head, holding her in place. She needn't have bothered. There was no place else Lana wanted to be at that moment. She continued sucking and licking until Ronnie pressed hard into her and her whole body froze, then collapsed on the bed.

Ronnie stroked Lana's hair, and Lana was proud of herself. She'd made Ronnie come and that bolstered her confidence tenfold.

"You were amazing, baby," Ronnie said.

Lana kissed up her body and curled against her.

"Thank you. So were you."

"Now, let's get some sleep."

"Sounds great."

Ronnie wrapped her arms around Lana, and Lana had never felt more safe.

CHAPTER SEVEN

Ronnie woke at seven the next morning as usual. She felt like the night before must have been a dream. A wonderful dream that symbolized new beginnings. Until she felt Lana stir next to her. Could she do this? Was she really ready to put aside her womanizing ways? She kissed Lana on the shoulder.

"Good morning, beautiful."

"Mm. Good morning."

Looking at Lana's naked body lying there got Ronnie hot and bothered all over again. She kissed her shoulder again, then rolled her on to her back so she could help herself to Lana's beautiful, firm breasts. She bent and sucked one nipple while she tugged and twisted the other.

"You're playing with fire, Ronnie Mannis."

"Well, as long as I put out the fire, we'll be okay, right?"

"Right."

Ronnie slid her hand down between Lana's legs to find her wet and ready for her. She slid her fingers inside and felt Lana quiver in there. She moved her fingers in and out until she felt her shivering more intensely. Ronnie slid her fingers out and pressed them into Lana's slick clit, rubbing slowly at first, but then picking up speed. Lana finally called her name and closed her legs, trapping her fingers. Ronnie smiled. She didn't need those fingers for anything else at the moment.

Lana finally opened her legs and Ronnie repeated what she'd just done, bringing Lana to another orgasm. Ronnie kissed Lana. Hard on the mouth. Lana opened her mouth and welcomed Ronnie in. But only for a moment.

"It's my turn now," she said.

"You don't have to. I'm okay."

"No way." Lana reached between Ronnie's legs. "You're drenched. No way I'm leaving you this way."

She teased Ronnie by dragging her fingers all over down there. She finally found her way to her clit, which she rubbed just as Ronnie had done for her. Ronnie felt her whole world burst into a million tiny pieces as the most powerful orgasm she'd ever had washed over her body.

"Now see?" Lana said. "Isn't that better?"

"Mm. Much."

Ronnie wrapped her arms around Lana and they dozed for a few minutes. When she woke up, Lana was gone. She sat up, panicked.

"Baby?"

"I'm here." Lana came walking down the hall.

"Oh, thank God. I thought you'd left."

"No way, Jose. No chance of that. I'm afraid you're stuck with me now."

Ronnie smiled.

"That works for me. So where were you and why are you dressed?"

"I got dressed because I always feel weird walking around the house naked. And I made coffee, which should be ready now if you want to get out of bed."

"Aw. Do I have to?"

"Only if you want coffee and a day at the beach."

"Okay. Okay. I'm coming."

"Not without me you won't."

"Very funny," Ronnie said. She put on her board shorts and muscle shirt and followed Lana to the kitchen.

"I don't have much here for breakfast," Ronnie said. "Would you mind pancakes again?"

"Not at all."

They sipped their coffee and kissed in the kitchen.

"You're not helping me get breakfast made," Ronnie said.

"Sorry. I mean, not really, but okay."

Lana sat at the kitchen table and Ronnie set about making breakfast. After they'd eaten, they did the dishes together and packed the ice chest for the beach. Ronnie was bummed that her time with Lana was drawing to an end but tried to maintain hope that this wasn't just a beach fling for Lana. Ronnie really wanted more. She believed she could cool her womanizing ways now that she and Lana were a thing.

They spent another fun-filled day at the beach, and Ronnie was sad when Lana said it was time to pack up and head back to Houston.

"When will I see you again?" Ronnie said.

"How about dinner tonight? I'll pack an overnight bag."

"Are you serious?" Ronnie couldn't stop smiling.

"Yes. If you want to."

"That would be wonderful."

"And I have a shoot with you tomorrow."

"You do? I haven't checked my schedule."

"Well, I checked mine," Lana said. "And I know."

"Great."

They said their good-byes and Lana promised to call as soon as she had her overnight bag packed so she could go to Ronnie's.

Ronnie got home, showered, then set about picking up her house. She wasn't a slob, per se, but she was a bachelor. Fortunately, she'd paid to have her house deep cleaned before her disastrous dinner party, so she only had to pick up a little.

She had just sat down and turned on the TV when her phone rang. She checked before she answered it. Lana.

"Hey there," she said.

"Hi. Are you ready for me to come over?"

"Totally."

Ronnie gave Lana her address and waited. It seemed like it took forever, but Lana was finally knocking at her door. Ronnie opened the door and stood to the side to let Lana in. She took the overnight bag down the hall to her room, then came back and kissed Lana.

"I've missed you," she said.

Lana laughed.

"I've missed you, too. Now, are you ready for dinner? Because I'm starving."

"Sure. What are you in the mood for?"

"I'd like another steak, to be honest."

"I know just the place. Let's go."

They enjoyed their dinner together, and on the drive home, Lana held her hand the whole way. Ronnie knew she was right where she belonged. She ran her thumb over Lana's hand and felt Lana squeeze her tighter.

"So, you're sure about staying at my place?" Ronnie said.

"Positive. That is, unless you don't want me."

"Oh no, baby. I want you. Don't worry about that. I'm just checking your level of comfort."

"It was my idea, wasn't it?"

"Yeah. I suppose it was."

"So, relax. I'm fine. Better than fine."

"Okay."

Ronnie wanted to believe her. It just felt too good to be real. She didn't want to do anything to scare Lana off. But if Lana said she was fine, then Ronnie had to believe her.

They pulled into her driveway and got out of the truck. Ronnie unlocked her front door and stood back to let Lana in first. She again admired the sway of her curvy hips as she walked past her. When she'd closed the door behind them, she pulled Lana into her arms.

"I've been wanting to do this for so long."

"It hasn't been that long since you did it last." Lana laughed.

"It feels like forever."

"You're so sweet."

Ronnie closed the distance between them and kissed Lana full on the mouth. Lana responded by letting her tongue meander into Ronnie's mouth. Ronnie moaned at the sensation and kissed her more passionately. She finally pulled away and came up for air.

"Dear God, woman," she said. "I need you. Now."

"Then take me, Ronnie. I'm ready for you."

They kissed again, and Ronnie took her hand and led her down the hall to her bedroom. Ronnie made short order of Lana's clothes, undressing her quickly and efficiently. When she was naked, Ronnie ran her hands over her satiny smooth skin and cupped her ass, pulling her against her.

"Wait a minute," Lana said. "You're not naked yet. Hurry, please. I want to see and feel you."

Never one to disappoint, Ronnie quickly stripped and pulled Lana to her again. She ground her pelvis into her and kissed her mouth, her cheek, her earlobe, and her neck.

"I need you now," Lana said. She climbed up on the bed and extended her hand to Ronnie who took it and climbed up next to her. She ran her hand over Lana's body and brought it up to cup her breast. She lowered her mouth and sucked on her nipple. Lana ran her hands through Ronnie's hair and moaned, letting Ronnie know she was on the right path.

She continued to suckle as she slipped her hand between Lana's legs, finding her wet and ready for her.

"You feel so good," Ronnie said.

"So do you. Please don't tease me. I need you."

Ronnie slid her fingers inside Lana and thrust them deep. She felt Lana trembling already and knew it wouldn't take long. She continued to move in and out and then brushed her thumb over Lana's clit. Lana clamped down on Ronnie and cried out as Ronnie didn't slow down and took her to several more orgasms.

"Better?" Ronnie said.

"Much." Lana smiled.

"Good."

"And now it's my turn."

Ronnie was happy to let Lana have her. Making love to Lana got her so worked up she needed release. Lana kissed down her body until she came to where her legs met. She kissed her lovingly, slowly licking all over. When Ronnie was sure she'd combust on her own, Lana kissed her clit, sucking it and licking all over it until Ronnie cried out as her body convulsed time and time again.

"We should get some sleep now," Ronnie said. "We have to be fresh for our shoot tomorrow."

When Lana woke the next morning, she was alone. It took her a moment to remember where she was. Ronnie's house. But where was Ronnie? She pulled on a pair of shorts and a T-shirt and went looking for her. She followed the scent of coffee until she found Ronnie at the kitchen table.

"I thought you'd left without me," Lana said.

Ronnie got up and kissed her.

"No way. We do things together now, remember?"

"Can I get a cup of coffee?"

"Sure."

Lana sat at the table and gratefully took the cup Ronnie handed her.

"This is what I need," she said. "How do you look so fresh when you first wake up?"

"Don't kid yourself, baby. You look amazing, too."

"That's very sweet of you, but I don't feel very amazing."

"The coffee will help."

"I hope so."

"So, baby, I wanted to talk to you."

"Uh-oh. You're tired of me already?"

"Oh no. Nothing like that. I just want you to know that just because we're together now, doesn't mean I'm going to go easy on you at a shoot. I'm still going to push you, maybe even harder now, to be the best you can be."

"And I appreciate that. You know I like perfection."

"Okay. Just don't get mad at me."

"I never have."

"Great."

Ronnie finished her coffee and went to take a shower. Lana sat sipping her coffee trying to wake up. She was starting to feel human. She was glad she hadn't looked in the mirror. She was scared of how she must look. But she'd feel good after one more cup, a shower, and some makeup.

She finished her second cup and was heading down the hall to the bathroom, when Ronnie stepped out of the shower looking absolutely delectable with a towel wrapped around her waist.

"Are you sure we don't have time to go back to bed?" Lana said.

Ronnie laughed.

"Sorry, sweetheart. It's a workday."

"Bummer." Lana pouted, and Ronnie took her lower lip between her lips and sucked on it.

"Now get in the shower."

Lana took a long shower and dried herself off in the surprisingly fluffy towels Ronnie offered her. She looked around for something, anything resembling a dressing table, but found none. She wiped off the mirror in the bathroom and set about applying her makeup.

When she was finished, Ronnie grabbed her keys and handed Lana's to her.

"We've got to get going," she said.

"Okay. I'm ready."

Ronnie kissed her.

"She you there."

Lana pulled her back for a longer kiss.

"Yes, you will."

When they got to the studio, Ronnie unlocked the door and let them in. She made more coffee and they sat having another cup as the hair and makeup artists showed up. When Lana had finished her coffee, she disappeared into the dressing room.

She got dressed, and when her makeup was being applied, she heard voices coming from the kitchen area. She recognized

Ronnie's, but not the other. The conversation didn't sound friendly and she couldn't wait to get out there to see what was going on.

She walked out to the kitchen to see Ronnie talking to a tall woman with short brown hair. She looked like a model.

"It's not that I don't appreciate it," Ronnie was saying. "It's just that I have a coffee maker here. You should save your money."

"But I like doing nice things for you."

Lana's spine tingled. She knew Ronnie's reputation and wondered if this was one of the women she'd slept with.

She cleared her throat and Ronnie jumped.

"Thanks again, Whitney, but I need to get to work now. I haven't even set up for the morning's shoot. I'm sorry, Lana. Give me just a second."

"No problem."

Lana sat at the table and watched as Ronnie went about setting things up. The woman named Whitney left, but Lana still felt her presence. She'd have to ask Ronnie about her later. Or would she? Yes. She had to know. Not that it mattered, she just needed to know. And then she would ask for reassurance that she and Ronnie were exclusive. Then she'd feel better.

The shoot lasted three hours. They retook shot after shot until they got every one down perfectly. When Lana was satisfied, she moved to go into the dressing room.

"You want lunch again?" Ronnie said.

"Sure. That would be great."

Ronnie sent Devon out and the sandwiches were there by the time Lana came out of the dressing room. They sat down to eat.

"So, who was that woman?" Lana said.

"What woman?"

"The one you were talking to when I came out of the dressing room."

"Oh. That's Whitney. Why?"

"Did you sleep with her?"

Ronnie sat silently chewing her sandwich.

"Did you?" Lana asked again.

"I did. But it didn't mean anything. I swear."

"Clearly, it meant something to her."

"No, it didn't. She likes sex. That's all. Trust me."

"So, answer me this, Ronnie. Are we exclusive or not?"

"We are."

"You swear?"

"I do. I don't want anyone but you now, Lana. You've got to believe me."

"Okay. Just making sure. So is Whitney going to be bringing you coffee anymore?"

"I don't think so."

"It doesn't make any sense anyway. You have coffee here."

"I've told her that several times. But don't you worry. There's nothing between us."

"Okay. I have to believe you, Ronnie. But please don't hurt me. I'm not used to opening myself up to someone, so this is really scary ground for me."

"It's scary for me, too. I played around because I didn't want to let anyone get to my heart. But I'm ready to commit to you. I promise."

They finished their lunch and Lana said good-bye. The next model was there, and she knew she deserved Ronnie's undivided attention.

"Wait," Ronnie said.

Lana turned back.

"Here." Ronnie slipped a key off her key ring and gave it to Lana. "So you can let yourself into my house."

"Thanks." Lana felt the wide smile on her face. She was happy and didn't care who knew it.

Chapter Eight

Lana drove to the modeling agency to see if Madeline was available, but she was in with someone, so she left. With a few hours to kill before Ronnie got home, Lana went to her house and packed more clothes to take to Ronnie's.

Still having plenty of time, Lana decided to do some grocery shopping. She didn't know what Ronnie had at home, but since they'd gone out to dinner the night before, she guessed there wasn't much. She got home and put everything away. She'd been right. The cupboards had been bare.

After she put everything away, she sat on the couch trying to decide what to do next. Her phone rang. She checked it. Madeline.

"Hello?"

"Hello," Madeline said. "I heard you stopped by. Is everything okay?"

"Everything's fine. I just wanted to have some girl talk with you."

"Well, I'm not doing anything now. What's going on?"

"I'm seeing someone," Lana said.

"Do tell."

"You're not going to like it, but you're going to have to trust me."

"Okay. I'm listening."

"I'm seeing Ronnie Mannis."

"Oh, Lana. Are you sure about that?"

Lana laughed.

"Quite sure. I'm sitting in her house right now waiting for her to come home from work."

"I want to be happy for you, Lana. I really do, but I'm scared for you instead. When did this happen? How? Last time we chatted, you assured me you wouldn't be sucked in by her charms."

"We spent the weekend at Galveston together, and one thing led to another. She promised me I wasn't just a notch on her bedpost."

"She said that?"

"Not in so many words."

"I don't know Lana…"

"Maybe you don't, but I do. I'm so happy, Madeline. She makes me happy. She's charming and attentive and wonderful."

"Sounds like you've got it bad."

"I do."

"Please be careful, Lana. Guard your heart," Madeline said.

"It may be too late for that."

"Oh, don't say that."

"I thought you'd be happy for you."

"I am. But I'm also worried. I've known Ronnie longer than you have."

"Did you ever sleep with her?" Lana said.

"What? No. How could you even ask me that?"

"I don't know. I know she's been with a lot of women, and I'm just curious who falls into that category."

"Well, I certainly don't," Madeline said.

"Good."

Lana heard Ronnie's truck in the driveway.

"Listen. She's home now so I've got to go. I'll keep you posted."

"Please do. Good-bye."

Lana got up from the couch and greeted Ronnie when she walked in. She hugged her and kissed her.

"I missed you," she said.

"Mm. I missed you, too. So, what have you been doing with your afternoon?"

"Well, for starters, I went grocery shopping. You had next to nothing here, so I went a little crazy. I hope you don't mind."

"Mind?" Ronnie laughed. "I appreciate it. Eating out all the time gets expensive. What kind of groceries did you buy?"

"You name it, I bought it. I bought salmon for tonight. I hope you don't mind grilling?"

"I'd love to. But I'm not real hungry right now, are you?"

"Not particularly."

"I know just how to work up an appetite." Ronnie pulled her close.

"Is that right?"

"Mm-hm."

Arm in arm, they walked down the hall to the bedroom. Ronnie undressed Lana slowly and deliberately. Lana stood shivering from the intensity of her gaze on her flesh. She shook with desire as Ronnie quickly stripped out of her own clothes and pulled Lana to her. The feel of their flesh on flesh made Lana dizzy with need. She kissed Ronnie passionately and Ronnie returned the kiss in kind.

Lana felt her knees buckle, and Ronnie was there to hold her up.

"Please. Let's lie down," Lana said.

"After you."

Ronnie helped Lana get on the bed, then climbed up next to her.

"You're shivering," Ronnie said.

"I need you."

"That bad?"

"Worse."

Ronnie kissed Lana's mouth, her cheek, her neck. Lana froze as Ronnie nibbled at the hollow at the base of her neck. She was so aroused, she thought she might come without Ronnie touching her. She took Ronnie's hand and placed it between her legs.

"Oh, my. Someone is ready," Ronnie said. She continued to nuzzle Lana's neck while her fingers found her center. Lana spread her legs and welcomed Ronnie in. Ronnie thrust her fingers deep inside.

"Yes. Yes, that's it," Lana said.

Lana arched her hips off the bed and met each thrust.

Ronnie slipped her fingers out of Lana and slid them over her clit.

"Oh yes," Lana cried. "Yes. Oh, dear God, yes. I'm so close."

Ronnie kept the pressure on Lana's clit and sucked and nibbled her neck. Lana felt her whole world go black, and then it exploded in color as the climaxes cascaded over her.

She lay there, breathing hard, and willing her heart to slow down. She'd never come that hard and she wasn't sure she was going to recover.

"Wow," she finally said. "I've never come that hard. You're amazing."

"I'm glad you enjoyed that."

"Give me a minute to catch my breath and I'll reciprocate."

"No hurry."

But Lana wanted to hurry. She wanted to take Ronnie and please her just as she'd been pleased. She didn't think she had the skills, but she certainly wanted to try. She finally took a deep breath and kissed down Ronnie's body. She stopped to suck on her nipples, which caused Ronnie to moan. Then she kissed down between her legs. She smelled the scent that was all Ronnie, and her mouth watered. She needed to taste her, to devour her. She needed to possess her.

She lowered her head and licked the length of Ronnie. She delved inside as far as she could reach, lapping up all the juices she was able to. She licked her way to her clit, which was hard and slick, and sucked it between her lips. She played over it with her tongue and soon Ronnie was pressing her face to her, so hard Lana could barely breathe. But that was okay. She was surrounded by the essence of Ronnie and she was happy. She flattened out her tongue, and dragged it over Ronnie's clit once, twice, three times, and Ronnie called out her name, tensed up, then collapsed onto the bed.

They dozed for a while, then Lana felt Ronnie stir.

"Mm," Lana said. "Is it time to get up?"

"I think so. I'm hungry."

"Okay. Let's do this."

Lana got up and put on a black silk kimono. She watched as Ronnie pulled on a pair of sweat shorts and a T-shirt. They went out to the kitchen to make dinner together. Ronnie grilled salmon while Lana steamed asparagus. They came together at the table on the patio and enjoyed their dinner with a bottle of white wine.

After dinner, they washed the dishes together then curled up on the couch to watch some television. Soon, the closeness of Ronnie was too much for Lana to stand. She slid her hand under Ronnie's shorts and felt how wet and warm she was.

"Someone's ready for me." Lana grinned.

"Always."

Lana pressed her fingers to Ronnie's clit. She circled it several times before pushing it into her pubis. Ronnie arched her hips and growled an animalistic sound as Lana took her over the edge.

"Damn, woman," Ronnie said. "You know just how to get me off."

"Good." Lana beamed. "I'm glad. I like making you come."

"I like making you come, too. Why don't we take this to the bedroom?"

Ronnie quickly divested Lana of the kimono she was wearing. She eased her down on the bed and knelt before her. She kissed up one inner thigh and then the other. Lana shivered and knew it wouldn't take long. Ronnie sucked her lower lips and ran her tongue over them. She licked her deep inside before she sucked her clit. Lana closed her eyes tight, reveling in the sensations Ronnie was causing. She kept her eyes shut tight and once again saw the lights burst forth as Ronnie took her to the most powerful few orgasms she'd ever had.

They slept, and Lana woke the next morning to an empty bed. Ronnie came out of the bathroom all dressed for her day.

"I have to get to work, baby. I should have a break around one. I'll call you then."

"Why don't I bring lunch to you?"

"That would be great."

"Okay. I'll see you around one."

Lana went back to sleep and woke up at ten. She showered and dressed, which included makeup and hair, which took her until noon. She wondered what she should do until one. She put last night's dishes away and then it was twelve thirty. She drove over to the sandwich shop and then to the studio.

She let herself in and heard Ronnie's voice.

"Your shoot is over, Whitney. I need to get ready for the next model."

"Ah, come on," the woman named Whitney said. "Just one kiss."

"No."

"Then promise me you'll come over tonight."

"I told you," Ronnie said. "I'm seeing someone now."

"What about me? What about us?"

"There is no us. There never was. You said yourself we were just having some fun."

"I gave myself to you, Ronnie Mannis. You can't just toss me aside like yesterday's goods."

Lana had heard enough. She walked closer to the kitchen and cleared her throat.

Both Ronnie and Whitney turned to stare at her.

"Hey, baby," Ronnie said. "You brought lunch. Thanks."

She walked over and put an arm around Lana.

Whitney stared at them with fire in her eyes.

"Are you a model, too?" she asked Lana.

"I am."

"Well, Ronnie fucks all her models, so don't think you're anything special."

"Get out of here, Whitney," Ronnie said.

"Fine. But you know where to find me when you're ready for someone who really gets you."

They watched her walk off.

"I'm so sorry," Ronnie said.

"It's okay. She's jealous. I get that."

"Do you? I mean, do you understand that you're the only one for me now?"

"Yes, Ronnie. I know that. Did I enjoy hearing that exchange? No. But I'm confident that you're not sleeping with anyone but me."

"Great. So let's eat."

Ronnie pulled out a chair for Lana, then sat next to her and they ate their sandwiches.

"What time is your next shoot?" Lana said.

"Not until three."

"Oh, good."

"Yeah. So we can relax and enjoy lunch. It sure was sweet of you to swing by. Especially on a day you don't have a shoot."

"I don't mind. I was missing you."

"Yeah?" Ronnie looked at her lasciviously. She moved closer to Lana and kissed her, running her hand up to cup a breast as she did.

"Ronnie," Lana said. "What about the makeup artist and hair stylist? They could walk out here any minute."

"They're gone."

"Really?"

"Really."

Ronnie unbuttoned Lana's shorts.

"I don't know, Ronnie."

"Mm. I do."

"Oh, my God. How can I say no to you? I want you so desperately."

"So I feel." Ronnie had her hand inside Lana's shorts. She pulled the crotch of her thong to the side and slid her fingers inside.

"Oh, God, Ronnie."

"Yeah?"

"Yeah. God. Please don't stop."

Ronnie had no intention of stopping. She slid her fingers to Lana's clit and pressed into it.

Lana cried out as she came and then came again. Ronnie slowly withdrew her fingers and licked them clean.

"You taste so good."

"You feel so good. Thanks for that. But what would you have done if that Whitney woman came back?"

"She's not coming back today, baby. I knew we had the place to ourselves or I wouldn't have taken you."

"Well, I'm glad you did. How hot was that to be so dangerous?"

Ronnie laughed.

"I do love your spirit."

"And I like yours."

"What time is it?" Ronnie said. She looked at the clock on the wall. "I hate to do this, baby, but I need to set up for my next shoot."

"No problem. I'll see you when you get home."

"Sounds good."

They kissed good-bye and Ronnie's heart was still thumping as she watched Lana walk out.

She got her shoot set up and waited as Christine was late. When she arrived in a flurry of apologies, Ronnie simply looked at her. She had no patience for tardiness.

"Just go to the dressing room," she said. "We'll shoot when you're ready."

Ronnie wasn't amused. She sent a text to Lana saying she'd be late because the model was late and then focused on the shoot when Christine finally emerged from the dressing room.

The shoot didn't go well. Christine seemed to have forgotten how to follow directions. Ronnie was frustrated but kept pushing her. They finally got some good shots and Ronnie told Christine she could change back to street clothes.

Ronnie waited impatiently and finally Christine was out.

"I'm sorry again I was late," she said.

"Just don't let it happen again."

"May I take you to dinner? To make up for it?"

"No, thanks. Just remember to be on time next time."

"Really. I insist. I'll take you anywhere. My treat."

"I'm going home, Christine. And so are you. Or not. Go wherever you want. But I'm going home. Now, good night."

Christine looked like she might cry, but Ronnie didn't care. She was still pissed. And she had a fine woman at home she wanted to spend time with. She didn't want to spend the whole evening at the studio. Those days were gone.

She left with the makeup and hair people and headed home. She couldn't wait to be in Lana's arms.

Lana greeted her at the door with a big hug and several stimulating kisses.

"Mm. Welcome home to me," Ronnie said. Lana moved out of the way and let her in. "I'm sorry I'm late."

"It's okay. You can't help it if a model is late."

"I know. It still sucks, though."

"Who was the model?"

"A young one named Christine. And then she wouldn't leave. She kept insisting she wanted to take me to dinner to make up for being late."

Ronnie shook her head.

"Have you slept with her?" Lana said.

"Nope. Never."

"Hm."

"Why?"

"Well, why would she be so intent on taking you out?"

"I took her out once. But nothing happened. I promise you."

"I believe you, Ronnie. I'll always believe you. I just hope that won't make me a fool."

"I'll always be honest with you, Lana. I promise you."

Lana moved into her arms and wrapped her arms around her.

"Good," she said.

She kissed Ronnie then, a slow, lingering kiss. She ran her tongue along Ronnie's lip, and Ronnie opened her mouth to welcome her in. They kissed for a few minutes before Lana stepped back.

"What's going on?" Ronnie said.

"Dinner is just about ready."

"Can't we have dessert first?"

"No. Sorry. Dinner first."

Ronnie followed Lana to the kitchen where she removed the lasagna from the oven.

"That smells amazing," Ronnie said. "But it's hot. We should let it cool."

"No. We'll eat it hot." Lana laughed.

They ate dinner, cleaned up, and then Ronnie took Lana to the bedroom.

"I didn't get enough earlier," Ronnie said.

"You're incorrigible."

"Thank you."

Ronnie quickly undressed Lana and waited impatiently while she undressed her. They fell into bed together, tongues dancing, limbs entwined. They kissed and stroked and pleased each other until they fell into a satisfied sleep. Ronnie held Lana tight, reveling again in the knowledge she was right where she belonged.

CHAPTER NINE

R onnie woke in the middle of the night with a need to have Lana again. She positioned herself between her legs and feasted on her glory. It didn't take long for Lana to wake up, and soon after that, she was calling Ronnie's name.

Ronnie climbed up next to Lana and kissed her.

"What time is it?" Lana said.

"Early. Go back to sleep."

They fell back asleep and Ronnie woke up at seven the next morning. She tried to disentangle herself from Lana so as not to disturb her. But it didn't work.

"Is it time to get up already?" Lana said.

"I don't know about you, but it is for me."

"No. I don't have anything going on today except a shoot with you at three."

"Then go back to sleep. I'm sorry I woke you."

"No. I'll get up with you. I don't want to miss a minute of our time together."

"That's sweet. But don't get up just yet."

"Why not?"

Ronnie kissed her and ran her hand down to where her legs met. She could still feel the wetness from their early morning lovemaking.

"You're going to spoil me," Lana said.

"Good. You deserve to be spoiled."

Lana's insides were trembling when Ronnie entered her. She plunged in and out, and when she knew Lana was close, she swiped her thumb over her clit and Lana clung to her as she called her name again and again.

"Can I have a turn now?" Lana said.

"Sorry. I need to get going. You can get me twice tonight."

"I'm going to hold you to that."

"Please do."

Ronnie kissed her again and got out of bed. She took a quick shower, dressed in her trademark black, ran some gel through her hair, and she was ready. She smelled coffee and smiled that Lana had made it for her. She could really get used to having Lana around. She really, really liked her.

She found Lana sitting in her kimono at the kitchen table. She was tempted to take her again, but knew she had to get to work. Instead, she sat and had a cup of coffee with her.

"Are you up now?" Ronnie said.

"No. I'll go back to bed once you leave. I need my beauty sleep."

"I disagree with that, but I won't fault you going back to bed. I'd do the same if I could."

They enjoyed their coffee and then Ronnie stood. She kissed Lana, a long, slow kiss and promised her more of the same at her shoot that afternoon.

Ronnie arrived at the studio and set about making coffee. She was sitting down with a cup trying to wrap her head around the first shoot of the day when Whitney showed up, coffee in hand.

"What are you doing here?" Ronnie said. "You don't have a shoot today."

"Do I need a reason to come see my favorite photographer?"

"Whitney, this is getting weird. You're bordering on stalking."

"Just because I bring you coffee? No. I'm patient. I'm biding my time. I know you'll come back to me. Whoever that trollop is you're sleeping with now won't hold your attention long. And then you'll want a real woman and you'll come back to me."

"Don't you dare call her a trollop! She's my girlfriend and I don't need you for that anymore. Now, take your coffee and leave before I call security."

"You wouldn't call security on me. Unless you wanted to see me in handcuffs, but that could be arranged without them."

"Whitney, you're trying my patience. Leave."

"Fine. I'll go, but I'll be back."

"Not unless you have a shoot."

"Whatever."

Ronnie watched her leave and let out a sigh of relief. What was she going to do about her? She could get a restraining order, but they had to be able to work together. Ronnie rued the day she'd ever slept with her.

She got everything ready for her first model of the day. She tried to calm herself down enough to photograph her, but she was still shaking with anger. She sat at the small kitchen table and took some deep breaths. Satisfied she could work, she grabbed her camera and waited for the model to come out of the dressing room.

The model, Tina, was tall and thin with shoulder length brown hair and blue eyes. She was a natural in front of the camera, and the harder Ronnie pushed her, the better she did. Ronnie was pleased when their shoot ended.

"You did great," she told her.

"Thanks. It felt good. I've worked with lots of photographers, but I think you're the best."

"Well, thank you."

"I hope we'll work together again soon."

"So do I. You're free to put on your street clothes now."

Ronnie's stomach growled and she was just about to send Devon out for sandwiches when Lana showed up bearing Chinese food.

"Yum," Ronnie said. "Chinese is my favorite. How did you know?"

"Lucky guess. It's mine, too."

"Great."

They ate their lunch at the table. They both said good-bye to Tina when she came out of the dressing room and left.

"How has your day been?" Lana said.

Ronnie thought about it. Should she tell her about Whitney? She decided to be honest.

"Well, Tina was great."

"But?"

"But Whitney brought me coffee this morning."

"Okay. I officially don't like her."

Ronnie laughed.

"You're not alone."

"Seriously. Why won't she leave you alone?"

"I don't know. Let's not talk about her anymore. I want to hear about your day."

"I slept until noon. Showered, got ready, picked up lunch, and I'm here."

"Sounds like a good day."

"So far it has been. And someone promised me treats tonight, so I'm excited."

"Don't look at me like that or I'm going to have to have my way with you right here."

"Oh, no. I'm ready for a shoot. It wouldn't do for me to be on wobbly legs."

"True."

"And speaking of the shoot…"

"Yeah. I suppose you should get ready." Ronnie kissed her. "I'll see you in a little bit."

Ronnie set up the shoot. She used a beach backdrop and had fans in position. She was all set when Lana came out in a one-piece blue bathing suit that brought out her eyes.

"You're beautiful," Ronnie said. She stepped in for a kiss, but Lana moved away

"My makeup, loverboi. You can't mess it up."

"Right. Okay, you ready?"

"Yep."

"Let's do this."

The shoot went smoothly, as Ronnie knew it would. They finished up, and Lana, as usual, asked to see the photos. Ronnie scrolled through the pictures for her.

"Perfect," Lana said. "You do such good work."

"Thanks. You're easy to photograph. The camera loves you."

"Okay. I'm going to get changed. Do you have any other shoots today?"

"Nope. I'm done. Get back into your street clothes and we'll head home."

Ronnie put away all the props and was cleaning out the coffee pot when Lana emerged in shorts and a golf shirt. She looked amazing, and Ronnie felt the familiar tug in her gut whenever she saw her.

"Are you ready to go?" Lana asked.

"I am. Let's get out of here."

They walked toward the door, but before they got there, Whitney burst in.

"Where are you going?" She looked at Ronnie and then Lana and then their hands joined together. "Oh. Is this your model for the night?"

"What are you doing here?" Ronnie said. She felt Lana try to pull away, but she held her tight.

"I came to give you another shot to sleep with me tonight. But I see you have other plans."

"Yes, I do. And I will continue to have other plans."

Whitney looked at Lana.

"Don't believe her if she says she'll be faithful. It's not in her genetic makeup."

"Actually, I do believe her," Lana said. "She may have made some mistakes in the past, but she knows where she belongs now."

"Mistakes?"

Ronnie thought Whitney was going to strike Lana. She released her hand and put both of hers on Whitney's chest.

"We're on our way home. Now get out of here."

"Hey, I know. Why not let me come with you two?"

"What?" Ronnie and Lana said in unison.

"Sure. We can have a threesome. Then you'll remember I'm the best."

"You're crazy, Whitney. Now leave before I call security."

"Afraid I'll show up blondie?"

"I mean it. Leave now."

Whitney looked down at Ronnie's hands, still on her chest.

"Fine. But anytime you want a threesome, my offer still stands."

She left, and Ronnie turned to Lana.

"You okay?"

Lana only nodded.

"I'm really sorry about her. She'll leave us alone now."

"I hope so," Lana said.

They stepped outside, and Ronnie locked the studio. They got in their cars and drove home. When Lana was in her car, she turned off the radio. She didn't want any noise. She needed to be alone with her thoughts. Was that Whitney woman right? Was it impossible for Ronnie to change? She hoped not. Ronnie seemed so into her. Was she being misled? She was more confused than ever when she pulled up at Ronnie's house. Part of her just wanted to go to her own house for the night to think things through. But that wouldn't be fair to Ronnie. She hadn't done anything to her to deserve that.

She got out of her car to find Ronnie waiting at the front door. She tried to smile but was sure it looked forced.

Ronnie reached for her hand.

"You don't look very happy," she said. "Do you want to talk about it?"

"Yeah. Maybe that would be a good idea."

"Great. Let's have a glass of wine and talk."

Lana sat at the kitchen table while Ronnie poured the wine.

"So, what's on your mind? Or do I even need to ask?"

"I don't know, Ronnie. Things are happening so fast between us."

"But we're good, right? I mean everything that's happening has been wonderful."

"It seems that way. But you have so many skeletons in the closet."

"No, I don't. I've owned being a womanizer before we got together. And I made it very clear that I want a relationship with you. Those days are over."

"But now I'm going to worry about every woman we run into together."

"Well, don't. None of them meant a thing. Honest."

"And did you tell them that? Clearly, Whitney got a different message."

"No. I was upfront with her. She assured me she was only in it for fun, too."

"Okay. I'll try not to be paranoid," Lana said.

"Thank you. Now let's go to bed where I can prove that you're the only one for me."

Lana's nether regions betrayed her. She felt herself grow wet at the prospect of making love with Ronnie.

"Okay. But I get you first."

"If you insist."

Ronnie got up and kissed her. It was a tender kiss that made Lana's heart flutter. She was crazy about Ronnie. And surely Ronnie was crazy about her, too?

They walked to the bedroom where they quickly undressed each other. Lana took her place between Ronnie's legs and licked and sucked everything she saw. She loved the flavor of Ronnie and couldn't get enough. Eventually, she positioned her tongue on Ronnie's clit and licked it until Ronnie came. Then she started all over. The tastes of Ronnie's orgasm fueled her on. She licked deep inside, running her tongue over every soft inch in there. Ronnie was gyrating on the bed, and Lana knew she was close. She lapped at her clit again and Ronnie cried out her name as she found her release again.

When Lana was in Ronnie's arms, she knew her doubts were for naught. She didn't have long to ponder it though, as Ronnie's lips quickly found hers as her hand skimmed down her body. She kissed lower and took a nipple in her mouth. She played over it with her tongue while her fingers probed deep inside.

Lana was in heaven. She loved the way Ronnie touched her. She felt full when Ronnie had her fingers inside her. She bucked against her, driving her deeper with each thrust. Ronnie slid her fingers out and teased Lana's clit.

"Please. I'm so close," Lana said. "Please, Ronnie."

Ronnie quit teasing her. She rubbed her clit until Lana's whole body tensed up. She knew what was coming and braced herself for it. The next thing she knew she was flying into orbit as a multitude of climaxes rocked her body. When she was back in her body, she held Ronnie close.

"What time is it?" Ronnie said.

"I have no idea," Lana answered sleepily.

"We need dinner."

Ronnie's stomach growled, emphasizing her statement.

"I don't feel like cooking," Lana said. "And I don't feel like going out."

"Fine. We'll order pizza."

"That sounds great."

Ronnie reached for her phone and called in the order.

They got up and got dressed so they'd be decent when the pizza arrived. They curled together on the couch with wine while they waited.

"So, are you feeling better?" Ronnie said.

"Much."

"Good. Because I'm crazy about you, Lana."

"Thanks. I hate to be so insecure. That's not like me."

"It's okay."

The pizza arrived, and they moved to the kitchen table to eat. Ronnie poured them some more wine. Between the lovemaking and the wine, Lana was feeling very mellow.

They finished their dinner, put the leftover pizza away, and Ronnie loaded the dishes in the dishwasher. Lana couldn't resist the sight of Ronnie's ass bent over like that. She walked up behind her and ground into her.

"Well, hello," Ronnie said.

"Hello. I love your ass. Do you know that?"

Ronnie stood straight and wrapped her arms around Lana. She kissed her, tenderly at first and then with more passion as the kiss lengthened. Lana opened her mouth and welcomed Ronnie's tongue inside.

"We should go back to bed," Lana said.

"Lead the way."

They hurried to disrobe and fell into bed together. Lana was on fire. She wanted, needed Ronnie to claim her. To show her how much she meant to her. She'd never responded to a woman like she did to Ronnie. But first, she had to taste her again.

She scooted down to where Ronnie's legs met. She threw Ronnie's knees over her shoulders and gazed at her.

"You're beautiful. I don't know where to start."

"Just start," Ronnie said. "I need you."

Lana dragged her nails over Ronnie and felt her shudder. She longed to enter her but feared her nails would cut her. So she again used her tongue to please her. She licked in and out and on her, each lick earning more begging from Ronnie.

"Oh, God, Lana. That's it. Oh God, please."

Lana continued to lick and suck Ronnie's lips while she pressed her fingers into her clit.

"Oh, shit," Ronnie said. "Oh shit. Oh God. I'm gonna come."

Lana kept at her pace and soon Ronnie arched off the bed, froze, and collapsed. Lana kept doing what she was doing, but Ronnie reached down and tapped her shoulder.

"I don't have any more, baby. Come on up."

Lana kissed her way up Ronnie's body. When their mouths met, her clit swelled. It was already rock hard from pleasing Ronnie, but the kiss was amazing. Ronnie kissed her way down

Lana's body until she was where her legs met. She thrust her fingers inside and placed her mouth on her clit. In no time, Lana was rocketing again as the orgasms crashed over her.

Ronnie moved up and held her.

"You sure know how to please a woman," Lana said.

"As do you."

"Thank you. We're going to be okay, aren't we?"

"We are if I have anything to say about it."

"Good. I feel better now."

"I'm glad," Ronnie said.

"Yeah. Me too."

CHAPTER TEN

The next morning, Ronnie had a later start time, so she got to hang out at home for a while. Lana got up with her and made her breakfast. They sat drinking coffee together. They were still basking in the afterglow of their early morning lovemaking when Lana's phone buzzed.

"Who's texting you?" Ronnie said.

Lana checked. Danielle. Should she tell Ronnie about her? Ronnie had been honest about her past. Lana surely owed her that much.

"Lana?" Ronnie said.

"Oh. It's a friend of mine from Galveston."

"Oh. What's she want?"

"We went to dinner a couple of times, Ronnie."

"Okay. So now she wants to see you again?"

"Yeah. Something like that."

"It's okay," Ronnie said. "We both have pasts. Even if yours isn't as colorful as mine. Just tell her you're with me now and can't see her anymore."

"Yeah. I'll do that."

Lana sent the text. She felt bad for Danielle, but she wouldn't have been honest if she hadn't told her about Ronnie.

"You okay?" Ronnie said.

"Yeah. Fine."

"Okay. Thanks for doing that. Hopefully, she won't go all Whitney on us."

"Oh, I doubt it. We'd only had a couple of dates."

"Good." Ronnie checked her watch. "I need to get a move on. You want to join me in the shower?"

"I'd love to."

Ronnie's shower was large enough for two. It even had two showerheads. It was luxurious to say the least. Lana dropped her kimono and stepped inside. Ronnie joined her soon after. She took the bath sponge from Lana and lathered it up. She washed every inch of her, paying special attention to between her legs. After she'd rinsed her off, she dropped to her knees and pleased her. Lana cried out and dug her fingers into Ronnie's shoulders to keep from falling over from the force of the climax.

Lana squeezed the shower gel into her hand and used her hands to massage and wash Ronnie. She slipped them between her legs and rubbed her clit until Ronnie screamed her name.

They got out of the shower and toweled off.

Lana watched as Ronnie got dressed and gelled her hair.

"You're so damned fine," Lana said.

"Thank you. You're not too shabby yourself."

"Gee. Thanks."

"You know I'm teasing. I think you're drop-dead gorgeous."

"That's better." Lana laughed.

Ronnie kissed her.

"Okay. I need to go. I'll be home early. I've only got this one shoot today."

"Sounds good. Have a good day."

"You, too."

And then she was gone, leaving Lana alone to contemplate her day. She went into the bathroom and did her makeup and her hair, then called Madeline to see if they could do lunch. Madeline said she could meet her at the bistro at one. Lana had another cup of coffee, cleaned up the kitchen, and it was time to meet Madeline.

She was sitting at a small table when Madeline walked in. She stood and kissed Madeline on each cheek.

"How are you?" Madeline asked. "How is everything with Ronnie?"

"Overall, things are really good."

"Overall? So, what's not good?"

"Some model she slept with won't leave us alone."

"Oh, no. Well, that's not good. But is it really surprising?"

"I think so. Ronnie said they both agreed to having fun. There was no mention of commitment."

"Well, obviously this model thought there was. Lana, are you being careful? Are you sure she's really committed to you? I'd hate to see you get hurt."

"But we spend every spare minute together. She wouldn't have time to be with anybody else. Trust me."

"Madeline!" someone called as they approached the table.

Lana turned to see Whitney headed their way.

"Hello, Whitney," Madeline said. "What are you doing here?"

"I went by the office and they said you were here. I wanted to talk to you."

It was then she looked at Lana, really looked at her, and the recognition showed in her eyes.

"Oh, it's *you*," she said.

"You've met?" Madeline said.

Lana got up, threw some cash on the table, and murmured an excuse about having to be somewhere. She sat in her car, shaking. She hated that Whitney woman. With every ounce of her being. She undermined all the faith Lana had in Ronnie. Why couldn't she simply disappear out of their lives?

She knew Ronnie had to work with Whitney. Unless Madeline could assign her to other studios. Maybe Lana could ask her to do that. Whitney was probably looking for Madeline to get more work with Ronnie. Lana hoped not.

When Lana felt she was under control, she headed to the mall. She needed some retail therapy and knew just what to buy. She pulled into the mall and walked to Victoria's Secret. She shopped until she was feeling much better, then took her goodies and went home.

She carefully unpacked her bags and loaded up a spare drawer at the bottom of Ronnie's dresser. Then she took another shower and dressed in a pair of blue satin boxers and a matching camisole. She put her new blue satin bathrobe over her outfit and settled in to paint her nails while she waited for Ronnie to get home.

Lana heard her truck in the driveway and got up to stand by the door. When Ronnie opened it, she pulled her to her for a warm embrace. Ronnie's hand moved up and down her side.

"I like this," Ronnie said. "It feels nice."

"Thanks. I bought it especially for you."

"Well, thank you."

Ronnie pulled her close and kissed her.

"Mm. It's so good to be home."

"How was your day?" Lana took her hand and led her to the couch.

"It was great."

"Did you see Whitney?"

"Surprisingly, no."

"I did."

"You did? Where?"

Lana told her about having lunch with Madeline.

"What did she want?" Ronnie said.

"I don't know. As soon as she recognized me I left."

"I'm sorry, baby. I wish I could protect you from her."

"I don't think she's going to hurt me."

"I know. But I'd like to make sure your paths never cross."

"Unfortunately," Lana said. "That's not possible based on the business we're in. Especially now that I know she uses Madeline, too."

"So how was the rest of your day?"

"It was great. I went shopping, which always helps my mood."

"So, is this new?" Ronnie tugged on Lana's belt.

"Yes, it is."

"Mm. And what's under this?" Ronnie opened Lana's robe and gazed longingly at her outfit.

"I like this outfit so much," Ronnie said, "that I think I want to take it off of you right now."

"You do, huh?" Lana smiled.

"Indeed."

Ronnie eased the robe off Lana, then lifted her camisole. She bent to take a nipple gently in her mouth. The feeling of her hot breath on her nipple made Lana shiver. Ronnie tenderly sucked and nipped at it, and Lana felt the contact directly in her nerve center between her legs. She wanted Ronnie to take her shorts off and please her, but Ronnie didn't seem to be in any hurry.

Lana tangled her hands in Ronnie's short hair, holding on for dear life as Ronnie switched to her other nipple and teased her some more. Lana eased back on the couch, aching with need.

Ronnie slid her hand down her body and under the waist of her shorts. Lana braced for contact, but none came. Ronnie brought her hand back up and cupped the breast she was suckling.

"Please, Ronnie," Lana begged.

"So soon?" Ronnie said.

"Yes. I need you."

Ronnie went back to sucking a nipple, but slipped her hand under Lana's shorts.

"You're so wet for me," Ronnie said.

"Of course I am."

Ronnie slid her fingers inside.

"More," Lana said.

"Are you sure?"

"Yes. I need more."

Ronnie slipped another finger inside, and Lana felt more full than she ever had. She moved against Ronnie, making sure all her favorite spots were hit. She slid her own hand between her legs and, while Ronnie continued to thrust in and out, she rubbed her own clit. The combination was out of this world, and she clamped hard around Ronnie as she had the hardest orgasm of her life.

"Damn," she said after she'd caught her breath. "That was amazing."

"Mm. I'm glad you enjoyed it. Now if you would just loosen your grip on my fingers I'll come out."

"Sorry."

"Don't be. It's actually hot."

Lana finally relaxed enough for Ronnie to pull out. She eased Lana's camisole back down and kissed her.

"You drive me crazy, you know that?" Ronnie said.

"Likewise, I'm sure. Are you ready for your turn?"

"I'm fine for now. Actually, I'm starving. I didn't have lunch today."

They heated up the leftover pizza and ate at the kitchen table. Lana poured them wine which they sipped with dinner.

"You have the best wine," Lana said. "Where did you learn so much about it?"

"Actually, my ex was really into wine. So, I learned from her."

"Ah. So there *is* an ex in your past. You haven't always been the womanizer you have the reputation for."

"No. Once upon a time I was in a relationship. Her name was Constance. You remind me a lot of her, actually. Except I hope you're not the type to come home one day and announce you're in love with someone else."

Lana placed her hand over Ronnie's.

"I'm so sorry. No wonder you turned into a player. It was all to protect your heart."

"Yes, it was. But now I have someone to share my heart with again. And that's a good thing."

"It's a wonderful thing."

Ronnie leaned over and kissed Lana and felt her heart swell. She was falling hard and really hoped Lana wouldn't hurt her.

Lana stood and offered Ronnie her hand. Ronnie took it and followed Lana to the bedroom.

"You know, you don't need to worry about me," Lana said as she unbuttoned Ronnie's shirt. "I'm not going to hurt you."

She pushed it off her shoulders and lifted her undershirt over her head.

"Never." Lana kissed her neck.

She unbuttoned Ronnie's jeans, and Ronnie stepped out of them, pulling her boxers with them. She lay back on the bed and Lana climbed on top of her. She kissed her passionately on her mouth, then nibbled down her neck before sucking on a nipple. Ronnie ran her hands through her hair.

"That's it, baby," she said. "Show me that you care."

Lana kissed lower until she was between her legs. Ronnie spread her legs wide to let Lana have at her. Lana buried her tongue inside Ronnie, and Ronnie arched her hips, urging her deeper. Lana continued to lick and suck on her as she ran her fingertips over Ronnie's clit, and Ronnie felt her world shatter into a million tiny pieces.

When she had finally recovered from her orgasm, she pulled Lana up next to her. It was early, but they dozed.

Ronnie woke up to a pounding on her front door.

"What's going on?" Lana said.

"I don't know. You stay here."

Ronnie pulled on some shorts and a T-shirt and crossed the living room as the doorbell rang.

"Hold your horses!"

She opened the door and there stood Whitney, wearing a long, red overcoat.

"What are you doing here? How did you find out where I lived?"

"Does that matter? What's important is that I'm here. Won't you invite me in?"

"No. I won't. Good-bye."

Before she could close the door, Whitney had side stepped inside and was in her entry hall. Lana came around the corner and stopped in her tracks.

"What's *she* doing here?" Whitney said.

"She's my girlfriend," Ronnie said. "She's always here."

Whitney looked Lana up and down, then untied the belt of her overcoat and let it fall to the floor. She was wearing nothing underneath it.

"This is what a real woman looks like," she said.

She took Ronnie's hand, but Ronnie quickly pulled away.

"Don't touch me," she said.

"But you know you want me. Look at me. Tell me you're going to deny yourself. Send your little friend home and we'll have a great time."

"My *girlfriend* isn't going anywhere. You, however, are leaving right now."

Ronnie picked up her overcoat and handed it to her.

"You don't really want me to leave. I know this. Let's go to your room where we can talk in private."

Ronnie looked over at Lana.

"Call the police, baby. They'll make her leave."

"Hold on. Don't get so pushy. I just thought we could have fun," Whitney said.

"Well, we can't. Not today. Not tomorrow. Not ever. Do you understand?"

"You'll come around," Whitney said. She put on her overcoat and stood looking from Ronnie to Lana and back. "I'll catch you when she's not around and I know you'll give in."

"Get out," Ronnie said.

Whitney left, and Ronnie locked and bolted the front door. She crossed over to Lana and pulled her close.

"I'm so sorry about her," Ronnie said.

"She scares me. Not that I don't think you can handle her, but I worry she's going to try to do something to me."

"I'll keep you safe, baby. You've got to believe me."

They went back to bed but sleep eluded Ronnie. She held Lana until she heard soft snores coming from her and knew she was asleep. But she was wide awake. She needed to get rid of Whitney and soon. How had she found out where she lived? She must have followed her home. The idea creeped her out. Everything about Whitney creeped her out. How was she going to keep her promise to Lana? To keep her safe? Was Whitney really dangerous?

Ronnie finally fell into a restless sleep. She woke up at seven and dragged her butt out of bed to make coffee before getting into the shower. She was lathering her hair when she heard the door of the shower open and close.

"Hey, baby," Ronnie said.

"Hey, gorgeous. I thought you might need some help."

"Oh, you did, did you?"

"Yep."

Lana lathered her hands and slid one between Ronnie's legs.

"I want to make sure you're good and clean here," she said.

"Oh, baby. You make me feel so good."

"Good. Now relax and let the feelings wash over you."

Ronnie had no choice. Her whole body was alive. Every nerve ending tingled as Lana pressed their bodies together and she teased Ronnie's clit.

"Oh, yeah, baby. That's it," Ronnie said as she closed her eyes and focused all her attention on Lana's fingers. She was close, so very close. "Just a little more. There. That's it."

Ronnie sank back against the wall to keep from falling as the powerful climax took her breath away. When she was back to reality, she dropped to her knees and pleased Lana with her mouth and fingers and was rewarded when Lana cried out and dug her fingernails into Ronnie's shoulders as she fought to maintain her balance.

They quickly rinsed, dried, and dressed, then went to the kitchen for coffee.

"So, what does your day look like?" Lana asked.

"My first shoot is with Christine again. She was the one who was late the other day. I hope she doesn't make a habit out of that. And then it's your turn."

"Should I come early and bring lunch?"

"That would be great."

Ronnie kissed her good-bye and headed off to work.

Chapter Eleven

Christine was late. Ronnie had the shoot all set up and was drinking her second cup of coffee when Christine came waltzing in, full of excuses.

"Save it," Ronnie said. "I have a schedule to keep. If you and your agency want me to keep shooting you, you'd better start being on time. I mean it."

Ronnie was mostly worried that the shoot would run late and cut into her time with Lana.

"Now go get changed."

Ronnie finished her coffee while she waited. As soon as Christine was out of her dressing room, Ronnie had her on the set, giving directions and taking shot after shot. After a few minutes, Ronnie was still frustrated.

"Are you even trying?" she said.

"Yes. I really am. I'm sorry. Let's try again."

"Fine."

They took it from the top, and Christine finally relaxed into following Ronnie's instructions. Ronnie was good, and she knew it. She just needed the stupid models to have faith in her. She didn't really want to work with Christine again. But she pushed her hard for a couple of hours and, satisfied, Ronnie let her go back to the dressing room.

Ronnie looked over the pictures she'd gotten. Perfect. She was sure the magazine paying for the spread would be pleased. She downloaded her pictures onto her computer and sent them off.

Happy with that shoot, and knowing she only had one more shoot that day, Ronnie relaxed with a cup of coffee and waited for Lana to get there.

Ronnie heard loud voices in the hallway and went out to see what was going on. There were Whitney and Lana in a shouting match. Shit.

"What the hell is going on out here?"

"I brought you lunch." Whitney was wearing the same overcoat as the previous night, and Ronnie was pretty certain there was nothing under it again. "And she says she brought you lunch and I should just go. I think we should see whose lunch you like better."

"I choose hers," Ronnie said. "Now beat it, Whitney."

"But you don't even know what I brought you."

"It doesn't matter. I planned to have lunch with Lana, and I'm going to. Now leave or I'll call security."

"You're no fun anymore," Whitney said.

"Whitney. Get out of here. I mean it."

Whitney left, and Lana and Ronnie walked back inside the studio. They set up lunch at the kitchen table and said good-bye to the rest of the crew who all left the building for lunch.

"I'm so sorry about Whitney," Ronnie said.

"It's not your fault. The woman has a screw loose."

"Obviously. If only I'd known that before I slept with her."

"You couldn't have known, Ronnie. Now relax and eat your lunch."

"You look very gorgeous today, by the way."

"So, do you."

Ronnie moved closer to her.

"I may have to have my way with you."

"Here?"

"Yep. We did it before and didn't get caught."

"I think you should cool your jets and eat your lunch."

"Mm. I don't think I can."

She ran her hand up Lana's leg.

"Ronnie Mannis!"

"Yes?" She unbuttoned and unzipped Lana's shorts.

"You're so bad."

"Ah, but I'm so good."

Ronnie slid her hand inside Lana's thong to find her wet and ready for her. She rubbed her clit until Lana buried her head in Ronnie's shoulder as she called out her name. Ronnie moved away, and Lana fixed her shorts. She'd just gotten them on when the hair and makeup people came in. Lana fixed Ronnie with a look, but Ronnie just smiled and ate her sandwich.

They finished their lunch, and Lana went into the dressing room to change. Ronnie was excited. It was another formal, black-and-white shooting, and she knew Lana could pull it off with flying colors. She got the studio set up for her, and her breath caught when she turned and saw Lana coming out of the dressing room.

"Damn, you're gorgeous," she said.

Lana smiled.

"Thank you. You're not so bad yourself."

Ronnie closed the distance between them.

"I want to tear that dress off you with my teeth."

"Careful, dear. This dress isn't mine and they might not like it returned with teeth marks."

Ronnie laughed, but couldn't loosen the tightness inside of her. She wanted Lana again. But she'd have to wait until they got home.

"Okay. Let's get this shoot over with," she said.

They worked well together, and Ronnie was happy with all the shots they had at the end of two hours. She showed them all to Lana, who agreed they were quality pictures. Ronnie downloaded the pictures to her computer and emailed them while Lana changed back into street clothes.

She was all ready to go when Lana emerged. The makeup artists and hair stylists and Devon were already gone, so she locked up the studio and they walked to their cars together.

They got home, Ronnie just minutes before Lana, and went inside. Ronnie pulled Lana to her and kissed her hard on her mouth.

"What was that for?" Lana said when they came up for air.

"Does a boi need a reason to kiss her girl?"

"No. I suppose not."

"Good. Now go get relaxed. I'm gonna grill a couple of steaks."

"What can I do to help?"

"You can make a salad."

"Sounds good."

Ronnie fired up the grill and seasoned the steaks. She had them ready to go on when Lana came out in her kimono.

"Are you wearing anything under that?" Ronnie said.

"You'll have to wait and find out. Now, go tend to the steaks and I'll make a salad."

Dinner was ready in no time, and they ate and drank wine on the patio.

"I love your backyard," Lana said. "I love all the plants and fountains. It's like a little slice of paradise."

"Thank you. That's how I feel about it, too. Now, speaking of paradise, let's see what's on under that kimono."

"All in due time. Let's get the dishes washed first."

Ronnie could barely concentrate on anything other than Lana, but she managed to get the dishwasher loaded. She turned to find Lana leaning against the kitchen counter.

"You're looking awfully sexy there," Ronnie said.

"I am, am I?"

She took Ronnie's hand and led her to the living room.

"So, come on," Ronnie said. "Untie that thing."

Lana untied it and, sure enough, was wearing nothing underneath. Ronnie growled her approval. She eased the kimono the rest of the way off her and laid her back on the couch. Ronnie lay next to her and dragged her hand all over the exposed flesh.

"I love your body," she said.

"It loves you."

"Good."

Ronnie nuzzled Lana's neck while her fingers found her hot center. She moved them in and out while Lana arched off the couch, meeting each thrust.

"I need more," Lana said.

"Are you sure? I don't want to hurt you."

"You won't. Please, Ronnie."

Ronnie slipped another finger in and was surprised when Lana slid her hand down to join hers. Lana rubbed her clit while Ronnie continued to thrust, and Lana clamped hard around her fingers while her legs wrapped around Ronnie.

Ronnie lay still until Lana relaxed enough for her to slide out. She replaced Lana's hand with her own and rubbed her clit until Lana cried out again.

"I could make love to you all night," Ronnie said.

"Unfortunately, we both work tomorrow."

"Oh, yeah."

"Come on. Let's go to bed. I need you naked and now."

Ronnie started down the hall, shedding clothing as she went. She kicked off her boots and stripped out of her jeans and boxers in the bedroom and she was ready for Lana. She lay on the bed and spread her legs. Lana settled in between them and Ronnie closed her eyes and focused on Lana's talented tongue.

In no time at all, Ronnie was writhing on the bed, praying for release.

"Oh, God. Please, Lana. My clit. Please, baby."

She felt Lana's tongue on her clit, and all thoughts flew from her head as she climaxed harder than she ever had before.

But Lana didn't stop. She went back to sucking her lips while her fingers rubbed her clit and, again, Ronnie lost all ability to think as one several orgasms racked her body.

They fell asleep in each other's arms, and when Lana woke the next morning, she heard Ronnie already in the shower. She stretched, put her kimono on, and went to the kitchen for coffee. She had a ten o'clock shoot with Ronnie that day, so she had a little time before she had to get ready.

Ronnie came into the kitchen with only a towel wrapped around her waist.

"Lookin' good," Lana said.

"So are you."

Ronnie kissed her, and Lana found herself dizzy with need.

"Do we have time to play before you go?" she said.

"Sorry. I have an early shoot today. Unfortunately, it's Whitney."

"Oh no. I'm sorry. Should I talk to Madeline and ask her to find someplace else to send her?"

"No. It's okay. She'll settle down. I just hope there's no funny business today since you two are probably going to see each other."

"Yeah. I hope not, too."

"Okay. I need to get dressed." Ronnie took her cup of coffee down the hall. Lana followed.

She watched Ronnie drop her towel and fumble through her drawer of boxers.

"You have the most amazing body," Lana said.

"Have you seen yours?"

"Very funny. Damn. I could stare at you all day."

"But you don't have time. You have a shoot at ten."

"I know."

She watched Ronnie get dressed, bummed to watch that body be covered up in clothes. Ronnie gelled her hair, kissed Lana good-bye and was out the door.

Lana hit the shower, applied her makeup, and dried her hair. She put on some shorts and a short-sleeved oxford shirt and finished another cup of coffee. It was time to go. She was excited to see Ronnie again, but she had to steel herself against seeing Whitney the psycho bitch.

She walked into the Studio and found Ronnie in the kitchen. She got up and greeted her with a kiss.

"Is it safe for me to go into the dressing room?" Lana said.

"No. She's still here."

"Damn."

"I'm sorry, Lana."

"It's not your fault." She looked at the clock. "But we've got a shoot to do. I need to get in there."

"I'll go urge her along," Ronnie said.

Lana helped herself to a cup of coffee while she waited for her turn. She heard yelling coming from the dressing room. She couldn't hear what was being said, but she knew from Ronnie's voice that she wasn't happy.

Ronnie was out a few minutes later.

"I take it that didn't go so well?" Lana said.

"No. But she should be leaving any minute now."

Sure enough, Whitney came into the kitchen a few minutes after.

"I'm going to have a cup of coffee," she said.

"Only if you take it to go," Ronnie said.

"Don't be silly. I want to watch the next shoot."

"Nobody watches my shoots," Ronnie said. "It's between me and the model. No one else. So leave."

"I used to like you a lot better," Whitney said.

"Like I care. Now, I'm calling security." Ronnie spoke into the intercom. With security on their way, she turned back to Whitney.

"Fine. I'm leaving."

She shot Lana a dirty look.

"You know, she fucks all her models. You're nothing special."

It was nothing Lana hadn't heard already. She didn't say a word, just watched as security arrived and Whitney turned on her heel and stormed out.

Lana was shaking on the inside but held it together. She was nothing if not a professional.

"I'm going to get ready now," she said.

"Great. I'll get the studio set up for you."

By the time she was through with hair and makeup, Lana had forgotten about Whitney. All she cared about now was Ronnie and her camera. And Lana was determined to make them both love her.

The shoot went wonderfully. Lana followed all Ronnie's directions and the shoot was over before she knew it. The three hours had passed quickly. She looked at the pictures over Ronnie's shoulder. Standing that close to her made her weak in the knees. She couldn't believe the effect Ronnie had on her. But she forced herself to concentrate. Happy that the pictures were perfect, she went to the dressing room and changed back to her street clothes.

"You want some lunch?" Ronnie said. "I can have Devon go get sandos."

"That would be great. Thanks."

While Ronnie was talking to Devon, Lana looked through the small refrigerator and found a diet soda. She popped it open and sat at the table. Ronnie came in and joined her.

"That was a great shoot, baby," she said.

"Thanks. It felt good."

"You're such a natural. I wish everyone were as easy as you."

Lana laughed.

"I don't know that I want other models being easy for you. Those days are over."

"That's not what I meant, and you know it."

She kissed Lana and Lana felt the earth shift off its axis.

"Mm. You're the best," she said.

"No. You are."

Devon was back with their sandwiches. They ate them in the silence of the empty studio.

"I really like our lunches," Lana said.

"Me, too. But sitting with you in the empty studio is awfully tempting."

"You're so bad. You can have me when you get home. I promise."

"I'm going to hold you to that."

"Please do. I plan to go home and get dinner prepped, so it'll be all ready to put in the oven when we're ready. So there will be nothing to do when you get home but make love."

"I do like the sound of that."

They finished their lunches and kissed some more.

"I'm kind of bummed I have to leave," Lana said.

"Yeah. But I'll be home soon."

"Okay. I'll see you at home."

Ronnie walked her to the door and kissed her good-bye.

Lana walked to her car, but before she got there, someone grabbed her arm. She held it bent up and tight against Lana's back. It hurt, but Lana wouldn't let on.

"Listen, bitch." She thought she recognized Whitney's voice but couldn't be sure. "You're gonna sashay out of Ronnie's life just like you sashayed into it. Do you understand me?"

Lana nodded. She wasn't about to argue with her. She was in no position. Her arm hurt and she just wanted to get away.

"Good," the voice said. She pushed Lana hard and walked off.

Lana ran her hand over her hurt arm. It wasn't seriously injured. She looked at the disappearing figure of her attacker, but whoever it was was wearing a sweat suit and ski mask. Lana walked to her car and turned to survey the street. She saw a familiar car. Danielle. What was she doing there?

She got in the safety of her car and drove home. Home. That's what she thought of Ronnie's house. Should she feel comfortable there, though? Whitney knew where it was. And she was threatening her. It went beyond mild annoyance.

She fought to control her racing emotions, tried not to think she'd be better without Ronnie. Nothing was making sense. She took a deep breath and began making dinner. It was a chicken enchilada casserole. When it was ready, she put it in the fridge to keep until Ronnie got home.

To pass the time until Ronnie got home, she ran a bath and soaked herself until she heard the front door close.

"I'm in here, Ronnie," she called.

"Hi, baby. How are you?"

The sight of Ronnie made all her fears seem ridiculous. People would kill for what they had. She'd be a fool to throw it away because of some psycho ex. Right?

"I'm okay," she said. "How was the rest of your day?"

"Easy. Nothing major happened."

"Lucky you."

"What's that supposed to mean?"

Lana launched into her tale about the incident in the parking lot.

"You really think it was Whitney? Damn her," Ronnie said. "Why the fuck won't she leave us, specifically you, alone? I'm going to call the cops. That's assault."

"I don't know. I thought about just going home to my house, but I don't want to. I like it here. With you. And you can't call the cops on her. I can't be certain it was her."

"I'm glad you came here. We'll get through this. Together. And who else would it be?"

"I can't imagine anyone else. What are we going to do about her, Ronnie?"

"I don't know. I'll have security watch the parking lot more closely. I know what kind of car she drives, and if it's seen in the parking lot, I'll have them call the cops."

"But she's a model and you work with her. She's allowed to be there sometime."

"I'll let them know. They can escort her in and out. Two can play at this game, Lana."

"And what about here? She knows where you live."

"She won't bother us here again. I'll call the cops."

"I just hope she doesn't escalate. She was pretty scary this afternoon."

"She won't. Besides, you could take her."

"Oh yeah. That's what I want to do. Get in a catfight with her. I need this face to make money, you know?"

"I know. I was only teasing. You're safe, baby. I won't let her near you again if I can help it."

"Thanks. Now I need to get out of this tub. I'm turning into a prune."

"Great. I'll meet you in bed."

"You will, will you?"

"If that's okay?"

"Kiss me."

Ronnie kissed her, and Lana forgot all her troubles.

"I'll meet you in bed," she said.

Chapter Twelve

They woke in the morning and made love again. It was slow, passionate lovemaking that Ronnie enjoyed as she brought Lana over the edge time and again. When Lana finally claimed she had no more in her, Ronnie got up and made coffee. She went back to get in the shower, and Lana joined her.

Lana pleased Ronnie in the shower to the point Ronnie was afraid her legs wouldn't hold her. She lowered herself to the bench that ran along the inside wall until she was sure she could rinse and not fall.

When they were clean and dry, they sat at the kitchen table and drank coffee.

"What are you going to do today?" Ronnie said.

"I have no idea. Maybe clean house, do some laundry, you know basic, domestic necessities."

"I'm sorry I won't be here to help you."

"It's okay. I don't mind. I'll enjoy it."

"Okay. If you say so."

"I do. Now, you'd better get going."

"Yeah. I just don't want to go to work today. I have a shoot with Whitney at ten. I really don't want to see her."

"But you're a professional, Ronnie. You've got this."

"I suppose."

"Now, kiss me and be on your way."

"Yes, dear," Ronnie said.

She kissed Lana. The kiss started as chaste but soon steamed up. Ronnie had to fight not to call in and stay home to take Lana again.

"Okay. Okay," she said. "I'm out of here."

"I'll see you this evening."

"Good-bye."

Ronnie's first shot of the day was Tina. She was a natural and a professional. The camera loved her, and she followed directions well, so they were done a half hour ahead of schedule.

"You were terrific," Ronnie said.

"Thanks. It felt good."

"Yeah. You did a great job. Why don't you go ahead and change? You're free to go."

"Thanks."

Ronnie downloaded the pictures and sent them off. She was reviewing them again, just because, when she heard Whitney beside her.

"So I understand condolences are in order," she said.

"What are you talking about?"

"Word on the street is that blondie left you."

"Word on the street is wrong."

She watched the anger flash in Whitney's eyes.

"What?"

"Yeah. Which reminds me, security will be monitoring the parking lot. If your car is ever there when you're not in a shoot, the cops will be called. The same thing goes for you. If you're ever in the building or parking lot and not scheduled for a shoot, the cops will be called. Basically, I'm not messing around anymore, and you need to know that."

"You're not being fair."

"I've been more than fair with you." Ronnie waved to Tina as she left. "Now, go get changed and let's get this shoot over with."

The shoot did not go well at all. Whitney was angry, and it showed in her eyes and her posture. After a few shots, Ronnie insisted they take a break.

"You need to relax. You need to let go of your childish attitude toward Lana. It's showing in the shoot and ruining it."

"I'm not childish."

"Yes, you are. You're acting like a petulant kid who can't get what she wants. Now lose the 'tude and let's get back to the shoot."

Whitney took a deep breath.

"Fine. I'm ready."

"You don't look ready."

"What the hell do you want from me?"

"I want you to be a professional. I'll do my best with what you've brought today, but I can't guarantee they'll like the pictures. And if they don't, I'm going to refer you to a different photographer."

"You wouldn't dare."

"Watch me."

If Whitney was still livid, she didn't show it in the rest of the shoot. She was pretty much professional and listened to Ronnie's instructions, and they finally had enough decent shots that Ronnie told Whitney she could go change back to her street clothes.

She came out of the dressing room and approached Ronnie in the kitchen. Ronnie had just poured a cup of coffee and was stirring it. Whitney was in her face, her arms around Ronnie's neck.

"Whoa," Ronnie said and set her cup down to disentangle herself from Whitney's arms. "What do you think you're doing?"

"Blondie isn't here. She'll never know."

"But I will."

"So?" Whitney pressed closer against Ronnie.

"It's time for you to go," Ronnie said.

"Just one kiss?"

"No. Security will be watching for you now."

As if on cue, a security agent walked into the kitchen.

"Everything okay, Ms. Mannis?"

"No. Actually. I need you to escort this woman off the property, please."

"You got it."

He took one of Whitney's arms and led her toward the door.

"This isn't over," Whitney said.

Unfortunately, Ronnie believed her.

Ronnie sat in the empty studio trying to figure out what to do about Whitney. She needed to be committed, she thought. She was clearly off her rocker. But how could Ronnie make that happen? To her, Whitney was an annoyance, but to Lana? She seemed to be a threat and Ronnie couldn't stand the thought that Lana wasn't safe.

She called home.

"Hello?" Lana answered, and Ronnie felt the moisture pool in her boxers. Damn, what she did to her.

"Hey Lana, it's me. I need you to do me a favor."

"Sure."

"Make sure the front door is locked and bolted and don't open the door for anyone until I get home."

"I can do that. I take it your shoot with Whitney didn't go well?"

"Not even close. Just be careful, okay?"

"Okay."

"I'll see you in a few hours."

Ronnie hung up the phone and greeted the makeup and hair artists as well as Devon. Lunch must be over, she thought. Her next model came in and Ronnie set up for the shoot. She grabbed her camera and noticed something missing.

Where was her SD card? She went back to the kitchen and looked all over. It was nowhere to be found. Shit. It had all Whitney's pictures on it. She'd have to call and reschedule the shoot. That wouldn't be fun.

She turned her attention to the model who was there. They worked well together and soon they were finished with some excellent photographs.

"You're a natural," Ronnie told the model.

"Thanks. I'm still fairly new."

"Well, you're great at this. You can go ahead and change back into your street clothes."

Ronnie took a deep breath and called Whitney.

"Hello?"

"Whitney, it's Ronnie."

"Oh, you've finally come to your senses? Would you like to come over?"

"No. This is a business call. I have misplaced the SD card with your shoot from this morning. I need you to come back in and do a reshoot."

"When?"

"Now?"

"I'll be right there."

Ronnie notified security that Whitney would be in and then called Lana. She wasn't looking forward to that phone call.

"Hey, baby, what's up?" Lana said.

"I hate to do this, but I've got to work late tonight."

"Why? What's up?"

"I lost my SD card with this morning's shoot on it. So Whitney has to come back in and I need to reshoot her." There was silence from the other end. "Lana? Are you still there?"

"Yes. I'm not happy about this."

"Neither am I. I'll be home as soon as I can."

"Okay. Be careful, Ronnie."

"Always,"

Whitney arrived a few minutes later looking triumphant even being escorted by a guard.

"I knew you'd see things my way eventually." Whitney approached Ronnie and tried to wrap her arms around her neck. Ronnie stepped back.

"We're here to reshoot you. That's all. Now, go change and get to makeup."

Whitney practically skipped to the dressing room. Ronnie felt sick. She hated having to spend additional time with her, but she had no choice. She had to do the shoot and send the photos off. What could she have done with that SD card?

The shoot went well and after, Whitney sidled up to Ronnie again.

"How about you pour me a nice glass of wine?"

"How about I don't? It's late. I want to get home. Go change and get out of here."

Whitney finally left and Ronnie waited until everyone else was gone, then she locked the door and headed home. When she was on the front porch, she called Lana.

"Hello?"

"Hey, baby. I'm on the porch. Will you let me in?"

"Sure."

Lana opened the door for her.

"Don't you have your keys?"

"I never carry my key for the bolt. I'll start doing that now."

"I'm sorry you had to deal with her this morning."

"She was a mess. She told me she'd heard that we split up and when I told her that was a lie, her eyes got crazy with anger. You should have seen her. And then it took her forever to shake it off and do a decent shoot." She shook her head. "I had to call security to remove her from the building afterward. It wasn't much fun. I'll tell you that."

"And then you had to reshoot her this evening? What happened again?"

"I lost my SD card. That's never happened before. It couldn't have just fallen out, but I have no recollection of removing it. I don't know where it got to."

"I don't like you spending extra time with her. I guess if I'm honest, I was a little jealous."

"You don't need to be jealous, baby. You're the only one for me now."

Lana moved into Ronnie's arms.

"Well, you're home now," she said.

Ronnie kissed her, and suddenly, the weight of the world was lifted from her shoulders.

"The place looks great, by the way," Ronnie said. "And something smells good."

"Good. I'm glad you think so."

"I feel bad, though, that you had to clean up on your own. I should have helped."

"Nonsense. I love housecleaning."

"You do?"

"Yep. Big time. And it's easier to do it on my own. So, don't give it a second thought."

"Okay. Well, did you make our bed?"

"Of course. Why do you ask?"

"Because I want to take you back there now and mess it up."

"Patience, my dear," Lana said. "Dinner is ready."

They ate dinner and did the dishes, then Ronnie took Lana's hand and led her back to the bedroom. She stripped off her silky robe and found yet another pair of boxers and camisole underneath. They were both satiny, and Ronnie loved the feel of them under her hands. She lifted the camisole and ran her hands over the soft skin underneath.

She took the camisole off and kissed all over Lana's body. She sucked on her nipples and trailed kisses down her belly. She pulled the boxers off and inhaled deeply of the scent that was all Lana. She lowered her mouth and licked and sucked all she saw. She moaned at her deliciousness. She ran her tongue over the length of her before licking deep inside her. She replaced her tongue with her fingers and moved her mouth to Lana's clit. She licked and sucked it, and soon, Lana was clamped down around her fingers as she rode out her orgasms.

When Ronnie was able to pull her fingers out, she did so and moved up next to Lana, who made short order of undressing her. Soon, she was lying naked there for Lana to do with as she pleased. And please Lana did. She ran her fingers over Ronnie's body until she came to where her legs met. She dragged her fingers all over before pressing them into her clit and rubbing. Ronnie felt her world tilt just before she launched into orbit from the power of her orgasms.

They fell asleep and Lana was awakened the next morning by Ronnie between her legs. She loved her as only she could, and soon Lana was wide awake and screaming Ronnie's name.

"To what do I owe that delicious surprise?" she said.

"I woke up a little early and you looked so beautiful lying there that I had to have you."

"Well, good morning to me."

"Mm-hm. Now would you care to join me in a shower?"

"Of course."

They made love in the shower, and they took turns pleasing each other until both were weak in the knees.

It was soon time for Ronnie to go to work and Lana to get ready for a shoot with a different photographer. It was Timothy. She'd worked with him before and found him lacking. But she got herself ready and headed out to her shoot.

As she'd expected, the shoot did not go well. The pictures were flat, not like Ronnie's.

"You need to reshoot me," Lana insisted.

"Why? These are fine."

"No. They're not. They're lacking. You didn't catch any exuberance, any substance. These are just pictures. A ten-year-old could have taken them. Now, I demand a reshoot."

Timothy rolled his eyes at her and murmured something about a prima donna. She didn't care. She went back out to the set and posed for him. He started taking pictures with more zeal and she responded in kind. This time when she looked at the pictures, she was happy with the results.

"Thank you, Timothy. These look great."

"Yeah, they do. But I'm behind on my schedule for the day."

"Well, I'd say I'm sorry, but I'm not. I'm a professional and want my pictures to reflect that."

"Fine. Go ahead and change. I'll see you next time."

Lana changed back to her street clothes and headed to Madeline's office.

"Lana, dear. Come in. Come in."

She greeted Lana with a kiss on each cheek.

"Hello, Madeline. I'm glad you have time to meet with me."

"Of course. What's going on?"

"I'd like to ask you not to schedule me with Timothy anymore. The man is anything but a professional."

"Oh, no. What happened?"

"I've worked with him twice now, and I've had to demand retakes both times. He's just not a good photographer."

"And I suppose you'd like me to set you up only with Ronnie Mannis?"

"In my dream world. And not just because we're an item. You've got to admit, she's one of the best in town."

"Yes, she is. But her schedule is normally booked for just that reason."

"I understand. Just please don't book me with Timothy again."

"Okay, dear. I won't."

"Thank you."

Lana opened the door to leave Madeline's office and saw Whitney sitting in a chair. She got up when she saw Lana.

"You!" She dove at Lana, who quickly sidestepped to avoid an attack on her face. Whitney went sprawling.

"What is going on?" Madeline stepped between the two models as Whitney got up off the floor and turned back to Lana. "I mean it. I won't tolerate such high school shenanigans."

"She's just mad that Ronnie's with me now," Lana said.

"She's holding her against her will," Whitney said. "And I intend to prove it."

Lana laughed sardonically.

"She's not being held against her will. We're a couple now and you just need to accept it."

"Yes," Madeline said. "You need to grow up, Whitney. I mean it. I won't tolerate this type of behavior from my models. Now, did you need to talk to me?"

"Yes."

"Then come into my office. Lana, I'll see you later."

Lana drove to her house and gathered some more clothes to take to Ronnie's. She drove home and pulled into the driveway just as Ronnie did.

"Hey, baby," Ronnie said.

"Hi."

Ronnie opened the door and stood to the side to let Lana and her suitcase in.

"Ah, I see you're getting more comfortable here, huh?" Ronnie said.

"I am indeed. Now kiss me hello, please."

"Gladly."

Ronnie kissed Lana tenderly at first, but soon the kiss grew hotter when Lana opened her mouth and urged Ronnie in. Ronnie pressed Lana against the front door and moved her knee between Lana's legs. Lana ground into it, feeling her desire growing.

Ronnie broke the kiss.

"I don't want to take you against the front door," she said.

"I think it would be hot."

"Duly noted."

Lana followed Ronnie into the kitchen where she poured them each a glass of wine.

"So, how was your shoot today?" Ronnie said.

"Ugh." Lana sat in a chair. "Timothy is so unprofessional. I made him redo the whole shoot. He was pissed, but he did it and it ended up being a good shoot. But then he was pissed that I'd made him late for the rest of the day. Oh, well. If he'd gotten it right the first time, he wouldn't have been late."

"I'm sorry, baby. It's hard for a professional like yourself to settle for anything less than perfection."

"I won't. This is my face and my body, and I want them looking their best."

"So, how about the rest of your day?"

"Believe it or not, Timothy was the highlight."

"Oh, no. What happened?"

Lana proceeded to tell her about seeing Whitney at Madeline's office and how she dove toward her, fingernails outstretched like she was going to mar her face.

"No shit?"

"No shit. I managed to avoid the attack, and she ended up lying sprawled out on the floor, but it wasn't fun. She scares me, Ronnie."

Ronnie got up and pulled Lana in her arms.

"I won't let her get you, baby. I'll keep you safe."

"But how? You can protect me here. And at the studio. But I'm often not at either of those places."

"Well, outside of the modeling agency, there's no reason for your paths to cross. I think you'll be okay, baby."

"I hope so."

Ronnie grilled salmon for dinner and Lana made green beans. They ate together, and Lana was starting to relax again after having told Ronnie about her day. She had another glass of wine while they cleaned up.

"Why don't I draw you a bath?" Ronnie said.

"That would be great. Thanks."

Lana submerged herself in the scented bubbles. It felt so good to be relaxing after such a hectic day. Ronnie left her alone for a while, then came in and washed her back for her. Lana rinsed off and took Ronnie by the hand.

They went to bed and Ronnie made love to her slow and steadily, not stopping until she'd coaxed four orgasms from her. Lana returned the favor and they curled up together on top of the covers. Lana believed, at that moment, Ronnie could keep her safe forever.

CHAPTER THIRTEEN

Ronnie held Lana through the night, which was hard because several times, Lana thrashed about in her sleep, clearly engulfed in a nightmare of some sort. Ronnie cooed her back to sleep each time, but when it was time to get up in the morning, Ronnie felt anything but rested.

She got up and made coffee, thinking she was careful to not disturb Lana. But Lana was soon in the kitchen with her.

"How are you this morning?" Ronnie said.

"I don't know. I'm really tired. I don't know why."

"You were having bad dreams last night."

"I was? I don't remember them."

"That's good," Ronnie said. "They seemed pretty out of control."

"Hm." Lana took the coffee Ronnie offered her. "Then I'm really glad I don't remember them."

"But if you did, you'd tell me, right?"

"Of course, I would. I have no secrets from you."

"Okay. Good. Just checking."

"Did I keep you up?" Lana said.

"Don't worry about it. It was no big deal."

"Aw. I feel horrible now."

"Don't. It was only a few times and I like to think I helped you relax and get back to sleep."

"Okay. If you say so."

"I do. Now. Why are you up so early? Our shoot isn't until three."

"I don't know. I felt you get up and wanted to be with you."

"That's sweet." Ronnie kissed her. "But you should go back to bed. I need to get in the shower anyway."

"Okay. I'll be by around one with lunch."

"Sounds great."

She kissed her and got in the shower. When she got out, Lana was sleeping peacefully. She finished getting dressed and headed off to work.

Her first shoot was with a new model, and she prepared herself for the unknown. She got the set ready and sat down to drink some coffee when she heard the front door close. She heard a few tentative steps on the floor, but then they stopped. She walked out to the studio area and saw a beautiful woman with fiery red hair that fell past her shoulders. She also had beautiful green eyes and high cheekbones.

"You must be Molly?" she said.

"Yes. Are you Ronnie?"

"I am. Come on in. Would you like a cup of coffee?"

"No, thanks. I'm ready to get things going."

"Excellent. The dressing room is right over there. Go on in and get changed."

Ronnie liked Molly so far. She wanted to get right to it. That made her happy. Now she just needed to follow instructions and she'd be a perfect model.

Molly came out of the dressing room looking stunning in a long green dress.

"You look great," Ronnie said. "Are you ready?"

"Yep."

Ronnie started telling Molly how to pose and which way to look as she took photo after photo of her. Molly was a natural. And the camera loved her. She followed instructions well, and their shoot ended a little ahead of time.

"You did great, Molly."

"May I see the pictures?"

"Sure."

Ronnie held the camera and scrolled through the pictures for her.

"Wow," Molly said. "You take really good pictures."

"Thank you. But these are all you. You really are a natural."

"So, am I through here?"

"Yep. You can go change into your street clothes."

Ronnie said good-bye to Molly and then the rest of the crew as they headed out to lunch. She was restless, excited to see Lana. She wondered what was taking her so long but checked the phone and realized it was just one.

Lana was there a few minutes later.

"Hey, baby," Ronnie said. She kissed her and took the Chinese food from her. "Chinese again? Thanks. It's my favorite."

"So you've said."

They sat in the kitchen and ate their lunch.

"You know we're here alone." Ronnie winked.

"No. Not today. There'll be plenty of time for that when we get home this afternoon."

"Are you sure?" Ronnie moved closer, longing to touch her.

"I'm positive. Behave Ronnie."

Ronnie moved away and pouted. Lana laughed at her and Ronnie soon joined in. She knew she had plenty of time to take her when they got home.

The rest of the crew showed up, and Lana went into the dressing room. Ronnie set up the shoot then sat down to finish her lunch. When Lana came out, Ronnie paused with a forkful halfway to her mouth. Lana was unbelievably gorgeous. She was wearing a form fitting blue dress that brought out her eyes and made Ronnie's clit swell.

"Damn," she said. "You're unbelievable."

"Thank you. Now be sure to capture it on film."

"Will do."

Ronnie started taking pictures and giving instructions, which Lana followed to a tee. The two hours flew by, and Ronnie called the shoot complete.

"Not until I see the pictures," Lana said.

"Sure. Come here and take a look."

She scrolled through the pictures and Lana deemed them exceptional.

"Good. I'm glad you like them."

"You're the best."

Lana nibbled on the back of Ronnie's neck, then disappeared into the dressing room. Ronnie dismissed her staff and waited for Lana. Lana came out dressed in her street clothes and looking just as stunning as before.

"You sure I have to wait to get home?" Ronnie whispered in her ear.

"Yes. Come on. The sooner we get there, the sooner we get naked."

Ronnie closed up the studio and followed Lana home. She pressed her against the door again and kissed her passionately. Lana opened her mouth, and Ronnie let her tongue meander in. She ran her tongue over Lana's, each swipe fanning a fire that already threatened to consume her.

She unzipped Lana's shorts and slid her hand inside. She continued to kiss her as she found her center wet and warm. She separated her lower lips and slid her fingers inside. She used her knee to help move her fingers in and out.

"Oh, God," Lana said. "Oh, yes, Ronnie."

Ronnie slipped her fingers out and slid them over her clit. Lana threw her head back and cried out as she shuddered through her orgasm.

Ronnie stepped back and Lana adjusted her clothes.

"Can we go to bed now?" Lana said.

"Sure. Sorry. I couldn't wait to have you."

"Don't apologize. It was beyond hot."

"Great."

They walked down the hall and quickly stripped and fell into bed. Ronnie took Lana over the edge time and time again until Lana claimed to have nothing left. Lana kissed Ronnie's neck and chest before stopping to suck a hardened nipple. Ronnie moaned, aroused beyond words by Lana's actions.

Lana kissed farther down Ronnie's body until she came to where her legs met. She put her knees over her shoulders and began to lick and suck all over. Ronnie moved against her, urging her on. Lana placed her fingers on Ronnie's clit and rubbed until Ronnie felt her whole body tense up, then she felt white heat shoot through her body as she came down from her orgasm.

Lana moved up Ronnie's body and Ronnie wrapped her arms around her.

"That was wonderful, baby."

"Yes, it was."

"But it's kind of early for sleep."

"Mm."

Ronnie laughed.

"I take it you disagree?"

"Not really. I'm just really content lying here with you."

"I agree. It's nice. But I'm hungry."

"I didn't take anything out of the freezer for dinner."

"Then we'll order out. What are you in the mood for?"

"Fajitas."

"Sounds good to me. Hand me my phone and I'll order."

Ronnie entered their order, then lay back down with her arms around Lana. Lana's skin was so soft, and she smelled so good that Ronnie had to have her again. She kissed her shoulder and nibbled her neck.

"What do you think you're doing?" Lana smiled.

"What do you think?"

She kissed lower and lovingly took a nipple in her mouth. She felt it harden as her tongue played over it. She skimmed her hand down to where her legs met. Lana opened her legs for her and Ronnie thrust her fingers inside. She moved them all around and pulled them back out, then plunged them in again. She did this until Lana was panting and quivering inside. Ronnie brushed her thumb over Lana's clit and was rewarded when Lana cried out her name again.

"I should get up," Ronnie said a few minutes later.

"Are you sure?"

"Yeah. Food's gonna be here soon and I want to be dressed."

"Fine. Let's get up and get dressed."

They had just finished dressing when the doorbell rang. Lana grabbed Ronnie.

"How do we know who it is?"

"Relax. It's our dinner. See?" She held up her phone to show Lana the food had been delivered.

"Okay."

Lana went into the kitchen to set the table. She smelled Ronnie come in with the food.

"I'm sorry I freaked out," Lana said. "I just still don't feel safe."

"But I told you, as long as I'm around, I'll keep you safe. And I meant it. So just relax and eat your dinner, okay?"

Lana kissed Ronnie, and everything felt right.

"Let's eat," she said.

They ate as much as they could, then Lana leaned back in her chair, stomach full.

"That was so good. But I couldn't possibly eat another bite."

"I hear ya," Ronnie said.

They put the leftovers away and made their way back down the hallway to bed.

"We should probably get some sleep," Lana said. "I have a ten o'clock shoot with you tomorrow."

"So no play time?"

Lana looked at Ronnie and saw the sadness in her eyes. But she was full and had a shoot in the morning.

"Sorry, Ronnie. Maybe in the morning?"

"Okay. Something to look forward to."

The snuggled together and Lana fell into a deep sleep. She awoke the next morning to Ronnie's hand between her legs and feathery light kisses on her cheek.

"Mm. Good morning to me," Lana said.

"Yay. I thought you'd never wake up."

Ronnie slipped her fingers inside Lana. Lana gasped and spread her legs wider. She wanted to feel Ronnie deep inside her. She arched her hips and took her in.

"You feel so good," Lana said.

"Mm."

Ronnie kissed lower and had a nipple in her mouth. Lana was losing her grip on reality as she teetered so close to the edge. Finally, she closed her eyes and screamed as Ronnie nudged her over into oblivion.

When Lana could breathe normally, she kissed her way to Ronnie's center. She licked and sucked her while she rubbed her clit with her fingers. Ronnie dug her fingers into Lana's shoulder as she rode out the waves of orgasms.

"We should get ready," Lana said.

"Yeah. Let's hop in the shower."

They made love in the shower, then rinsed off and got dressed. Lana put on a pair of shorts and a pink golf shirt while Ronnie dressed in her usual black outfit. They enjoyed a cup of coffee, then Lana followed Ronnie to the studio.

The shoot went wonderfully and when it was over, Lana changed back into her street clothes. Ronnie had Devon go pick up lunch for them, which they ate in comfortable silence.

"So, what are you going to do this afternoon?" Ronnie finally said.

"I don't know. Laundry, probably."

"Well, my next shoot should be pretty easy, so I should be home around five."

"Great. I'll do some grocery shopping and get dinner started."

"That'll be great."

The rest of the crew was back from lunch, and Lana knew it was time to go. She wished she could stay with Ronnie but knew she had work to do.

Ronnie walked Lana to the door and kissed her gently.

"I'll see you in a couple of hours," she said.

"Okay. Don't work too hard."

One more kiss from Ronnie and Lana let herself out of the studio. She looked around the parking lot, not wanting to get accosted again, and seeing the coast was clear, headed for her car. When she got to her car, she wanted to scream. All four of her tires had been slashed. Damn security. They were supposed to watch for Whitney. She had no doubt she'd done it.

Lana sat on the bench in front of the building and called the cops. She was determined to file a report and hopefully send Whitney to jail. The police showed up and took her statement, as well as pictures of the tires.

"Do you know if those cameras work?" one of the officers asked her.

"I don't, but I'd assume they do."

"Do you have any idea who might have done this?"

"Yes, I do. A woman named Whitney. She's been harassing me for a while now."

"And what's her last name?"

"I don't know. But Ronnie would."

"Who's Ronnie?"

"She owns the studio inside."

The officer looked at her partner.

"Go find this Ronnie person and find out if these cameras work."

"You can't bother Ronnie now," Lana said. "She's in the middle of a shoot."

"Well, she's just going to have to postpone the shoot. We need to speak to her."

The officer disappeared inside the building. Lana sat shaking on the bench. She hated to disturb Ronnie, but they were right. She might have answers for them.

In no time, Ronnie was outside. She knelt in front of Lana.

"Are you okay, baby?"

"I'm fine. Just a little shaken up."

"So, what happened? Your tires are slashed?"

"Yes. And you and I both know who did it."

Ronnie dropped her head.

"Yeah. I suppose we do."

"So you agree with Ms. Ferguson?"

"I do. I think it was probably Whitney."

"Does Whitney have a last name?"

"LaRoche."

"And do you have her address?"

"I don't. But I know where she lives."

Lana listened as Ronnie gave directions to Whitney's apartment. She felt like she was in the middle of a bad dream. And she would wake up any moment. It wasn't that she was worried about the costs of new tires. Lana made excellent money and had substantial savings. It was the feeling of being violated. And unprotected. And the studio was supposed to be one of the two places she would be safe. That and home. Clearly, that wasn't the case.

The other officer was back.

"Any news on the cameras?"

"Yeah. They work, but the person was wearing an overcoat and hat, so it's impossible to see them."

"Damn," Lana muttered.

"It's okay. We'll still question this Whitney person. But just know, it's not looking good."

"Thank you, though," Lana said. She looked at Ronnie. "You should get back to work."

"I think I'll cancel my afternoon so I can spend it with you."

"That's not necessary. I'll just have my car towed and have four new tires put on. I can do that. You get back to work."

"Are you sure?"

"Positive."

Ronnie kissed her, then disappeared back into the building.

"Okay, well, I think we've got all we need for now," the officer said. "We'll get back in touch with you if we learn anything."

"Sounds good. Thanks for coming out."

"No problem."

One of the officers gave Lana her card, then got in her car and they drove off. Lana sat on the bench for a few minutes longer, trying to gather herself. She called a tow truck and told them which tire shop to take her car to.

She got out of the truck and waited for the tires to be put on. It didn't take long, and soon she was on her way. She went to the grocery store and got home just as Ronnie was pulling into the driveway.

"Hey, baby," Ronnie said.

"Hi."

Ronnie helped Lana unload the groceries and carry them inside.

"Hey, I'm really sorry about your tires," Ronnie said.

"It's not your fault."

"But I feel like it is."

"No. It's Whitney's. She's clearly unstable."

"Right. But if I'd never slept with her, this wouldn't be happening."

"You couldn't have known, Ronnie. I appreciate what you're saying, but please don't blame yourself."

"I'll try not to."

"I just realize now that we need better safeguards in place. I thought the studio was safe."

"So did I."

"And what's she going to do next?"

"That's what I'm afraid of."

"Me, too."

CHAPTER FOURTEEN

The following morning, they made love leisurely since Ronnie didn't have to be at the studio until just before ten. Lana stretched next to Ronnie, feeling completely satiated.

"So, what are you going to do today?" Ronnie said.

"I don't know. I know it's silly, but I probably won't leave the house. I don't want to run into Whitney."

"Oh, baby. I don't blame you. I just hate you having to live in fear."

"Yeah. Me, too. But I do, so I'll just stay home. I can do some laundry and file a claim with my insurance company for what happened yesterday. I'll find things to do to keep me busy."

"And I should be home a little after three."

"Yay."

Ronnie smiled.

"I sure am crazy about you, baby."

"I'm crazy about you, too, Ronnie."

"Okay. I'd better get in the shower."

"I'll get your coffee started."

Lana made coffee and was sipping her first cup when Ronnie came down the hall looking handsome and smelling faintly woodsy. She made Lana's heart race.

"Do we have time for me to take you back to bed?" Lana said.

Ronnie laughed.

"I wish. You save that thought for this afternoon."

Lana pouted, and Ronnie took her lower lip in her mouth and sucked on it.

"Better?" Ronnie said.

"No." Lana laughed. "But I'll survive."

"Good."

"Now I've got to get going. I'll see you this afternoon."

"Sounds good to me."

"Enjoy your day."

"You, too."

Lana closed and locked the door behind Ronnie. She padded down the hall and ran a hot bath with extra bubbles. When she was relaxed in the tub, she played over their morning's lovemaking. She hadn't been kidding when she'd told Ronnie she needed her again.

She skimmed her hand down her body and found herself wet and ready for action. She leaned her head back and closed her eyes while she teased her clit. She dragged circles around it again and again until she could stand it no longer. She rubbed her clit until she called Ronnie's name as she rode out her orgasm.

Lana relaxed in the tub for a while afterward. The bath water was tepid when she rinsed off and got out. She grabbed a load of laundry and got it going. Then she made some popcorn and settled in front of the television with a movie.

She must have dozed at some point because she awoke to the sounds of the neighbor's dogs barking and squealing tires. Wondering what was up, she peered outside. There was a gash that ran the length of her car.

"Shit."

She put on some clothes and called the cops. She found her report number from the previous day's incident and gave it to the officers when they arrived.

"Are you sure those scratches are new?" one officer said.

"They're not just scratches. They're gashes. And yes. I'm sure they're new."

"They couldn't have happened at the tire store yesterday?"

"No. Absolutely not."

"Do you have any enemies, Ms. Ferguson?"

"Just one. Whitney LaRoche."

"And why is she your enemy?"

Lana sighed.

"It's a long story."

"Try me."

"She used to sleep with my girlfriend. Since Ronnie and I have been together, she's been insanely jealous."

"What else has she done?"

Lana recounted every event from the slashing of the tires to her showing up in a trench coat demanding a threesome. She was sure to include her attempt to scratch Lana's face at Madeline's.

"Wow. Sounds like she's got a screw loose, for sure."

"Yes. And now this. But I don't know how to prove it was her."

"Well, we've dusted the car for fingerprints, so we can compare hers with any we lift."

The other officer walked up.

"Looks like whoever did this wore gloves. There aren't any fingerprints at all."

Lana felt like she'd been punched in the gut. There had to be something they could do to catch her.

"Can you think of anyone else who might have a grudge against you?"

Lana shook her head.

"No one."

The officer gave her his card and said to call if she had any other issues. She took it and watched them drive off, feeling naked and vulnerable.

She called her insurance company and filed a comprehensive claim. They told her the name of the body shop they used and gave her a claim number.

"Remember, you'll be responsible for your deductible which is two hundred and fifty dollars."

"Thank you," Lana said and hung up the phone. She called the body shop and made an appointment for the following day. Then she called the rental car company to pick her up from the auto shop. By the time everything was done, she was still shaking, and checked to see that Ronnie should be home any minute.

She poured a glass of wine and sat on the couch, trying to soothe her frayed nerves. She heard Ronnie's truck in the driveway, but it was a few minutes before she let herself in.

"Baby, have you seen your car?"

"Oh yeah. The cops have been here, and I have an appointment tomorrow at the body shop."

"This has gone too far," Ronnie said.

"Tell me. But there's no way to prove it's her."

"That can't be true."

"It is. And there's no way to stop her."

"Shit." Ronnie sat next to Lana on the couch. "I'm so sorry, baby."

"Yeah. Me, too."

Lana handed her wine to Ronnie who took a sip and handed it back.

"I feel so helpless and I'm not used to that feeling," Ronnie said.

"I know. It's frustrating and unnerving to say the least. I never know where she's going to strike next. I'm not safe in my own home."

"At least she can't get to you," Ronnie said. "It's bad enough what she's doing to your car, but she can't touch you."

"I hope you're right. I really hope you're right. She's got me afraid to leave the house."

"Don't. Be brave. She's not gonna get you."

Lana burrowed against Ronnie, feeling instantly safer. She took another sip of wine.

"You want a glass of wine?" she said.

"I'll get it. And I'll bring you a refill."

"Thanks."

"No problem, baby."

Lana thought back to their morning and the promise of an afternoon of lovemaking. And now, thanks to Whitney, she wasn't in the mood. Whitney was winning and that pissed her off. She took her glass of wine from Ronnie who sat back down on the couch next to her.

"I wish I had something to say."

"I think we need to forget about it. She's disrupting our life, and that's what she wants to do. We can't let her win."

"Well, what can we do to forget about it? You wanna watch some TV?"

"No. I want you to kiss me."

"Gladly."

Ronnie leaned in and brushed Lana's lips with hers. Lana held on tightly and ran her tongue over Ronnie's lips. Ronnie opened her mouth and their tongues tangoed together. Lana lost herself in the kiss. Soon her pulse was racing with a familiar need.

Ronnie broke the kiss and stood. She set her wine glass down and took Lana's from her.

"Shall we take this to the bedroom?"

"We shall."

They walked hand in hand to the bedroom where Ronnie stripped Lana before quickly undressing herself. They fell onto the bed together. This was just what Lana needed. To be taken by Ronnie and claimed as hers. Ronnie ran her hand over Lana's body before slipping between her legs. She delved inside her, and Lana moaned her appreciation. Ronnie moved in and out over and over, and Lana felt the tension grow. She knew she was close. Her muscles in her stomach tightened as she fought to maintain control. But it was a losing battle. One swipe on her clit from Ronnie sent her soaring high above her body. When she was back, she couldn't fight the desire to please Ronnie.

She kissed down her body, pausing briefly to tease and please her small breasts. She kissed lower until she was where her legs met. She licked the length of her before plunging her tongue deep inside as far as it would go. She lapped up all the juices flowing there. Her face was covered in Ronnie's essence before she moved to her clit, which she licked ferociously until Ronnie pressed the back of her head against her and called her name as she came.

They lay together like that until Ronnie's stomach grumbled.

"Oh yeah," Lana said. "I guess it's time for dinner."

"I hate to get out of bed, though."

"We'll be getting back in soon enough," Lana said. "Now, come on."

They got up and dressed.

"Oh, by the way," Ronnie said as they walked out to the kitchen. "While I was getting wine earlier, I called and cancelled my first couple of shoots in the morning. I want to go with you to the auto body shop."

"That's not necessary, Ronnie."

"It may not be necessary, but it's what I want to do. Besides, Whitney was my first shoot."

"Ugh."

"Tell me. I'd rather be with you. Besides, you're gonna need a lift back, right?"

"No. I made arrangements for a rental car to be delivered."

"Oh. Good idea. Well, I'd still like to go with you."

"Okay. I'd like to have you there. I just feel bad about you missing work."

"Don't worry about it. I'm not sure I can photograph Whitney objectively. I may have to talk to Madeline and tell her I won't photograph her anymore."

"I think that would be wonderful."

"Yeah," Ronnie said. "I thought you would like that."

Ronnie went out to fire up the grill. She seasoned the steaks and drank her wine while she supervised the cooking of them. Lana was in the house making a salad. Ronnie thought how happy they were. They were completely blissful or would be if it weren't for Whitney. Damn her!

She'd been surprised Lana was in the mood to make love that afternoon. Ronnie sure hadn't been. Until they'd kissed. That always put Ronnie in the mood. She smiled at the thought of their lovemaking that afternoon. Even after everything Lana had gone through, they'd still come together in bed. And it had been wonderful.

Lana was out with the salad and plates and silverware.

"How are those steaks doing?" she said.

"They're ready. Thanks for bringing the plates out."

"Thanks for cooking dinner."

They ate in the warm summer evening, and Lana poured them each another glass of wine.

"I'll take mine while I do the dishes," Ronnie said.

"I'll help."

"No. You go relax. I've got it. Honest. I'll meet you in the living room in a few."

Lana kissed her and walked out of the room.

Ronnie wanted to be alone with her thoughts again. She had to figure a way to get back at Whitney. She could refuse to photograph her, but she was popular and people paid big bucks for her. Still, it wasn't like Ronnie didn't have enough models to keep her busy.

She finished the dishes without a solution. She sat on the couch with Lana.

"What's on your mind?" Lana said.

"This whole Whitney fiasco."

"I thought I'd gotten your mind off that earlier."

"And you did. But now it's back. I think I'm going to call Madeline and let her know I won't photograph Whitney again."

"Are you sure? Doesn't she bring in a lot of money?"

"Sure. But I'm so busy I'm turning models away anyway. This way I'll have room for more."

"Okay. I just think it may cause her to go even more ballistic."

"What more can she do?"

"I suppose you're right."

They finished their wine and went back to bed where Lana curled up against Ronnie, and she held her all night long.

In the morning, they made slow, passionate love in bed before continuing it in the shower. Ronnie was in a fantastic mood by the time they got out and dressed. She was relaxed from all the sex, but also happy to have time to spend with Lana. They were sipping their coffee when there was a knock at the door.

"Don't answer it," Lana said.

"Baby, relax. I'll go get it. You stay here."

She opened the door to find Whitney standing there.

"What the hell are you doing here?"

"You cancelled my shoot this morning. I demand to know why."

"Personal reasons. If you have a problem, take it up with Madeline."

She went to close the door, but Whitney put her foot in the way.

"Bullshit. You never cancel shoots."

"I have some personal business to take care of this morning, thanks to you."

"What's that supposed to mean?"

"If you must know, we're taking Lana's car to the shop this morning to take care of your handiwork."

"I don't know what you're talking about."

"Bullshit. Now, leave my house or I *will* call the cops. I'd love to see you taken away in handcuffs."

Whitney stood as if trying to decide her next move.

"Well, when are we going to do our shoot?"

"I don't know. I may never photograph you again if you don't grow up."

"I am a grownup. And don't you dare threaten me like that."

"Never mind. I'm going to call Madeline as soon as I get a chance."

"You wouldn't dare."

"Watch me. Now get out of here."

She slammed the door in Whitney's face and locked and bolted it.

Ronnie walked back to the kitchen where she saw tears in Lana's eyes.

"She scares me, Ronnie."

"Don't be scared. I've effectively just cut her out of our lives. Relax, baby."

"You sure she's not going to be angrier?"

"She'll get over it. We won't have to deal with her anymore. Now, come on, we need to get to the body shop."

They drove in silence, with Ronnie lost in her thoughts about Whitney. She sure hoped she wasn't poking the bear by deciding not to photograph Whitney anymore. She prayed she'd made the right decision. She'd feel sick if Whitney escalated. But what more could she possibly do?

They arrived at the body shop, and Ronnie stood with Lana while the repairman looked over her car.

"Wow. Someone really wanted to mess up your car," he said.

"Yeah. It was someone with a vendetta," Lana said.

"I guess. Okay. If you two want to wait inside, I'll be in in a minute with an estimate."

While they waited, the rental car arrived. Lana filled out all their paperwork and was given the keys. The driver got into a waiting car and drove off.

"At least you have a nice ride while yours is getting fixed," Ronnie said.

"Yeah. At least there's that."

The repairman came in and went over the costs for repairing her car. Ronnie held Lana's hand while he went over everything.

"That's a lot of money," Lana said.

"At least you have good insurance," he said.

"True."

"Okay, if you'll sign here and here, we'll get started. It should be ready in a few days."

"Thank you."

"No problem. And don't worry. She'll be as good as new."

Lana signed the forms and handed the clipboard back to him.

"Great," he said. "You're free to go."

They drove back home.

"How do you like your rental?"

"It's nice. I hope she doesn't attack it."

"Yeah. Me, too."

Chapter Fifteen

Ronnie got to the office a little past twelve. She'd stayed and had lunch with Lana before leaving her alone. Lana was still shaken up and Ronnie hated leaving her alone, but she had work to do. The first thing she did was call Madeline.

"Hello?" Madeline said.

"Madeline, it's Ronnie Mannis, the photographer?"

"Of course. To what do I owe this pleasure?"

"Well, unfortunately it's not really a pleasure call."

"Oh dear, what's going on?"

"I'm calling to tell you that I can no longer work with Whitney LaRoche."

There was silence on the other end.

"Are you sure?" she finally said.

"Positive. I'm sure someone else would love to pick up her shoots but it can't be me."

"Would you mind telling me why?"

"It's personal. She won't leave my girlfriend alone. She's attacked her and her car here at the studio and attacked her car in my driveway. I'm afraid of what she'll do if I continue to have contact with her."

"I'm so sorry to hear that. Okay. I'll let her know."

"Thank you."

Ronnie hung up and took a deep breath. She needed to get Whitney out of her head so she could focus on her job.

She still had an hour before her shoot, so she called everyone and cleared her weekend. She thought Galveston would help Lana relax.

Her model arrived, and Ronnie got the set ready while she changed. It was all set when she came out of the dressing room. Ronnie gave the model instructions, and she followed them well. Ronnie worked the camera as did the model, and after an hour and a half, they were done.

"You did great work," Ronnie said.

"Thank you."

"You can change back to your street clothes now."

The model left, and Ronnie told everyone they were through until Monday. She locked the door behind her and headed home, excited as usual to see Lana.

"Hey, baby, I'm home," she called as she locked the door behind her. There was no answer, so she walked through the house looking for her. She found her sound asleep on the bed. Ronnie couldn't blame her for sleeping. It was a nice escape from everything that had happened lately. Ronnie climbed into bed and wrapped her arms around her.

Ronnie had just dozed off when she felt Lana stir. She checked to make sure she was okay only to find her wide-awake.

"Hey, baby."

"Hi. When did you get home?"

"A little while ago. How long were you asleep?"

"I don't know. Longer than I'd meant to be. I'm sorry I wasn't awake when you got home."

"It's all good." Ronnie kissed her forehead. "Hey, I had an idea today."

"Yeah? What's that?"

"I thought we'd go to Galveston. How does that sound?"

"You don't work this weekend?"

"I cleared my schedule. I work enough hours. I need to think about not working weekends anymore. I mean, now that we're together and all. Wouldn't it be nice to spend our weekends together?"

"If you think you can afford to."

"I do. Believe me, I'm not hurting for money. And I won't do it all at once. I'll start by cutting back, okay?"

"Sounds great to me."

"So, Galveston?"

"Yeah. When do you want to leave?"

"As soon as we can get packed."

"Oh. Okay. That sounds good. It'll be nice to get away from everything for a couple of days."

Ronnie got a suitcase and they packed for the weekend. She put the suitcase in the back seat of her truck. She came back in and found Lana reaching for her keys.

"What are you doing? We only need one car."

"I don't feel comfortable leaving the rental here. I want to drive it, too."

"Okay. That makes sense. I'm sorry you're living in fear, baby."

Lana shrugged.

"You're not responsible for her actions. I just wish there was something we could do to put her away."

"We've threatened her enough. And the cops have been on her case. She's probably learned her lesson by now."

"I hope so."

"Well, I don't mind leaving my truck here, so we can ride together in the rental."

"I really think I'd feel safer if you bring your truck, too. I don't want you taking any chances, either. Let's just bring both cars."

"Okay, baby. If that would make you feel better."

"Thanks."

They kissed good-bye and Ronnie headed off down the road with Lana following close behind. They pulled onto Seawall and Ronnie rolled down her window and inhaled the salty air. She smiled to herself. She loved Galveston, and it made sense that she'd share it with her favorite woman.

She drove to their subdivision and pulled into her driveway. Lana pulled in behind her.

"Hey, baby," Ronnie said. She kissed Lana, who snaked her arms around her neck and pulled her close.

"Hey back," Lana said when the kiss had ended.

"Let's get upstairs," Ronnie said.

She carried the suitcase and the ice chest upstairs while Lana opened the blinds and made the place homey. Ronnie took the suitcase into the bedroom. She turned to see Lana standing behind her.

"What's up, baby?"

"I need you, Ronnie."

"You've got me."

"You know what I mean."

Ronnie looked into Lana's eyes, dark with lust, and felt her insides melt. She was happy to give her just what she needed. She took her in her arms and kissed her passionately, letting her know she was the only one for her.

She pulled Lana's shirt over her head and unhooked her bra. She brought her hands up to caress and knead her firm breasts, making her nipples pebble. She skimmed her hands lower and unbuttoned Lana's shorts, then unzipped them and pushed them to the floor. Lana stood only in her thong, and Ronnie thought she would explode at the beauty of her.

Lana stepped back and took Ronnie's shirt and undershirt off. She bent to lovingly lick her nipples while she fumbled with the buttons on her jeans. She finally got them undone and Ronnie sat on the bed and kicked off her boots, then took her jeans off. She stripped out of her boxers while Lana made short order of her thong.

They fell into bed together, and Ronnie lay on top of Lana with her knee pressed into her wet center. Lana ground into her, further aroused Ronnie. She moved her knee and replaced it with her fingers. She used her knee to force her fingers in deeper and deeper, and Lana was soon writhing on the bed. Ronnie slid her thumb over Lana's swollen clit and Lana cried out as she clamped around Ronnie over and over again.

When Lana had settled down, Ronnie slid out of her and held her close.

"Don't ever leave me," Lana said.

Surprised by the statement, but pleased by the sentiment, Ronnie responded. "I never will."

"Promise?"

"I promise."

Lana made love to Ronnie, tenderly yet passionately. The connection between them was more apparent than ever as Ronnie climaxed.

They lay there after, relaxing in each other's company until Ronnie's stomach growled.

"You're hungry," Lana said.

"Yeah. Aren't you?"

"I could eat."

"I brought salmon and steak. Which would you prefer?"

"Ooh. Steak sounds good."

"Great. I'll get the grill going."

She got out of bed and pulled on a pair of shorts and a muscle shirt. Lana got dressed as well and headed to the kitchen to make a salad. Ronnie contemplated their lovemaking while she cooked. There was something different about it. The intensity was deeper than usual. Something had definitely shifted between them. Were they falling in love?

She didn't have time to ponder it any longer, as dinner was ready. They ate at the picnic table and sipped some wine.

"So, are you okay, baby?" she said.

"I'm great. Why?"

"Did it seem like there was something different about our lovemaking to you?"

"Yes. Like there was more emotion involved or something. I don't know. But I liked it."

"Me, too."

After dinner, they refilled their wine glasses and went for a walk along the beach. It was a warm evening and the wind had died down some, making for a lovely walk. They held hands and passed several other couples out for an evening stroll as well. When it started getting dark, they turned around and headed back to the house.

They got inside and sat on the couch together.

"It's nice to be where it all began, isn't it?" Lana said.

"It really is."

They kissed for a while, and when their wine was finished, made their way to bed.

Ronnie took Lana to three solid orgasms and then Lana returned the favor. They lay together after, and Ronnie contemplated the way her heart felt so full around Lana. She finally had to admit what she'd been afraid to for so long.

She waited until she heard even breathing from Lana and then whispered in her ear.

"I love you, Lana."

"I love you, too, Ronnie," came the sleepy reply. Ronnie's heart raced. What did this all mean? She contemplated it until she finally fell into a restful sleep.

Lana woke up the next morning and stretched, finding the bed next to her empty. She frowned, got up, pulled a robe around herself, and made her way to the kitchen. No Ronnie. She poured a cup of coffee and looked outside to see Ronnie sipping coffee on the picnic table. She went out to join her.

They sat in companionable silence for a few moments, but Lana finally had to say what was on her mind.

"Did you mean it?" she said.

"Mean what?"

"You know what. Did you mean it?"

"Yeah. Yeah, I did."

"Good. Me, too."

Lana linked her fingers with Ronnie's. She brought her hand up and kissed her knuckles. Ronnie smiled at her. Lana could never remember being happier.

"You should come back to bed," Lana said.

"There will be plenty of time for that later. I'm itchin' to get in the water."

"Okay." Lana smiled. Ronnie could be so childlike. And she was adorable. "Can we at least have breakfast first?"

"Sure. Pancakes coming up."

Lana sat outside enjoying the morning breeze and thinking about their declaration of love. It felt so right, but was it too soon? Was it the stress from Whitney that had pushed them to say it? No, she thought. She did love Ronnie. With every ounce of her being. She smiled. It felt good to know she was with someone who loved her. She wondered if she should sell her house and move in with Ronnie. She figured that would be the next step, but something held her back. She wasn't quite ready for that step.

Ronnie brought out pancakes and syrup and they dug in.

"I think pancakes will always remind me of Galveston," Lana said. "I think this is the only place I ever eat them."

"I could make them at home sometime, you know."

"Yeah, but they're a bit decadent and I do have a figure to watch."

"Don't worry about that, baby. That figure isn't going anywhere."

"It would if I ate pancakes every day."

They laughed. Lana loved the sound of Ronnie's laughter. It was so easy and genuine. Ronnie worked so hard, she deserved to have time to laugh and relax. They cleaned up the dishes, put their suits on, and headed for the beach.

Once again, Lana had the ice chest filled with sandwiches, soda, and beer. And Ronnie had the towels and the chairs. They staked out a spot right in front of Ronnie's house and made their way out into the water.

They walked out past the second sand bar again, then dove into the water. Lana gazed lovingly at Ronnie with her short dark hair slicked back from the waves.

"You look so cute," Lana said. She closed the distance between them and kissed Ronnie's mouth. She tasted the gulf on her lips.

"You're pretty beautiful yourself," Ronnie said. She pulled Lana against her body and slid her fingers under the crotch of her bathing suit.

"Ronnie!" Lana looked around, but the people on the beach were mere specks and Ronnie's hand was underwater, so she knew no one could see what she was doing.

"Yes?" Ronnie said. She slipped her fingers inside Lana.

"Oh, God. Yes. Just like that."

"I thought you'd be okay with this." She smiled.

Lana rocked against Ronnie's hand until she could take no more. She reached her own hand between her legs and stroked her clit until she buried her face in Ronnie's shoulder to keep from screaming too loudly as wave after wave of orgasm racked her body.

When she trusted her legs again, she moved away from Ronnie and they took turns diving in the water and playing on the sandbar.

"I don't know about you, but I'm starving," Ronnie said.

"Yeah. I could go for some lunch."

They held hands as they walked through the surf back to the shore. They dried off and ate their sandwiches. Ronnie had a beer and Lana had a soda. She couldn't remember a time she'd felt so relaxed. Until she thought of Whitney.

"I hope your house is safe," she said.

"Hm? Why wouldn't it be?"

"I don't know. I worry about Whitney."

"Baby. You're not supposed to be thinking about her here. That was the whole purpose of this weekend."

"I know. And I'm sorry."

"She can't get to us here," Ronnie said. "We're safe. And she wouldn't dare mess with my house. So go back to relaxing, okay?"

"Okay."

She finished her sandwich and sipped her soda as she watched the waves crashing before her.

"You about ready to get back in the water?" Ronnie said.

"Sure."

She finished the last of her soda and stood, waiting for Ronnie to take her hand. She was right. All was right in the world right at that moment. There was no reason for Lana to worry about anything.

They played in the waves the rest of the afternoon, and Lana finally claimed exhaustion, so they could go back to the house. She decided a shower before dinner would be nice. Ronnie decided to join her.

She lathered up Lana's back and rubbed her shoulders. Then she slipped her sudsy hands between her legs. Lana opened her stance so Ronnie could have easier access. Ronnie slid inside her, and Lana braced herself on the wall while Ronnie made perfect love to her. She moved her fingers in and out until Lana was begging for release. Ronnie reached around with her free hand and rubbed Lana's clit until she screamed as the orgasms cascaded over her. When she trusted her legs again, she finished rinsing off and turned her attention to Ronnie.

She dropped to her knees and buried her tongue inside her. She flicked it over her clit a few times and Ronnie cried out as she came.

They toweled off and dressed and Ronnie fired up the grill for dinner. They ate on the picnic table to the sight and sound of crashing waves.

"It almost makes me want to get back in the water," Lana said.

"We could do that. If you're serious."

"I think I'll be satisfied with a walk along the shore."

"Great. I'll top off our wine and we can head out."

They walked in the water while they sipped their wine. Lana felt the love in Ronnie's constant touches. She hoped Ronnie felt her love as well. Just in case, she said it out loud.

"I love you so much, Ronnie."

"Thanks. I love you, too. And I think we should start walking back so I can show you just how much."

Chapter Sixteen

Sunday night they were back in Houston. They'd had an excellent weekend at the beach, and Ronnie was relaxed and rejuvenated and ready to take on the world. They made love that night. It was slow, unhurried, and they brought each other over the edge time and again.

Monday morning, Ronnie woke Lana up when her internal alarm went off. Lana would be her first shoot, so she had to get up. Ronnie started the coffee while Lana took her shower. Ronnie longed to join her, but knew Lana needed to get in and out and on with her makeup, so Ronnie sipped her coffee and waited until it was her turn.

When Lana came out looking gorgeous and ready for her day, Ronnie jumped in the shower and quickly dressed.

"Do you want to ride with me?" she said.

"No, thanks. I'll take my own car."

"Okay. I'll see you there."

Ronnie headed out to open the studio. She enjoyed the peace and quiet, but soon the makeup artist and hair stylist were there, along with Devon.

"We're out of bottled water. Go pick up some, please." She handed Devon the company business card and watched as she left the studio. Ronnie set up Lana's shoot and had just sat down with a cup of coffee when Lana showed up.

Fortunately, Devon was back with water, so she could offer it to Lana, who took a bottle gratefully. She drank half of it down, then disappeared into the dressing room. Ronnie couldn't wait to see her come out in the bathing suit that had been provided for the shoot. It was a bikini, and she knew Lana would rock it.

When Lana came out, Ronnie had to hold herself back from peeling the bottoms off with her teeth.

"You look amazing," she said.

"Thank you. I feel naked, but if this is what the shoot calls for."

"It is indeed."

They worked together for the next two hours, and after Lana had agreed she liked the photos, Ronnie called it a success. Ronnie went to the kitchen while she waited for Lana to come out of the dressing room.

While she waited, Whitney appeared. She got right in Ronnie's face.

"How dare you?" she said. "You can't refuse to shoot me."

"I can and I did. Now get out of here or I'll have you arrested for trespassing."

"You wouldn't dare."

Just then, Lana came out of the dressing room.

"You!" Whitney said. "This is all your fault."

"Actually, it's all *your* fault," Ronnie said. "You wouldn't leave us alone, which left me no choice but to stop using you at my studio. There are plenty of other studios in town. Use them. Now leave."

Lana just stood there watching the exchange. Ronnie kept a close eye on her out of the corner of her eye in case Whitney did something and she'd need to protect her. Whitney turned to go, and then everything happened in slow motion. She grabbed the carafe of coffee and threw it at Lana's head. Lana ducked, and the coffee pot shattered on the wall behind her.

"Get the fuck out of here!" Ronnie said. "Now!"

"I'm leaving. I'm leaving. But you haven't heard the last from me."

When she was gone, Ronnie took Lana in her arms and held her as her tears fell.

"I'm so sorry, baby. She's not supposed to be able to get in here. I'll make sure security knows that."

"She tried to physically hurt me, Ronnie. Not my tires. Not my car, but me."

"I know, baby. I'm so sorry."

"It's not your fault. I know that, but now I'm even more afraid of her than before."

"I wish there was something I could say to make you feel better." But the truth of the matter was, Ronnie was scared for her, too. She no longer knew what Whitney was capable of, and it terrified her.

"Call security. Please? Let's make sure she doesn't get near us again."

"Excellent idea. You have a seat and I'll call them."

Security came and Ronnie ripped them a new one for letting Whitney in.

"She's not allowed on the premises at all. Not in the parking lot and definitely not in the building. Do I make myself clear? If I see her here again you'll be looking for new jobs."

When security had left, Ronnie sat next to Lana and pulled her close. She sat holding her until the next model showed up and Lana excused herself.

"I need to get out of here so you can work."

"No. Stay."

"But no one is allowed to be in here when you're doing a shoot."

"I'll make an exception for you. It's my last one of the day, so get comfortable and I'll get to work."

Ronnie called Devon to clean up the mess and to go and buy a new coffee pot.

"But be careful out there, Devon. I hope Whitney is gone, but I don't know for sure."

"You got it," Devon said. "You really got yourself into a fix with that one, didn't you? I hope you've learned your lesson by now."

"I did and I have. On second thought, take a security guy out to the parking lot with you."

"Are you sure?"

"Yeah. I don't trust her, and I don't want anything happening to you."

"Okay. I'll be back soon."

"Do you want a bottle of water?" Ronnie asked Lana.

"Yes, please."

She handed it to her, then set up for her next shoot. She gave her model her undivided attention as she took picture after picture. The shoot lasted several hours, but when it was done, Ronnie was happy with the results.

"You're free to get changed now." Ronnie told her and headed to the kitchen where she found Lana engrossed in a book on her phone. "Good book?"

"Hm? Yeah. It's a great book. Is your shoot over already?"

Ronnie laughed and kissed her.

"Yep. It's over and now we can head home. Well, once everyone leaves."

She texted Devon to see where she was, and Devon walked through the door.

"I'm right here, boss."

"Great. Perfect timing. I'll take that and you're free to go."

"Yeah? We're through for the day?"

"Yep."

The model came out of the dressing room followed by the hair and makeup artists.

"You all have a good day, okay? We'll see you here early tomorrow."

Everyone said good-bye, leaving Ronnie and Lana alone.

"You ready to head home now?" Ronnie said.

"Yeah. Do you think she's gone?"

"I sure hope so. But if not, don't worry, I'll be with you."

They made it to their cars with no incident and Ronnie got home just before Lana. She opened Lana's door for her and kissed her when she got out.

"Thank you," Lana said. "I needed that."

"Yeah? Me, too."

They entered the house and went to the living room to sit on the couch.

"Did you lock the door?" Lana said.

"Yes, I did."

"Thank you."

"No problem. Baby, I'll do everything in my power to keep you safe."

"I know you will. But there's a lot that's not within your power. She's clearly unstable and violent, and I can't help but be afraid."

"I'm sorry, baby." She pulled Lana close to her and kissed her forehead. They snuggled for a while until Lana's stomach growled. "Have you eaten today?"

"No. Have you?"

"No. You want me to make some sandwiches?"

"That would be great."

Lana followed behind Ronnie and leaned on the counter while Ronnie made their lunch. Ronnie put the sandwiches on plates and handed one to Lana.

"Do you want to eat outside?" she said.

"Yes. I think I'd like that."

"It's gonna be hot."

"That's okay. Your backyard is like a refuge to me."

They finished their lunch, and Lana stood and straddled Ronnie's leg. She slowly unbuttoned her own shirt and slipped it off. She stared into Ronnie's eyes, which darkened with lust.

"Let's get inside," Ronnie said. She took Lana's hand and led her down the hall to the bedroom.

Ronnie sat on the bed and Lana stood in front of her. Ronnie unhooked her bra and let it fall to the floor. She leaned forward and took first one and then her other nipple in her mouth. She sucked them in as far as she could and flicked them with her tongue. Lana held on to Ronnie's shoulders as her knees began to feel weak and she wasn't sure she could stand much longer.

She dropped onto Ronnie's knee and Ronnie groaned.

"You're so wet," she said. "I can feel you even through all these clothes."

"Let's get naked."

"Okay."

They quickly undressed, and Lana lay on the bed with Ronnie next to her, running her hand all over Lana's body.

"You're so beautiful," she said.

"So are you. Except you're more handsome."

Ronnie kissed her hard on her mouth while her hand slipped between her legs. She moaned into Lana's mouth as her fingers found her center. Ronnie thrust her fingers deep inside, and Lana arched off the bed, meeting each thrust. Ronnie had Lana breathing in short gasps. She was close. So very close. She reached down between her legs and rubbed her clit, and soon she was soaring into oblivion.

When she came back to her body, Lana kissed Ronnie on her mouth before kissing down her chest to her small but firm breasts. She took one into her mouth and played over it with her tongue. Then she kissed lower until she came to where Ronnie's legs met. She got comfortable between them and licked and sucked all over before thrusting her tongue as deep as she could. She lapped at Ronnie's satin walls before licking her way to her clit. She sucked it between her lips and flicked it with her tongue. Ronnie pressed her face into her.

"Oh, shit, baby. Oh, God, yes."

Lana kept at it until Ronnie arched off the bed, froze, then collapsed.

Lana moved up next to her and kissed her tenderly.

"I love you," Ronnie said.

"I love you, too."

Lana curved back against Ronnie who wrapped her arms around her, and they took a little nap.

She woke up later to Ronnie sucking and nibbling her inner thighs. She spread her legs farther, urging Ronnie upward. Ronnie took the hint, and Lana soon felt Ronnie's talented tongue on her most sensitive spots. She moved around on the bed, meeting each stroke. Ronnie finally moved her tongue to Lana's clit, and that was all it took for Lana to launch into orbit again.

When Ronnie was lying next to Lana, she wrapped her in her arms again.

"So, what would you like to do with the rest of the afternoon?" Ronnie said.

"You mean we can't just keep doing this?"

Ronnie laughed.

"Well, I suppose we could."

Lana stretched.

"I don't know. What do you want to do?"

"I feel like going somewhere. Wanna catch a movie or something?"

"I don't know. Why not go to the Black Hole and have some drinks? Maybe shoot some pool?"

"You shoot pool?"

"Not very well." Lana laughed. "But I enjoy playing it."

"Great. Let's get dressed and go."

They arrived at the bar and it was fairly empty. Ronnie went to the bar to get some quarters and drinks. Lana leaned against the pool table lest someone else decide they wanted to play. But no one did. Ronnie put quarters in and racked the balls.

Lana admired Ronnie's fine form as she did that. She felt that usual tug deep inside her and wished she'd had Ronnie one more time before they left. Oh well. The balls were racked, and Lana took her best shot at them.

She scratched. They laughed together, and Lana was embarrassed but determined. Ronnie knocked in two balls and it was Lana's turn again. She knocked a ball in and released a whoop. Ronnie took her in her arms and kissed her. Lana went again and missed.

Ronnie bent over the table, but before she could shoot, someone yelled, "What are *you* doing here?"

Lana looked from Ronnie to see Whitney standing there. She felt fear gather in the pit of her stomach.

Ronnie straightened up.

"We're shooting pool. What are you doing here?"

"I'm meeting friends. You never come here. Why are you here now? Who's stalking who now?"

"We're not stalking you." Ronnie laughed mirthlessly. "We just came here to have a couple of drinks and shoot some pool. Now, go meet your friends and leave us alone."

"We always play pool," Whitney said.

"There's another pool table. Knock yourself out."

Whitney glared at Lana.

"This isn't over."

"Sure, it is. You've done enough damage. So, unless you want me to call the cops right now, I suggest you move along," Ronnie said. "Now, go on."

They watched Whitney walk off. Lana moved into Ronnie's arms.

"I'm scared."

"Don't be. She's not gonna do anything in a public place."

"I hope you're right."

"I am. Now, stand off and let me run this table on you."

"Oh yeah, right." Lana smiled. She wanted to believe Ronnie about Whitney, but she just couldn't relax. She sipped her wine and tried to watch Ronnie, but she kept looking over at Whitney. It wasn't until Whitney's friends showed up that she settled down and enjoyed her game.

"You want another glass of wine?" Ronnie said.

"You think we should stay?"

"I think we shouldn't live our life in fear."

"Okay. I'll have another glass. And I'll rack the balls for another game."

Ronnie gave her quarters, then went up to the bar. Lana racked the balls and leaned against the table. She chanced a glance at Whitney who was shooting daggers her way. Lana turned away. She shuddered inwardly. Whitney had been an inconvenience, even with her slashed tires and keyed car, but that morning when she'd thrown a pot of hot coffee at her, she'd become someone to fear. She was beyond unstable and she was dangerous. Lana didn't want to find out just how dangerous she was.

Ronnie was back with their drinks, and Lana sipped her wine while Ronnie broke. They laughed and joked and enjoyed their second game of pool. Lana had almost forgotten Whitney was there. Almost.

"How are you doing?" Ronnie said.

"I'm okay."

"You still worried about her?"

"I'm sorry. I can't help it."

Ronnie kissed her.

"Better?"

"Much."

"Good."

They finished their drinks and Lana suggested they leave.

"Okay. If you're sure," Ronnie said.

"Yeah. I'm sure. I want to go out for Chinese food."

"That sounds delicious. Let's go."

Ronnie took Lana's hand and led her out into the bright sunlight.

"I forget how dark that place is," Ronnie said.

"Yeah, but it's nice. I like it there."

"Good. We'll have to come here more often."

They drove to their favorite Chinese restaurant and went inside. It was early, so they were seated immediately. They ordered and then sat back with their drinks.

"You're awfully quiet," Ronnie said.

"I'm sorry. I had fun. I really did. I just wish Whitney hadn't shown up. After what she did this morning, I'm really scared of her. I mean, seriously."

"And I'm telling you, you have nothing to be afraid of. I'm sure she got it out of her system this morning. I mean, she threw coffee at you. What more could she do?"

"I don't know. And that's what scares me."

Ronnie reached out and took her hand.

"Baby, there's nothing she can do to you. She won't be at my studio anymore, and she'd damned well better not be seen around my house. If she is, we call the cops. It's as simple as that."

"I know. But still, I feel unsettled when it comes to her."

"What can I do to convince you?"

"Nothing. This is something I'm going to have to work through on my own. But I appreciate you."

"I'm always here for you, baby."

They ate their dinner and drove home. Ronnie grabbed a beer and poured Lana a glass of wine. They snuggled together on the couch. They watched some TV and then it was time for bed. Ronnie kissed Lana passionately and Lana responded, then pulled away.

"Would you mind just holding me tonight?" she said.

"Are you sure?"

"Yeah. I'm sorry, but I really think I just need to be held."

"Whatever you need, baby. Whatever you need."

They climbed into bed and Lana backed into Ronnie, who held her close. She lay awake for quite a while. She heard Ronnie's breathing become even and knew she was asleep, but sleep eluded Lana. She couldn't turn off her brain and her brain was focused on Whitney.

CHAPTER SEVENTEEN

The following morning, Ronnie awoke at her usual time. Her first shoot of the day was with Lana at three, and she was looking forward to spending the morning with her. She was feeling amorous after having simply held Lana the night before, but she opted not to wake her by pleasing her. Instead, she got up and put the coffee on.

She heard Lana walk up behind her before she felt her arms around her waist and her luscious breasts pressed against her back.

"Good morning. I didn't expect you up this early," she said.

"I couldn't sleep without you. You want to come back to bed?"

Ronnie's heart soared. Heat coursed through her body. Nothing would make her happier. As she turned to kiss Lana, her phone rang.

"Shit. Work."

She picked up the phone and answered it. The person on the other end sounded frantic.

"Ronnie? It's Tiaza from Mademoiselle Houston. The photographer for our shoot today just called in sick. The nerve, I know. But we need these women photographed. I immediately thought of you. You're the next best thing to Pierre. We'll pay you well, and you can use your own studio. And, of course, you'll be credited in the magazine."

Ronnie was silent for a moment. What an opportunity. But what about her morning with Lana? And the promises it held?

"Ronnie? Are you there?" Tiaza said.

"I'm here. Just thinking."

"Well, think fast. We're running out of time."

"Okay. I'll do it," she heard herself say. "I'll be at my studio in an hour."

"Thank you so much! And believe me, we'll make it worth your while."

"I'm sure you will. Thanks for thinking of me."

She hung up and turned to see the look of disappointment on Lana's face.

"Sorry, babe. But this is a huge opportunity."

"It's okay, I guess. I'll go back to bed. Alone."

"Don't be that way. This is for Houston's premiere women's magazine. They need a photographer. And I'm available."

"But you weren't really available. We had plans."

"I'm really sorry."

"It's okay. I do understand. But I'm still bummed."

"I'll make it up to you." She took Lana in her arms. "I promise."

"I'll hold you to it." Ronnie kissed her, hoping to convey her need in the kiss. "And I'll bring you lunch around one."

"That'll be great. I'll see you then.

Ronnie showered and headed for the studio. She felt guilty for not spending the morning with Lana, but she'd have been a fool to say no to Tiaza.

She arrived at the studio and stopped at the security desk. She handed them one of Whitney's head shots.

"Just in case you lost the other photo I gave you. This person is not allowed on site," she said. "If you see her, make her leave or call the cops. It's up to you, but do not let her in."

When she was sure they understood, she went back to her studio and made coffee and set up for the morning's shoot. The models were familiar to her, and she was sure everything would go smoothly. Ronnie spent the time waiting for her drinking coffee and thinking about Lana. She was so happy to have Lana in her life. They balanced each other very well. She'd only been away from her for an hour or so, but she already missed her. She thought about calling her just to hear her voice, but she didn't want to wake her. She imagined her sleeping there in her bed, looking like an angel. She took a deep breath. Enough of those kinds of thoughts. She needed to focus on work.

The first model, Cynthia, came out of the dressing room and Ronnie went to work photographing her. Cynthia listened well and followed instructions. The shoot went smoothly, and after a couple of hours, Ronnie called it good.

She reviewed the pictures with Cynthia before dismissing her to the dressing room. They were both satisfied.

"You can go change into your street clothes now," Ronnie said.

She went to the computer and uploaded the pictures. Cynthia came out and thanked Ronnie for the shoot and left. Ronnie took down the set and set up for the next one. Christine. She hoped she wouldn't be late, but she was sure she would be. She sat down with a cup of coffee and waited.

Surprisingly, Christine was there right on time. She went into the dressing room and emerged all ready for the shoot a short time later. They went through the shoot, having to stop several times.

"Your head just isn't in this," Ronnie said. "You need to focus and listen to what I'm saying, okay?"

"You seem determined to make my life miserable. I only hope I can return the favor one day."

"Don't threaten me."

"Oh, it's not a threat. It's a promise."

Ronnie didn't worry about idle threats. She had a job to do. Ronnie hoped Christine understood and started the shoot again. Finally, Christine seemed to get it. She relaxed into the pictures and did just what Ronnie said. The shoot lasted a couple of hours, but finally, they had some great pictures and Ronnie was satisfied.

The final model of the day, Aaliyah, exited the dressing room looking fantastic in her red ball gown. She was a natural in front of the camera. Ronnie took picture after picture of her and was almost sad when the shoot ended.

"Thanks so much for doing this on such short notice," Aaliyah said after she'd approved the shots.

"My pleasure. If you ever need a freelance shoot, you know where to find me."

"Do you have a card?"

Ronnie reached into her back pocket and pulled out her card case. She handed a card to Aaliyah.

"Call me anytime," she said.

"Thank you." Aaliyah went into the dressing room to change

Ronnie settled in with a cup of coffee and waited for Lana to show up with lunch. Aaliyah left, as did the hair and makeup artists.

"Do you want me to stick around?" Devon said.

"Nope. You're free to go. Lana should be here any minute now."

She checked her watch. It was almost one thirty. Where was Lana?

She was surprised yet again at how much she missed her when they weren't together. This being in a relationship was easier than she'd anticipated. She looked at her watch again. Lana was never late. She picked up her phone to call her.

Lana stretched and woke up slowly. She had plenty of time before she had to be at the studio. She was bummed Ronnie had taken that job this morning but had to admit the extra sleep felt good. She took a nice long shower and took her time applying her makeup and drying her hair. She went to her house and loaded up two more suitcases and brought them back to Ronnie's.

She put her clothes away and checked the time. She was right on schedule. She was all ready so she grabbed her keys and stepped outside.

She saw the movement in the corner of her eye and instinctively ducked. Something hit her cheek and neck, and it burned like a son of a bitch. She was in agony but managed to see a tall figure running away. She didn't know what had been poured on her, but she called 9-1-1. She told the operator she thought she had been splashed with acid and to please hurry.

The fire truck showed up first. They tried to get her calmed down, but she was frantic. She hurt so bad. They poured water on it and told her she needed to be in a burn unit. Their diagnosis was an acid burn, but it would take a doctor to know for sure.

They poured more water over it as they waited for the ambulance. Lana could hardly stand the pain. She was about to black out when the ambulance arrived. They loaded her up and she gave in to the blackness on the way to the hospital.

She came to in a cubicle with a kindly older gentleman looking down at her. He wore goggles, a gown, and rubber gloves.

"Ms. Ferguson? I'm Dr. Bremer. Can you hear me?"

Lana nodded.

"It looks like you were hit with sulfuric acid. How did this happen?"

The pain had subsided to a degree.

"Someone threw it at me."

"Someone did this to you on purpose?"

She nodded but stopped due to the pain.

"Yes. I think it was someone who hates me."

"We'll need to call the police."

"Please."

"Is there anyone else we should call?"

Lana thought of Ronnie, but she was sure she was deformed. She couldn't let Ronnie see her this way. But surely, Ronnie would worry if she didn't hear from her. She was probably angry at her for being late as it was.

"Ronnie," she said. "Please call Ronnie. Her number's in my phone."

"Okay. I'll have the nurse call her for you. We've been irrigating the burn, but we really need to get you out of those clothes. I'll have a nurse come in to help you undress. At least take off that shirt."

A nurse came in, similarly outfitted as the doctor. She helped Lana get her shirt off, then threw it away. She gave Lana a gown and helped her put it on.

"It's time to irrigate your wound again," the nurse said.

Lana tried to relax while the nurse washed her cheek and neck with cool water. It felt good on her burning flesh.

"How bad is it?" Lana said.

"It's bad." Dr. Bremer was back. "I'm not going to candy coat this for you. You have substantial burns on your cheek and neck. It's going to take some time for them to heal. We're going to keep you here for a few days."

Again, Lana went to nod but caught herself. She felt her eyes well with tears, and before she could stop them, they spilled over and trailed down her cheeks to her ears.

"Ah, kiddo," Dr. Bremer said. "We'll do all we can for you. And you can always get a skin graft if you choose once this is healed."

Lana suddenly felt very cold, and she started shivering.

"Poor kid. You're going into shock. Get her a heated blanket, stat."

Lana drifted out of consciousness and finally came to feeling warm and toasty. She tried to look around, but her neck hurt too bad. The nurse came in and irrigated her cheek and neck again.

"We'll be transferring you to a bed on our burn unit soon. Until then, you just relax."

"I'll try."

Left alone to her thoughts, Lana's brain went to Ronnie. What time was it? She was sure it was past one. Ronnie must be worried. Or pissed. But she couldn't think about that. She'd have to let her feel her feelings. Besides, Ronnie was likely out of her life for good now that she was a freak show.

Her career was over. The thought hit her like a ton of bricks. She'd never be able to model again. What was she going to do? She felt overwhelming despair.

The nurse came back in.

"You feel up to filling out some paperwork?" she said.

"Sure."

Lana filled out the intake form to the best of her ability. She filled in Ronnie's information as her emergency contact. And in the space that asked for her employer, she started to write down the agency, but realized that wouldn't be the case any longer, so she left it blank.

The nurse looked over the forms and looked at Lana, then back to the forms.

"You're not employed?" she said.

"I was a model. Clearly, I can't be anymore."

Lana's eyes teared up again.

"Do you have insurance?"

"Yes. My card is in my wallet in my purse."

The nurse got her bag from the chair and deposited it in her lap. Lana went through it until she found her wallet. She got it out and found her insurance card. She handed it to the nurse.

The nurse asked for her driver's license as well. Lana handed that to her.

"I'm just going to go make a copy. I'll be right back."

And she was back in no time. She irrigated Lana's burn again.

"I think they have a bed ready for you so I probably won't see you again. Good luck."

"Thanks."

Another nurse came into Lana's room, pushing a wheelchair.

"Hi. I'm Monica. I'm from the burn ward. I'm going to take you up there and get you settled."

Lana didn't say anything. She climbed out from under the warm blanket and sat on the edge of the bed. Monica brought the wheelchair over to her and she sat in it. She held her purse in her lap.

"Do you have everything you need?" Monica said.

"I think so."

"Great. Let's go."

How could she be so chipper, Lana wondered. She knew she had to look a fright, yet Monica didn't shy away from her. Lana decided she liked her. Lana tried to keep her face hidden from anyone they passed, but it hurt too bad. Fortunately, they only passed nurses and doctors, so no one showed signs of shock and horror. They stared a moment too long, but there was no look of disgust on their faces.

Lana still hadn't seen herself. She was curious but terrified. Her whole life had just been taken away from her. She couldn't wait until the police got there so she could tell them, and they'd arrest whoever did this, probably Whitney, and lock her away for good.

The walls inside the elevator were polished metal, but she still couldn't see herself. She figured that was for the best. The elevator opened on the eighth floor, and she was wheeled to her room. Fortunately, due to risk of infection, burn unit rooms only had one bed each. She didn't want to share a room with anyone. She just wanted to be left alone. She started shivering again.

"Climb into bed," Monica said. "I'll get you a heated blanket to help with the chills."

Lana did as she was instructed and was grateful when Monica was back with the blanket. She snuggled under it and lay patiently while Monica washed her burns again. The cool water felt good, although the intense burning from the beginning had subsided to a dull roar. After Monica cleansed her, she used some gauze to cover her cheek and neck.

"We don't want any infection getting in there," Monica said. "You're really lucky that acid didn't splash higher and get your eye."

"I guess I ducked just the right way."

"So, the police are outside. Are you up for talking to them?"

"Yes. Please. I want them to arrest the woman who did this to me."

"Okay. I'll show them in. But don't overdo it, okay? You're in a fragile state. If their questions get too much, you just ask them to leave. They can come back later, okay?"

"Okay."

Two officers came in. They were the same two who had come out about her slashed tires. She was happy her face was covered.

"Hello again, Ms. Ferguson," the woman said. Her badge said her last name was Winthrop.

"Hello, Officer Winthrop."

"Does this have anything to do with whoever slashed your tires?"

"It has everything to do with her I believe. I'm sure it was Whitney LaRoche."

"Ms. Ferguson, that's a very serious charge."

"I saw someone tall and thin. She's tall and thin."

"You must have been in a lot of pain, Ms. Ferguson. So, are you sure that's what you saw?"

"Positive."

Lana felt tears of frustration forming in her eyes. She tried to blink them back, but they spilled over, running down her cheeks and dampening the gauze covering her burn.

"Okay. Here's a clipboard. I want you to write down what happened, what you saw, then sign and date it, and give it back to me."

"Gladly."

She wrote down the details of the attack, signed, dated it, and handed it back to Officer Winthrop.

"I hope this will get her put away for a long time," Lana said.

"We'll certainly investigate it to the best of our abilities."

"There's nothing to investigate. I *saw* her."

"Is there any reason she would have to do this?"

"She's crazy." Lana drew a deep breath. "I'm sorry. She's jealous. She used to sleep with my girlfriend, but once we got together, obviously, that didn't happen anymore. Then, after she kept harassing me by slashing my tires and keying my car, Ronnie, my girlfriend, told her she wouldn't photograph her anymore."

"What does that mean?"

"Ronnie is a photographer. She takes pictures of models. She called Whitney's modeling agency and told them she wouldn't work with Whitney anymore. Whitney showed up at the studio the other day and threw a glass coffee pot filled with hot coffee at me."

"So you're thinking she's escalated."

"Yes."

"Did you file a report about the coffee pot incident?"

"No. I just chalked it up to a temper tantrum. I never dreamed she'd go this far."

Lana felt the tears threatening again. No matter how hard she fought to keep her composure, it was no use. The tears flowed freely.

"Okay. Well, thank you for your information. We'll be in touch."

"Please arrest her."

"We'll do our best."

They left and Lana sobbed. What was the big deal? Why didn't they believe her and go arrest Whitney?

Monica came in and saw Lana crying.

"Was that too much for you? You didn't have to put up with it if it was."

"No. It was fine. Just frustrating. I mean, I saw who did this to me. You'd think that would be enough. But no. They have to investigate? What the hell does that mean anyway?"

"Sh. Calm down. You've had a bad day and the frustration isn't helping. But I need you to try to stop crying if you can. Your gauze is wet and I'm going to have to change it, okay?"

Lana drew another deep breath. She managed to stem the flow of future tears.

"I think I'm okay now," she said.

"Good. Now you just relax, and I'll be right back with some more water and gauze."

Monica was back in a few minutes.

"I'm sorry," Lana said.

"For what?"

"For crying."

"Aw, honey, that's to be expected. You've been through hell today. Now lie back and let me take off this wet gauze."

Lana did as she was instructed. The cool water Monica rinsed her with felt good on her hot flesh. She covered it with gauze again. Then she pulled a little table up next to Lana's left side.

"What's that?" Lana said.

"We're going to get you started on IV fluids and antibiotics. We don't want to take any chance of infection. I'm also going to give you some pain meds to help ease the throbbing, okay?"

"Sure. That sounds good. What time is it, by the way?"

"It's a little after four. Now sit tight. This might sting a little."

But it didn't sting at all. Monica was obviously adept at what she was doing.

"All done. Now, I'm going to leave. If you need me, there's a button by your bed. I suggest you try to get some rest now, okay?"

"Okay."

She left Lana alone with her thoughts. By now Ronnie knew she wasn't going to show up. She wondered if they'd called her. Don't be ridiculous, she told herself. Of course they'd called. She should have left Ronnie out of this. She should have just let her go. It would have been easier than facing the rejection when Ronnie saw her disfigured face.

The pain meds had started to take effect. She was feeling a little woozy, but not in a bad way. She pulled the warm blanket around her and drifted into a drug-induced sleep.

Chapter Eighteen

R onnie was beside herself with worry. Lana hadn't shown up for her shoot and wasn't answering her phone. She dismissed everyone at the studio and hurried home to check on her. Maybe she'd just overslept, but that wasn't very likely. Lana was a professional. If she had a shoot, she'd make it. If she could.

Ronnie was surprised to see Lana's rental car sitting in the driveway just as it had been before she'd left for work. She opened the front door.

"Hey, baby. It's me," she called.

No answer. She went down the hall to the bedroom. The bed was made. She walked into the bathroom. No Lana, but all her cosmetics were in their place on the sink. She looked around the house for her purse but couldn't find it. So she had it with her. Where had she gone?

Ronnie pulled out her phone and called Madeline's office. She had to wait a few minutes before Madeline picked up.

"Ronnie? To what do I owe this pleasure? No problems with another model I hope?"

"No, ma'am. Nothing like that. Um, the thing is, Lana didn't show up for her shoot today. I'm at the house and she's not here. Her car's here, but her purse isn't. I don't suppose you've seen her today?"

"Oh. That doesn't sound like Lana to just disappear without a trace. I wish I could say I've seen her today, but I haven't."

"Hm. Okay. Thanks."

"And she's not answering her phone?"

"Nope. And now it's just going straight to voice mail."

"When was the last time you saw her?" Madeline said.

"This morning before I left for work. She was supposed to come by the studio at one with lunch."

"I'm really sorry, Ronnie. If I hear from her, I'll be sure and let you know."

Ronnie left her number, thanked Madeline, and hung up. She had no idea where to even start searching for her. She thought of Galveston, but she would have needed to take the rental car for that.

She sat on the couch and rested her head in her hands while she tried to think. She almost didn't register the knock on the door.

She opened it, hoping to see Lana. It was two police officers. Her stomach curdled. What if something really had happened to Lana?

"Hello. How can I help you?"

"Are you Ronnie Mannis?" Officer Winthrop said.

"I am. What's going on? Why are you here?"

"May we come in? We have a few questions for you."

"For me? Why? Is this about Lana? Is she okay?"

"We need to ask you about Whitney LaRoche."

"Come on in," Ronnie said. "And what do you want to know about Whitney?"

"Anything you can tell us."

Ronnie relayed every story she could think of about Whitney's animosity to Lana, including the coffee pot incident.

"Why would she behave that way?" Winthrop said.

"Because she's nuts."

Winthrop simply raised an eyebrow.

"I guess it all started when I was sleeping with Whitney. Which I did. Twice. She promised me it was all fun and games with no strings attached. And then I started seeing Lana and she got all jealous. After she'd slashed her tires and keyed her car, I decided I didn't want anything more to do with her. So I called her modeling agency and told them I wouldn't photograph her anymore. That's when she threw the pot of coffee at Lana. Now, will you tell me, is Lana okay? Do you know where she is?"

"Ms. Ferguson will be fine," Winthrop said.

"Oh, sweet Jesus, what has Whitney done now?"

"Thank you for your time, Ronnie. If we have any further questions, we'll be in touch."

Ronnie closed the door behind them and bolted the lock. Where the hell was Lana, and why were the cops investigating Whitney finally? Ronnie had an idea. She got in her truck and drove over to Lana's house. She pounded on the door until her hands hurt, but there was no answer.

With no other options, she drove home. It was then she noticed her favorite rose bush looked dead, almost burnt. She wondered what happened and reasoned nothing was going right for her that day.

She opened a beer and sat on the couch. She dialed Lana's phone again. Still no answer. Surely if something bad had happened to her, like if she had ended up in the hospital or something, she would have listed her as an emergency contact. So, she would have heard from them, right? She reasoned with herself there was no real reason to panic. Lana probably went somewhere and lost track of time. But without her car? None of it made any sense.

She had another beer and thought some more. That was all she could do. She felt impotent. Her mind whirled like a cat chasing its tail. She couldn't come up with anything. She finally finished her beer and decided she had better eat, even though she wasn't hungry. She went to their favorite Chinese restaurant, wondering if maybe she'd see Lana there. No joy.

She ate her dinner then went home. She turned on the television but couldn't focus. She couldn't imagine what had happened. She and Lana had seemed so solid. What could have made her disappear without a trace?

Finally, her eyelids were growing heavy so she went back to her room. She hated the idea of spending the night alone, but clearly Lana wasn't coming back. She tossed and turned all night, hating the empty feeling of the bed. She finally gave up around five and got in the shower. Regardless of where Lana was, she had a job to do. Maybe Lana would show up at the studio. If she was just leaving Ronnie, she could show up and break up with her there. The thought made Ronnie sick to think of, but at least she would know she was okay.

She had just stripped and was climbing into bed when her phone rang. Lana? She grabbed it. Unknown number. Should she even bother answering it? What if it had something to do with Lana?

"Hello?" she said.

"Hello. Is this Ronnie Mannis?"

"Yes." Ronnie told herself to calm down. "Who is this, please?"

"I'm calling from the Memorial Hermann Hospital Burn Unit. Did you not get the message I left on your phone earlier?"

Ronnie had a cold fist in her gut. This couldn't be good.

"Why are you calling me?" Though she already knew the answer. She was getting dressed while she waited for an answer.

"One of our patients who was admitted today requested that we call you."

"Oh, God. Not Lana. Please, not Lana."

"Yes. A Lana Ferguson."

"I'm on my way."

Ronnie hung up, tossed her phone on the bed, and finished getting dressed. She grabbed her phone and her keys and drove to the hospital. Her stomach was in knots the whole time. What had happened to Lana? Was Whitney somehow involved? No. That didn't make sense. She'd just have to find out when she got to the hospital.

She punched the elevator button ten times, wishing it would hurry up and arrive so she could see Lana. She was shaking with fear. What had happened, she asked herself for the millionth time. The elevator finally arrived and took her to the eighth floor. She practically ran to the nurses' station.

"I'm here to see Lana Ferguson," Ronnie said.

"And who are you?"

"I'm Ronnie Mannis. I believe you just called me?"

"Do you have some ID, Ms. Mannis?"

Ronnie fished out her driver's license and handed it to the nurse.

"Thank you. Sign in on this visitors form, please, and I'll have someone take you to Ms. Ferguson's room."

Ronnie felt like she was in a bad dream. Lana was really in the hospital. Why? She wished she could wake up and start the day all over again.

A nurse approached Ronnie.

"I'm Monica," she said. "I'll take you to see Lana now. Have you been briefed on what happened?"

Ronnie simply shook her head.

"Well, I'll let her tell you. There's a strong chance of infection so I'm going to have you scrub as soon as we get in her room. And, please, don't touch her face."

"Her face?"

"Are you ready? Come on."

What the hell did her face have to do with anything? She followed Monica down the hall, more confused with each passing minute.

Lana was asleep when they arrived and, as promised, Monica watched as Ronnie scrubbed her hands and arms. When she'd been approved, Monica led Ronnie to Lana's bed.

"It's best to let her sleep," Monica said. "But you can wait here."

"I'm awake," Lana said weakly. She opened her eyes, and Ronnie saw pain and fear in them.

"Lana, baby." Her heart dropped as she took in the dressing on Lana's face and neck and the emotions in her eyes. She went to the bed, leaned over it, and ran her fingers through her hair.

"Remember what I said about touching her face," Monica said.

"Oh, yeah." Ronnie straightened.

"I'll leave you two alone now." Monica left the room.

"What happened?" Ronnie said.

"Whitney threw sulfuric acid on me. I'm now deformed, so I can't be with you anymore. And I can't model either. My life is ruined."

"Damn her! How dare she? And fuck! If I'd turned down that job this morning and we'd spent the morning together like we'd planned, none of this would have happened."

"This isn't your fault, Ronnie."

"The hell it isn't. It's all my fault. I never should have left you alone." Ronnie's eyes grew wide. "And wait a minute. What did you say about us?"

"I can't be with you, Ronnie. I'm deformed. Mutilated. I can't burden you with that. Besides, you deserve someone who's attractive, not disfigured."

"But it's you that I want. I don't care about a little scar tissue."

"It's not a little. I haven't seen it yet, but it feels like hamburger under there. Not something I want you looking at for any foreseeable future."

"I think that's my choice. But I don't deserve you."

"How do you figure?" Lana looked genuinely surprised.

"I should have been with you. I shouldn't have left this morning."

"So we'd both be here in the burn unit? How would that have helped anything?"

"I don't know. I just feel so bad about this. I'm so sorry, Lana. How can I make this up to you? Can I ever?"

"You need to stop beating yourself up. This is Whitney's fault. No one else's."

Ronnie's stomach burned with guilt. She needed to prove to Lana how sorry she was.

"I know what I'll do," she said. "I'll go kick Whitney's ass."

"You'll do no such thing. Let the police handle this."

"But I can't sit idly by."

"You don't have to. You can leave, Ronnie. And I think you should. You don't have to stand by me. I'm a freak of nature now."

"I can't leave you, Lana."

"You have to. I won't have you tied to an unemployed, deformed version of my former self. Now go. Fly. Be free."

"Lana..."

"This isn't open for debate. Go find someone who's beautiful for you to spend your life with. Good-bye, Ronnie."

Lana turned away from her, and Ronnie knew she had no choice but to leave. Crushed and guilt-ridden, Ronnie walked out of the hospital room. She drove home and climbed into bed. It was the middle of the night, but sleep wouldn't come. She couldn't get over everything that had happened. She vowed to make it up to Lana. Somehow. Some way.

It was a rough night for Lana. The nurses were in and out all night, monitoring her vital signs and checking on her wound. It was just as well, as sleep escaped her. She lay awake pondering her future. She became overwhelmed at the thought of never modeling or seeing Ronnie again. Eventually, she cried herself to sleep, only to be woken up to have her soggy dressing changed.

She dozed again and was awakened when Monica came in with breakfast. Lana forced herself to eat, knowing she needed to keep her energy up. When she'd finished she decided to do what she'd been dreading the whole time.

"May I ask a favor?" Lana said.

"Sure. What?"

"Can I see myself?"

"You haven't looked at your burns yet?"

"No."

"Are you sure you want to?"

"I'm sure."

Monica seemed hesitant but went out and brought back a mirror.

"Now, remember, they haven't started to heal."

"Okay."

Monica held up the mirror and Lana's whole world spun. She felt the bile rise in her throat. She tried to stop it, but it was no use. She threw up all over Monica.

"I'm so sorry," she said.

"That's okay. You're not the first patient to do that, and I doubt you'll be the last. Now, let's get those burns dressed."

Lana lay there mortified. She couldn't believe what she looked like. She was disfigured beyond words. Her cheek and neck looked like raw hamburger. She knew she'd never work again. She heard Monica talking, obviously trying to soothe her.

"What?" Lana said. "I'm sorry. I wasn't paying attention."

"I asked what you do for a living."

Tears welled in Lana's eyes.

"Are you going to cry again?" Monica said. "Because I'll hold off on the gauze."

Lana fought to keep the tears in check, but they rolled down her cheeks, burning her raw skin.

"I was a model. I guess I'm not one anymore," she said.

"Oh, honey." She patted her arm. "I'm so sorry."

She handed Lana a tissue.

"I'm sorry. I'm just feeling sorry for myself," Lana said. "I'll get it together so you can apply new gauze."

She took a deep breath and let it out. Confident she wasn't going to cry anymore, she nodded at Monica.

"You sure?" Monica said.

"For the moment."

"That's all we can ask for."

She dressed Lana's wounds and then promised she'd be back to check on her, thus leaving Lana alone with her thoughts again. Time was passing so slowly, but the pain meds Monica had injected into her IV were starting to work their magic. She leaned her head back and closed her eyes and let the medication lull her to sleep.

❖

Ronnie hardly slept at all that night. She tossed and turned all night thinking first of Lana in that hospital room and then of Whitney, presumably walking around free. But was she certain it was Whitney? She flashed back to Christine's comment. Had it been an idle threat? It made her stomach hurt. She finally got out of bed at four and made some coffee and hopped in the shower.

She finished her shower and dressed and gelled her hair. She was ready to go, but it wasn't even six yet. She sat in the kitchen and drank some coffee. But she couldn't stand being home alone, so she headed for the studio.

She opened the studio and started the coffee. Then she set up for her first shoot of the day. She had nothing to do but wait. She poured a cup of coffee and sat at the kitchen table, absently flipping through the pages of a magazine.

She needed to get busy, to take her mind off Lana. She wanted desperately to assuage the guilt that consumed her for not being there to keep Lana safe. On top of that, she tried to process the fact that Lana had kicked her out of her life. It was too much to bear. Not that she deserved Lana, after what she'd done, but it killed her that Lana didn't think she deserved Ronnie.

Devon finally showed up.

"You look like shit, Boss. Are you okay?"

"Rough night. That's all."

"Is everything okay with Lana? Why didn't she show up yesterday?"

"Whitney." It was all Ronnie could say without choking up.

"Huh? What does that even mean?"

"Lana's in the hospital. That bitch Whitney threw acid on her face."

"Holy shit! Are you serious? How is Lana?"

"Not good. Not only is she in pain, she thinks she's too disfigured to model again."

"Oh no," Devon said. "Modeling is her life. Outside of you, I mean."

"That's the other thing. She doesn't think she's worthy of me anymore. She says I need to find someone beautiful to spend my life with. She doesn't think she deserves me."

"That's just crap. And shouldn't you make that decision?" Ronnie simply nodded. "So how are you doing? Should you take some time off?"

"No. I'll be okay. I need to work. I have to keep busy. I'll go see her tonight."

"Are you sure you're okay to work? Shouldn't you be with her? Does she have anyone else?"

"Not that I know of."

Ronnie sat silently thinking of Lana alone in a hospital bed and felt sad. Then she remembered who put her there and her anger boiled. She vowed to kick Whitney's ass, to make her pay for what she'd done. She was roused from her reverie when her morning model showed up for her shoot.

"Hi," Ronnie said. "We're all set up so go ahead and get changed."

Ronnie picked up her camera, determined to focus on the task at hand. The model came out of the dressing room, and she shot her for the next two hours, calling out instructions and making love to her with the camera. When they were through, they were both happy with the pictures.

Well, at least that was a good way to pass the time, Ronnie thought. She hadn't been able to think about Lana at all during the shoot. And another model had just walked in. It was good to be busy.

❖

Lana lay alone in her room with frequent check-ins by Monica. Finally, she came in to check her vitals one last time and bring her some dinner.

"My shift is over now," she said. "But the night shift nurse's name is Jackie and she's sweet as can be. If you need anything, don't be afraid to ask her, okay?"

"Okay."

Monica left and Lana had never felt more alone. She almost wished she had a roommate, someone to talk to at least. But then, she wouldn't want anyone to see her in the shape she was in. It was bad enough the nurses had to.

She managed to eat the horrible hospital food. She wasn't hungry, but reasoned she had to keep her strength up if she was going to heal. She turned the television on and tried to focus on a program, but all she could think about was all the times she'd watched TV with Ronnie. She missed her so much. The thought made her cry again. She could feel the gauze getting wet from her tears but was at a loss to stop them.

Jackie came in a few minutes later to get her empty plate.

"Oh, honey," she said. "You've been crying."

"I'm sorry."

"Oh, no. It's okay. I know this can't be easy for you."

"No. It's definitely not."

"Okay, well, let me take the tray away and I'll be back to rewrap your burns. Can't have wet gauze on them, you know."

She disappeared but was back a few minutes later. She unwrapped Lana's face and neck.

Lana awoke later. Her room was darkish. Jackie was there to take her vitals again.

"What time is it?" Lana said.

"It's nine o'clock. Do you need anything?"

"No. I don't think so."

Lana fell back asleep but didn't sleep peacefully. She had nightmares about disfigured beasts attacking her. She also was woken up every four hours to have her vitals checked. She finally gave up on sleep at some point when the room was still dark. She lay there listening to the sounds of the hospital around her.

She missed Ronnie. She wanted to call her, to tell her she'd changed her mind, that she wanted nothing more than to be with her forever. Again, she realized that wouldn't be fair to Ronnie, who would have no desire to be with her anymore. She started when Jackie came into her room.

"Good morning. You're up awfully early."

"Yeah. I had all sorts of nightmares, so I didn't want to sleep anymore."

"Oh. I'm sorry. That's not good. You need your rest to heal."

"Maybe I'll sleep some during the day."

"I sure hope you do. Okay. I'm going to put some salve on your burns now and redress them."

"Okay."

She held her breath while Jackie uncovered her burns. The fresh air hurt, but she gritted her teeth and dealt with it. She wouldn't cry. Not anymore.

The salve Jackie put on her wound was cool and felt good. She redressed them, and Lana was all set.

"Breakfast won't be served for another couple of hours," Jackie said. "But I might be able to get you a snack if you're hungry."

"No, thanks. I'm fine. I do hurt though."

"Yes. You're due for more pain meds. I'll go get them."

Lana leaned back and breathed carefully to try to keep the pain at bay. But Jackie was back with her pain meds shortly. Once they were in her system, Lana closed her eyes and dozed again.

She woke up next when Monica was there with her breakfast.

"I'm sorry to wake you," she said.

"That's okay." Her stomach growled. "I guess I'm hungry."

"Good. We've got to keep that strength up."

"Yeah. That's kind of what I figured."

"How's the pain?"

Lana thought for a moment.

"It's a dull roar. Not too bad."

"Well, you'll be due for more meds after you finish breakfast. And I'll check your wounds then, too."

She left, and Lana ate the scrambled eggs that she was sure were powdered. She ate the apple and drank her juice. She actually felt better, almost human.

Monica was back with her pain meds. She also changed and redressed her burns.

"Do they look any better?"

"You're a long way from healed. You've got a long way to go before they look better."

"Great. Just wonderful."

Monica patted Lana's arm.

"It's okay, Lana. It's hard to take sometimes."

"Yeah. I can't believe you guys can look at it day in and day out."

"We're a burn unit. Believe it or not, we've seen a lot worse. That doesn't minimize yours, though. Believe me."

Lana dozed some more and woke up when Monica came in to check her vitals.

"How are you feeling?" she said.

"Depressed."

"I can understand that. You know, it's visiting hours. Will someone be coming to visit you? That would help with the depression."

Lana thought again of Ronnie and wondered if she'd come by to visit. She doubted it. She wished she could call her, but it wasn't fair to think like that. Tears welled in her eyes again.

"There's no one," Lana said.

The tears spilled down her face, and Monica patted her arm as they fell.

"It's okay to cry, Lana. We'll just change your dressing when you're through."

"I'm sorry. I don't mean to make you do all that extra work."

"It's nothing. Now, are you okay?"

"Yeah. I think so."

"Okay I'll go get some more gauze."

Lana lay patiently while Monica administered to her.

"I gave you some more pain meds, too," Monica said.

"Thank you."

With more pain meds in her system, Lana closed her eyes and let sleep overtake her. She woke a couple of times when Monica came in to check on her, but outside of that, she slept like the dead.

She had no idea what time it was when she woke up to find Ronnie sitting in the chair by her bed.

"What are you doing here?" Lana said.

"I came to check on you."

Lana's heart melted. She was so crazy about Ronnie and was thrilled to see her. Besides which, she longed for some company other than the nurses'. But she had to be strong. She couldn't accept Ronnie's pity or anything else she had to offer.

"Thank you," she said. "But I gave you your walking papers. You're free to go. Don't feel obligated to come by the hospital."

"I don't feel obligated, Lana. I care and want to see how you're doing. Please don't try to push me away. I'm not going anywhere."

"Is this some way to rid yourself of guilt? You did nothing wrong, you know."

"I feel horrible about what happened to you. And, yes, I blame myself. But that's not why I'm here."

"You sure you're not doing some form of penance?" Lana said.

"I'm positive. Now, how are you feeling?"

"Like someone threw acid on me. How long have you been here?"

"Not long."

"What time is it?"

"It's about six."

As if on cue, Monica came in with dinner.

"Oh, good," she said. "I see you have company."

"Yes." Lana tried not to let her excitement and relief show. "What's for dinner?"

"Meatloaf, mashed potatoes, and peas. I want you to eat every bite."

"But I'm really not that hungry. And look at that mountain of potatoes. I'll never be able to eat all that."

"Carbs are important with burn victims. They help you heal. Now, eat up. I'll be back to get your tray and give you your pain meds in a little while."

Lana watched her leave and felt the tension between Ronnie and herself. It wasn't good. She needed Ronnie to understand she didn't want to see her again. But she missed her so much, it hurt almost as much as the burns.

"Eat up," Ronnie said. "Do you need some help?"

"No, thanks. I've got this."

She tasted the meatloaf. It wasn't bad. In fact, it was really good. And the potatoes were creamy and buttery. Before she knew it, she'd cleaned her plate. She sat back and patted her stomach.

"That was good," she said.

"Good. It was good to see you eat so well."

"Ronnie. Thank you so much for coming. I mean it, but you need to leave. You can't see me like this. I won't allow it."

"Who else is visiting you? Who else have you told? I can't stand the thought of you being here all by yourself."

Monica was back and cleared Lana's tray. She injected her pain medicine into her IV and told her good night.

"Jackie will be here to take care of you soon. I'll see you tomorrow."

"Good night, Monica."

"Thanks for everything," Ronnie said.

Monica paused at the door and looked from Ronnie to Lana and back, as if trying to gauge their relationship.

"You're most welcome. Thank you for being here for Lana. She really needs that right now."

After she left, Lana leaned back in the bed and closed her eyes.

"Did you hear that?" Ronnie said. "You need someone right now. Let that someone be me."

"I don't want to get your hopes up." Lana kept her eyes shut. "And there's no future for us now."

"I accept that. But I'm not going to just walk out of your life. That's not my style."

Lana opened her eyes and looked at Ronnie. She could feel the pain meds kicking in and knew she'd be asleep soon. She had to get rid of Ronnie before she said or did something that wouldn't be good for either of them.

"I'm going to rest now," she said. "You should leave."

Ronnie looked at her watch.

"Are you sure?"

"Positive. The pain meds kick my butt."

"Okay. I'll go. But I'll be back tomorrow."

"Ronnie. No. Please."

"You can't keep me away. Rest well."

She kissed Lana's forehead and left. Every nerve ending in Lana pulsated at the contact. She tried to be strong, but as soon as the door closed, she started crying.

CHAPTER NINETEEN

Ronnie pushed herself hard the next day. She'd booked four models so she wouldn't have any down time. She pushed her models hard and herself harder. At the end of the day, she was exhausted. She collapsed into a chair in the kitchen and opened a beer. Devon sat next to her with one of her own.

"So what's the story with Lana?" Devon said.

"I don't know. She's still in a lot of pain and she keeps trying to push me away. I can't leave her, though, you know? I mean, every time I look at her I'm reminded that it's all my fault, but I still can't stay away."

"It's not your fault, Ronnie. We all know it's all on Whitney. Which reminds me, have they caught her yet?"

"Not that I know of. Even though she seems tired of me, I think Lana would tell me if the cops contacted her with news."

"Yeah. I suppose you're right about that. So were you ever going to make an honest woman out of Lana? Or was she just another of your conquests? Maybe this was for the best."

"The best? How can you say that?"

"It kept you from breaking her heart."

"You're talking crazy.'

Ronnie took a good long look at her assistant. She was tall and thin with dark hair. Had Lana maybe seen her instead of Whitney that day?

"I'm just saying. Someone might have been protecting her from you."

"No. It was Whitney. It had to be."

"How can you be sure? You can't, can you?" Devon said.

Ronnie buried her face in her hands.

"I can't believe I let this happen to her. I should never have come into work that morning. I should have stayed home and protected her. Then none of this would have happened."

"You don't know that. Look, if someone wanted to hurt Lana or protect her from you, which they obviously did, they would have found a way."

"I don't know that I believe that. I don't think she would have done it in front of me. I really don't."

"She might have doused you both with acid. And then where would you be?"

"You sound like Lana," Ronnie said.

"I always thought she was a smart woman." Devon grinned.

Ronnie felt sick to her stomach. Lana was lying there in the hospital in pain with no company but the nurses and here she sat drinking a beer. She chugged the remainder and stood.

"I need to get going. I'm going to go see Lana."

"Tell her hey for me."

"I will."

Before she could leave, a security guard walked in.

"Hey, Joe," Ronnie said. "What's up?"

"Hey, Ronnie. I just wanted to tell you. You know that Whitney woman you told us to be on the lookout for?"

Ronnie felt her skin crawl.

"Yeah."

"Well, she was just here. We caught her before she could get down the hall. She made quite a scene and raised holy hell insisting she needed to talk to you. We called the cops, but she was gone before they got here."

"Thank you for keeping her away, Joe."

"No problem. It's what we're here for. I stayed out in the parking lot until I was sure she was gone, so she shouldn't be there to bother you when you leave."

"Great. Thanks."

Joe left with Devon right behind him. Ronnie locked up the studio. She walked past the security guards on her way out.

"You want me to walk you out, just in case?" Joe said.

"No, thanks. I think I can handle it."

She walked to the parking lot, her eyes peeled for Whitney's car. It wasn't there. She wasn't sure if she was relieved or disappointed. She was glad she hadn't seen the scumbag, but was almost disappointed. She would have loved to beat the crap out of her.

As she drove to the hospital, it hit Ronnie that, since Whitney had been at the studio, she was still free as a bird. She hadn't been arrested yet. Ronnie's stomach muscles tightened. She couldn't believe Whitney was running around unharmed while Lana was in the hospital, scarred for life.

Lana was eating dinner when Ronnie arrived.

"Am I interrupting?" She poked her head in the room.

"Come on in, as long as you're here."

Lana didn't sound too happy to see Ronnie. Not that she blamed her. Look where she was, and it was all Ronnie's fault.

"How are you doing today?"

"I hurt and my neck and cheek look like hamburger. That's how I'm doing."

"I'm so sorry," Ronnie said for the millionth time. The words sounded hollow even to her. But she truly was sorry. She wished she could make it up to Lana, but didn't know how.

"Look, I'll be going home soon I hope. When I do, I really don't want you coming over, okay? I get lonely in the hospital. I admit that, but you need to step away, Ronnie. You need to find your way out of my life just like you found your way into it."

"Not gonna happen. Who's going to check on you once you're at home?"

"I'm perfectly capable of taking care of myself. Now, don't just stand there. Have a seat."

Ronnie sat and rested her elbows on her knees. She placed her face in her hands and took a deep breath.

"You can't just kick me out of your life, Lana. Please."

"I have to. So I will."

Ronnie looked up and met Lana's gaze.

"Look, I get that you're pissed. I would be too if I was in your situation. I let something horrible happen to you. But I swear, I'll never do it again."

"You need to stop that." Lana went back to her dinner. "This isn't your fault. None of it is."

"Yeah, right. I'm the one who left you alone. I'm the one who slept with Whitney. This whole thing is my fault."

"As I've said." Lana sounded distant. "You couldn't have known what would happen. I don't blame you for any of this. Now, stop the pity party and just leave. I'm glad you came to visit me, but I really need to get used to my life without you in it."

"Please. Let me make it up to you. Please."

"Good-bye Ronnie. For good this time."

Knowing from Lana's tone that it was pointless to argue, Ronnie let herself out. She didn't blame her at all. She'd let this happen. She'd let Lana down. And Lana had every right not to want to see her again. But Ronnie still didn't know if she could stay away.

The next day was much the same for Ronnie. She woke up and texted Lana and asked if she could come by the hospital that night. There was no response, but Ronnie figured maybe she was sleeping. She could hope anyway. She took her shower and got ready for work. It would be another busy one with four shoots scheduled. She didn't know how long she could keep up the pace but was determined to try to make it the norm. She had nothing left in her life but her job.

She got to the office early and set up the first shoot. She made coffee and sat drinking her first cup when Devon walked in.

"Any improvement on the Lana front?" she said.

"No. She kicked me out of the hospital last night. I can't blame her. I'm the reason she's there, after all. Still, it's hard to believe she doesn't want me in her life. Although maybe if I don't see her, some of this guilt will subside. Maybe, but I doubt it."

"Hey, I'm really sorry, Ronnie. You seemed like you were really into her."

"Yeah I was. I still am. And I thought she was into me, too. It hurts on so many levels that we're not together any more."

Devon stood awkwardly, as if searching for something to say.

"It's okay, Devon. I'll recover someday. For now, I'm sure you have better things to do than watch me wallow away in self-pity."

"Yeah. I'll get to work."

Ronnie was glad to have Devon. She was an excellent assistant. She fielded calls well and did a great job of scheduling the models for Ronnie. Still, Ronnie couldn't get her words out of her head. What if Devon had done this to Lana to protect her in some twisted way?

Ronnie poured herself another cup of coffee as the first model of the day came in. Ronnie greeted her and told her to go ahead and get ready. And so another day began.

Ronnie pushed her models hard again that day, demanding perfection and receiving nothing less. She was halfway through her day when it was time to shoot Christina. She showed up late, and Ronnie had no tolerance for that.

"I told you if you continued to be late, I'd quit shooting you. This is your last warning."

Christina fought tears as she walked toward the dressing room. She turned back to Ronnie.

"I've told you before. You're not the only one who can make people miserable. Remember that."

What the hell was that supposed to mean? Could Christine be behind Lana's attack? She was tall and thin. But she was blond. Maybe Lana was wrong about the color of her attacker's hair.

"Hey, Ronnie," Devon interrupted her thoughts. "You were awfully hard on her."

"She keeps showing up late. It throws my whole schedule off."

"Still. You didn't have to sound like such an asshole. Look, I know you're going through a tough time, but don't take it out on the models, okay?"

"Okay. I'm sorry. But I meant what I said."

"Fair enough."

Devon left her, and Christina came out of the dressing room.

"Okay Ronnie," she said. "I'll work my ass off for this shoot."

"Sounds good. Let's get to it."

The shoot went perfectly, with Christina following every direction Ronnie gave. They even finished with a few minutes to spare.

"You did great," Ronnie said. "Thanks."

"Thank you. And I'll be here on time next time."

"Thanks."

The rest of the day went off without a hitch, and Ronnie finished the day with a beer in the kitchen. Devon joined her.

"What are you doing tonight?" Devon said.

"I don't know. I want to go by the hospital, but don't think Lana would welcome me. Maybe pick up some takeout and go home."

"I thought maybe you'd like to come over. We could order a pizza and play video games."

"It's been forever since I played a video game."

"It's just like riding a bike."

"You sure?"

"Positive."

"Okay then. Let's go."

❖

Lana was waiting to be released from the hospital the next day. She had her salve, gauze, and pain pills in her purse. She was just waiting for Monica to come in with her discharge paperwork. The doctor had told her as long as she continued to care for her burns the way he'd instructed her she should be fine. And they'd talked about a possible skin graft plastic surgery in her future.

Monica came in and Lana signed the paperwork. Monica helped Lana into a waiting wheelchair, then wheeled her downstairs.

"Did you call someone to come get you?" she said.

"No. I'll just call a cab."

"I'll have the nurse call for one for you."

"Thank you. That would be great."

"It's been a pleasure caring for you, Lana. You take care of yourself."

"Thanks for all you did. And don't worry. I will."

Monica walked off and Lana sat in her wheelchair waiting for the taxi. It finally showed up, and she gave the driver Ronnie's address. She figured Ronnie would be at work at that hour in the morning.

She got to Ronnie's house, and sure enough, her truck was gone. She let herself in the house and fought the tears that threatened as she walked through it one last time. She went into the bedroom and filled her suitcases and overnight bag, then took Ronnie's key off her ring and set in on the kitchen counter. With everything packed, she loaded her rental car and drove home.

She was hungry when she got there. She'd gotten used to the regimented feeding schedule at the hospital. She didn't want to go anywhere, though. Not looking like she did, with her face and neck all bandaged up. And knowing she had raw hamburger underneath the gauze didn't help.

She ordered Chinese food and sat on the couch to watch TV while she waited. The driver arrived, and it was one of the regular waiters that Ronnie and she had had on their many visits to the restaurant.

"Are you okay?" His face showed genuine concern.

"I'm fine. Just had an accident."

"I'm sorry. I would have thrown in extra fortune cookies if I'd known that."

"That's very sweet. And thank you for the food."

She tipped him some more and he drove off. She took the food to her dining room and laid it out. She was sure she wouldn't be able to eat it all, but it had all sounded so good when she'd ordered it.

She ate what she could and boxed the rest for later. It was time to tackle the reality she'd been avoiding. She unpacked her suitcases and hung her clothes in her closet. She set up her makeup on her dressing table. She was at least happy to have that back. Her stomach was sick as she unpacked. She knew how final it was. She would never see Ronnie again.

She was hurting by the time she was through, so she took some pain pills and lay down for a nap.

Her dreams were filled with Ronnie. Ronnie shooting her at the studio, making love to her, and lounging around the house with her. She woke up with a powerful need between her legs. She missed Ronnie something fierce. She slid her shorts and thong off and slipped her hand between her legs. She was wet with desire. And with no one to take care of it but herself.

She ran her fingers over herself, playing with her lips before going inside. She moved her fingers in and out until she was too close. She dragged her fingers to her slick clit and rubbed it until she came. She lay there catching her breath and then the tears came. She missed Ronnie so much.

She didn't try to stop the tears. She sobbed long and hard, letting everything out that she'd tried so hard to keep in at the hospital. She knew her eyes were swollen and her face blotchy without even looking in a mirror. But worst of all, she'd gotten her bandages all wet. She'd have to change them on her own. For the first time. Which meant she'd have to look at the burns.

She waited until she was sure the tears had stopped, then went into the bathroom to treat her burns. She carefully removed the gauze and, when she saw what lay under it, lost her lunch.

She spent several minutes vomiting, but soon had herself under control. She steeled herself for what she had to do and straightened up and looked in the mirror. The hamburger flesh staring back at her made her want to cry again, but she didn't. She stayed strong. She applied some salve and then the gauze. She thought she'd done a pretty good job. None of the burnt flesh was exposed. She brushed her teeth, got dressed, and went out to watch television.

She knew she'd have to decide what to do with her life now that her modeling career was over. Although, the idea of skin grafts and possible plastic surgery meant there was potentially hope. She was sure she'd have to go through all that if she ever wanted to look human again, but she knew she'd have scars. She feared she'd always have scars that would prevent her from working. She didn't need to decide right then, though. She had plenty of money to live on.

She stared at the TV, not really seeing, until it was time for her pain pills. She ate a little more Chinese food then popped her pills. As she watched the television, she became drowsy. She dozed on the couch.

Lana woke up a short time later. It was dark outside. She knew she should go to bed but wasn't looking forward to spending another night alone. She began missing Ronnie again. She wondered what she was doing and how she was. She wondered if she missed Lana at all, or if she was just overwhelmed with guilt. She wished she'd let her come by the hospital the night before. But she was too embarrassed. It was hard to have Ronnie see her that way. She was deformed beyond description and Ronnie didn't deserve that. Ronnie deserved someone beautiful. That's why she'd been with Lana to begin with. She'd have her pick of other models now, and although it pained Lana to think of Ronnie with someone else, she knew she had to let her go.

Lana washed her dishes, then went to bed. She was just slipping into her nightgown when she heard pounding on her front door.

"Lana! It's Ronnie! I know you're in there. Open up."

Lana's heart beat faster. She froze. She couldn't answer the door. She had to stay strong and let Ronnie go on with her life.

"Lana, your car's in the driveway. I know you're home. Please open the door."

She sounded so pathetic, Lana almost caved, but she didn't.

"Lana! Please!"

Ronnie rang the doorbell a few times. Lana put her hands over her ears, trying to block it all, but it didn't work.

Ronnie pounded a few more times, then apparently accepted defeat because Lana was left in deafening quiet.

CHAPTER TWENTY

Ronnie had enjoyed playing games with Devon. She'd eaten some pizza, drank a few beers, and actually relaxed. But it soon got late and she had to head home. When she pulled up to her house, she noticed Lana's car was gone. So she was out of the hospital. She rushed over to see her. She had hopes Lana would let her visit her, even though she'd already said no. Still, she refused to give up. Until she knocked on the door.

She pounded as hard as she could. She pounded the door until her fists hurt. She'd even rung the doorbell. She knew Lana was inside. Why was she avoiding her? She walked around to the side of her house and peered in. There was no sign of her. But she had to be there, right?

Ronnie finally gave up. Depressed, she got in her truck and drove home. She opened the door and turned on the lights. She went to the kitchen to get a beer. There, on the kitchen counter was Lana's key to her house. She walked back to her bedroom and checked her dresser. All Lana's clothes were gone.

She took her beer to the couch and collapsed into it. She fought tears. She wasn't a crier, but this hurt, damn it. Lana was gone. They were through. Okay, she could take a deep breath and accept that. But why?

That's the question that niggled in the back of her brain. They had seemed so good together. They were in love. Weren't they?

Had it all been some kind of a joke to Lana? Had the whole thing been a lie? No. Ronnie couldn't believe that. It had felt so real. She had loved Lana like no woman before. Even Constance. She refused to believe Lana had taken her for a ride.

She was probably just pissed at Ronnie for what had happened to her. And rightfully so. Ronnie knew she didn't deserve her, but she still wanted to be her friend. Why wouldn't Lana let her in?

Ronnie finished her beer and went to bed. She still wasn't used to sleeping in her bed all by herself. She held Lana's pillow to her, taking in the scent of her perfume that still lingered. She missed her so badly. An errant tear slipped out just as she fell asleep.

She woke up the next morning at seven and did her morning routine. She was out of the house by eight and at the studio shortly thereafter. She made the coffee and sat down with a cup and waited for the rest of the crew to get in. Devon came in shortly after the coffee was made.

"How's it going today?" Devon said.

"Terrible."

"Terrible? Why?"

"Lana came home yesterday."

"What?" Devon said. "That's great."

"No. She came home to move out. All her stuff is gone."

"Oh, Ronnie. I'm sorry. Man, that bites. But like I said before. Maybe it's for the best. It kept you from breaking her heart. You know as well as I do you're not the settling down type."

"That's where you're wrong. I did settle down. I promised myself to Lana. And now she's rejecting me. Anyway I stopped by her house on the way home and I saw her car wasn't in my driveway. I knocked on the door, but she wouldn't answer."

"That doesn't make any sense."

"No, it doesn't. I mean, on one hand, I'm glad she's out of the hospital, but on the other, why the hell won't she talk to me?"

"I wish I had some answers for you," Devon said.

"Yeah. Me, too."

The first model of the day had arrived, so Ronnie pushed Lana out of her mind and set up the shoot. The model looked great in a long black dress, and Ronnie forced herself not to think of the time she photographed Lana dressed similarly.

Ronnie started calling out instructions and the model followed them to a tee. The shoot was over in a couple of hours and Ronnie dismissed the model. She set up the next shoot and settled down with another cup of coffee.

The rest of the day went smoothly, and soon the last shoot was over. Ronnie and Devon sat with their beers while they waited for the hair and makeup artists to go.

"So, are you going by her house again tonight?" Devon said. "Or are you just going to leave her alone now?"

"I don't know. Part of me wants to, but part of me asks, why bother?"

"It might be for the best. But then again, she might talk to you tonight, though."

"Yeah, but she might not."

"Still, are you willing to accept defeat that easily?"

Ronnie stared at Devon.

"I don't know. It just seems so futile. She won't even talk to me. And I don't totally blame her. Look what I did to her."

"You didn't do anything to her. That was all Whitney. You know that as well as I do."

"Still. But why won't she let me be her friend? Does she hate me that much now? I tell you, between the guilt and the rejection, I'm a mess right now."

"I'm sure you are. I wish I had words to help you. I don't know. Maybe just consider it fate. That's all I'm saying."

Ronnie thought hard about what Devon said. She didn't want to accept it as fate. She didn't want to give up. She wanted Lana in her life. At least in some capacity.

They finished their beers and Ronnie drove over to Lana's house. Her rental car was in the driveway, just like before.

Ronnie knocked on the door. She rang the doorbell. She called out to Lana to please open the door. But just as the previous night, there was no answer. She left, determined to come up with a way to make Lana talk to her.

She got home and made some dinner, but it wasn't the same without Lana. Nothing was. She ate but barely tasted her food. She did the dishes, missing the way she and Lana had done them together. She poured herself some whiskey and plopped down on the couch.

She sent Lana a text asking if they could please talk. But she got no answer.

Damn it! It was so frustrating. She poured another whiskey and turned on the television, hoping to find something to keep her mind occupied. But it was no use. All she could think about was Lana. She finished her drink and went to bed.

❖

Lana had had a rough day. She'd been in a lot of pain and had spent most of the day in bed. She finished her leftovers early and was pondering ordering more food when Ronnie had shown up.

She felt horrible leaving Ronnie stranded but knew it was for the best. Ronnie didn't need to see her this way anymore. She'd never get to see her again. Why didn't Ronnie just accept it and move on?

Lana ordered some dinner and while she waited for it to arrive, she got a text from Ronnie. It was so tempting to respond. She wanted to tell her she still loved her. That she'd always love her, but that they just couldn't be together anymore. But she knew any conversation would give Ronnie false hope. And that would just be cruel.

Her dinner showed up, and she embarrassingly opened the door to pay. The delivery woman gave her bandages an odd look but didn't say anything. It just reinforced to Lana that she was now a freak. She took her food inside and ate a few bites. She felt the loss of Ronnie heavily, and she started to cry.

"Damn it," she said.

But she couldn't stop. The tears flowed like rivers down her face. She finally stopped and went in the bathroom to change her bandages. Which she could do without throwing up now, she thought proudly. She got her wet bandages off and applied some salve, then new gauze. She had done a good job.

She was starting to hurt again, so ate some more dinner before she took some pain pills and went to bed.

She had horrible dreams. Giant cameras with teeth were chasing her, trying to catch her. She had to run away and tripped and fell and they got closer and closer. And then she woke up. She was breathing heavily and covered in sweat. She got up and got a glass of water. She sat back down on her bed, knowing she needed more sleep, but afraid to close her eyes.

Lana went out to the living room and turned on the television, but her head was too messed up from the pain pills to allow her to focus. She finally gave up, turned it off, and went back to sleep.

The next morning, she woke a little after ten. She felt much better. She made some coffee and sat sipping her first cup. She tried to decide what to do with her day. She knew she wasn't going to leave the house. But she had to come up with something to do before she lost her mind.

One thing she had to do was call Madeline. She called the office and was put right through.

"Lana, dear? Are you okay? You had us worried sick about you."

"How do you mean?"

"I've been trying to reach you. You've been MIA for a few days. I was getting scared something awful had happened to you."

"I'm sorry to have scared you."

"But you're okay? That's what's important."

Lana didn't answer. She was anything but okay. She was a deformed mess.

"The reason I'm calling is I need to get out of my contract."

"You what? Why?"

"I'd rather not say. I just don't want to continue modeling."

"Very well. I'll look at your contract and see what the ramifications are for breaking it. I'll call you back."

"Thank you," Lana said. "I look forward to hearing from you."

She hung up and fought tears. She couldn't believe she was canceling her contract. It seemed so final. But she couldn't model anymore, so why put off the inevitable? She sat on the couch and let the tears fall. She was so tired of crying, but that seemed to be all she could do.

When she was through, she changed her dressing and went into the kitchen to get something to eat. She ate her leftovers, which meant she'd have to order out again. Which meant someone else would see her deranged self.

She shuddered at the thought. She hated the way she looked. Her whole life had been based on her looks. Life decisions like careers, etcetera, were all based on her physical presentation to the world. And now that had changed. Drastically.

She finished her lunch just before Madeline called her back.

"Hello?" Lana said.

"Lana? It's Madeline. So, I checked your contract. It was almost time for renewal, so I can let you out of it without charging you anything. I'm really sorry you're doing this. Are you with another agency now?"

"No. I'm through modeling."

"What? Why? You're a natural."

"Things happened. I can't model anymore. I'm sorry."

"Lana?"

"Yes?"

"Are you sure about this? I mean, absolutely sure?"

"I am."

"What are you going to do with yourself now?"

"That's something I need to decide. Thank you for the information about my contract. Good-bye."

She hung up the phone. Her face was starting to hurt so she popped some pills and turned on the television. She awoke a half an hour later, feeling groggy. She decided to go lie down for a while. She slept fitfully and woke up two hours later.

Lana was tired of sleeping her life away, but she needed the pain pills, so she took them. She wasn't about to let the pain take over. The doctor had advised against just that. So she would continue to take them, even if that meant sleeping for long periods of the day. Besides, what else did she have to do?

She put in a DVD and watched a movie. It was one of her favorites, and she actually laughed out loud at it. It was the first time she had laughed since the incident. And it felt good.

When the movie was over, Lana was feeling hungry again, so looked on her phone for a place that delivered. She was actually in the mood for Chinese again, so she ordered it and sat down with a new movie.

She was about a half hour into it when her doorbell rang. Thankful that her food was there, she opened it. And there stood Ronnie.

"Lana, we need to talk."

She was staring at the gauze covering Lana's cheek and neck. Lana tried to close the door, but Ronnie's foot was in the way. She forced the door open and let herself inside.

"Ronnie, no," Lana said, but Ronnie wasn't listening.

"Baby—"

"No. Don't call me that. I'm not your baby. We're through."

"Okay. Fair enough. We're not an item anymore."

"Right. And I told you I didn't want you coming to my house."

"But I can't stay away."

"You need to." Lana hoped her voice didn't betray her relief at having Ronnie there.

"You need to let me help you. Who else do you have around here?"

"That's not important. I can take care of myself just fine."

"Lana, stop being so stubborn."

"Look." She peeled the tape and gauze off her face so Ronnie could see her burns. "This is my reality now. This is what I look like. I'm a freak. You deserve a beautiful woman. I know you feel bad about what happened to me. You blame yourself. I get that. But it's not your fault. I absolve you, okay? Feel better? Now, go."

She opened the door for Ronnie to leave and saw a man on the doorstep. It was her dinner. She closed the door after tipping the driver.

"So, my dinner is here. Will you excuse me?"

"No. I need to be sure you're okay. I'm not going anywhere."

"Ronnie, please. Don't you understand? I'm a freak now. You deserve so much better."

"No. What I do deserve is not to be shut out. It looks to me like you're at the beginning of a long journey. I really wish you'd allow me to travel it with you."

"Why are you making this so hard?"

"Because I love you."

"But you can't."

"Don't tell me how to feel, Lana."

"I'm sorry. I just can't be with you anymore."

"And I can't accept that. That leaves us at a bit of an impasse."

"Please, Ronnie. I can't be with you. You need to move on."

"I can't do that, Lana. I just can't turn off my feelings for you. I love you and want to be with you. Even if you have scars on you. Especially because you have scars."

"Don't be that way. I don't need you to be a martyr. I need you to understand what I'm saying. To pay attention to my wants and needs. And to leave."

"I'm not being a martyr," Ronnie said. "I'm just not willing to throw away what we had, have, because of some scars."

"Ronnie, I don't want to ask you again. Please leave."

"Fine, but I'll be back. Tell me it's okay to at least check in on you to make sure you're okay."

Lana sat silently staring at Ronnie, her mind whirling.

"Sure," she said. "You can come by to check on me. But don't do it with the belief that we'll get back together."

"Yes, ma'am. I'll try to remember that."

Ronnie left and Lana collapsed onto the couch, bawling her eyes out. Denying Ronnie had been the hardest thing she'd ever done. And damn it, she still loved her so.

CHAPTER TWENTY-ONE

Ronnie got in her truck and drove off. She was filled with mixed emotions. Lana was home from the hospital and doing okay. Overall anyway. Sure, she had those burns, and damn but they looked painful, but outside of that, she was fine. Ronnie was flooded with relief at that fact. But she was bummed that Lana didn't want to be with her anymore. Ronnie still loved her and needed her. And she didn't like being turned away. At least Lana had said she could still come by. Maybe she'd be able to win her heart again.

She stopped by the Chinese restaurant and picked up some food to go, then went home and, for the first time in days, ate with gusto. She actually tasted the food. And it was good. She washed it all down with a beer, then went to the couch to watch some TV.

She began to doze, so she went to bed. She pulled Lana's pillow close against her and fell sound asleep. She awoke with a smile on her face. She planned to go see Lana after her day at the studio. Lana had agreed to let her do it, and she planned to go every single day until Lana took her back.

Ronnie got ready for her day then headed to the studio. She couldn't wait to see Devon and tell her the good news. She had another action-packed day planned, but she was used to them now. She made her coffee and had the first shoot all set up by the time Devon showed up.

"Good morning," Ronnie said.

"You look good. Did you finally get some sleep or something?"

"I saw Lana."

"You did? That's awesome. She let you in?"

"Not exactly. She thought I was someone else, so she answered the doorbell. She tried to close the door in my face, but I was too quick."

"How is she?"

"Overall, she's okay. But you should see what that bitch Whitney did to her."

"Did you actually see the burns?'

"Yes. She showed them to me. She thought it would freak me out or disgust me or something."

"And it didn't?"

"Well, I'd be lying if I didn't say they're pretty gnarly looking."

"So how are things on the couple front? Did she agree to take you back?"

"Not yet. She thinks she's not worthy of my love just because she's got those burns."

"Oh man, Ronnie. I'm sorry to hear that. For your sake. But then again, like I've said, it may all be for the best."

"No, it's not for the best. It sucks." Her suspicions about Devon crept in again.

Their conversation was interrupted when the first model of the day walked out of the dressing room.

"You ready?" Ronnie said.

"Yep."

"Let's do this."

Ronnie's day went very well. Her models were on time and listened to her instructions. She was through just after five.

"You going to have a beer tonight?" Devon said.

"No. As soon as everyone clears out, I'm heading to Lana's."

"Okay. I'm out of here. Good luck."

"Thanks."

Ronnie didn't have to wait long for everyone to leave. She locked the door and drove to Lana's.

Lana answered the doorbell when she rang it. She looked beautiful in plaid shorts and a pink golf shirt. Ronnie wanted to sweep her into a hug and kiss her. She slid her hands in her pockets to prevent herself from doing just that.

"May I come in?" Ronnie said.

"Sure. Why not?"

"Am I interrupting something?"

"Not a thing."

"Great. Do you want a glass of wine or something? I'll get it."

"Yes. That actually would be nice. The wine is in the kitchen."

"Okay. I'll be right back."

Ronnie took a minute to collect herself as she walked to the kitchen. She poured them each a glass of Malbec and walked to the living room where Lana was on the couch. She handed Lana her glass and sat at the other end of the couch, lest she be tempted to touch her.

"How was your day?" Ronnie said.

"It was okay. Actually, it was rough. I was in a lot of pain and didn't get out of bed until not too long ago."

"I'm sorry to hear that."

"How was your day?"

"My day was great. I started scheduling four shoots a day. Mostly to keep my mind off of you in the hospital. It's nice, though. It keeps me busy."

"Wow. That's a lot of models to shoot. Is the demand that great?"

"It sure is. So, can I ask you something?"

"Sure."

"Do you know if they got Whitney?"

"I haven't heard anything. I wish they would lock her up for life."

"Yeah. Me, too."

"She came by the studio after she attacked you, you know?"

"No, I didn't know."

Lana exhaled loudly.

"By the way, you look beautiful today."

"How can you say that?" Lana's eyes filled with tears.

"Oh, no. Don't cry."

"I'm sorry." She blinked back the tears. "It's just that I know I'm hideous."

"But you're not."

"I'm a deformed freak."

"No. You're a beautiful woman with some burns."

"Thank you, but I know that's not true. I see myself every time I change my dressing."

"I don't know what to say to change your mind."

"There's nothing you can say."

"Okay then," Ronnie said. "Are you hungry? You want me to order a pizza?"

"You sure you want to hang around that long?"

"I'd love to. Unless, I mean, if you're not up to it."

Lana smiled, and Ronnie's heart melted.

"Actually, pizza sounds really good."

"Great."

Ronnie called in the pizza order.

"It should be here in about forty-five minutes. You want me to top off your wine?"

"Yes, please," Lana said.

Ronnie went and got the bottle of wine and brought it to the living room. She filled their glasses, then set the bottle on the table. Everything seemed so right. But it wasn't. Lana still wasn't letting her in. She wished she could figure out how to get her to do that.

"So, what kind of pain pills are you on?" Ronnie said.

"Vicodin. Why?"

"Just curious. They don't mess with your head, do they?"

"No. I don't even know what you mean."

"I had a model once on Vicodin. It caused mood swings in her. It was scary."

"No. Nothing like that. It just makes me sleepy. I probably shouldn't be drinking wine in case I need some Vicodin tonight."

"I'm sorry. I wouldn't even have suggested it if I'd thought about it."

"Don't worry. I wanted some wine. I'm a big girl. I'll deal with the consequences."

"How are you feeling right now? I mean pain wise."

"Not bad. Which is hard to believe based on how I felt earlier."

"It really hurts, huh?"

"Yes," Lana said.

"I'm sorry. I'm so sorry you went through any of this. I blame myself."

"So you've said. Like a hundred times. Let it go, Ronnie. Let the guilt go."

"If I'd never slept with her, none of this would have happened."

"No. Don't do that. This is all Whitney. No one else."

"But still…"

"No. But nothing. Whitney is not stable. We knew that. We just didn't know how unstable she really was.'

"God, I hope she's locked up."

"That would be great," Lana said.

"Yeah, it would."

There was a knock on the door, and Ronnie said she'd get it.

"I'm sure it's the pizza," she said.

She opened the door to see Officer Winthrop and her partner standing there.

"Officers. What can I do for you?"

"We're actually here to see Ms. Ferguson."

Ronnie remembered she wasn't at her house. She stepped aside and let them in.

Lana got up off the couch.

"Officers, what's up? Did you catch Whitney?"

"We have a suspect in custody," Officer Winthrop said. "We need you to come down to the precinct and identify her."

"When? Like right now?"

"No. Tomorrow. Say two o'clock?"

"I'll be there."

"Great. Thank you."

Ronnie walked the officers to the door and said good-bye. She went back to check on Lana.

"You okay?" she said.

"I'm great. They caught Whitney."

"And you're going to be okay seeing her?"

"I have to be," Lana said. "I have to make sure she's put away and doesn't get out."

"You'll probably have to testify at trial."

"Then I'll testify. I need to know she won't hurt me again."

"You're a very strong woman."

"I don't feel strong. I just feel determined."

The doorbell rang again, and Ronnie went to get the pizza. She tipped the driver and took the pizza to the dining room. Lana joined her there.

They ate their dinner, and Lana found herself relaxing in Ronnie's company. She seemed to really want to spend time with Lana, which surprised her. She didn't seem disgusted by Lana's face, but Lana was sure she must be deep down. She knew she looked horrific. Ronnie was just being nice.

When dinner was over, they went back to the couch with another glass of wine.

"That was good," Ronnie said.

"It was. Do you mind if I keep the leftovers or do you want to take them home?"

"You can keep them. I don't mind at all."

"Thanks."

"So, you want to watch a movie or something?" Ronnie said.

"Actually, I'm getting tired. And my face is starting to hurt, so I think I'll have to take a Vicodin. I'm sure I'll be out like a light once I do. Sorry."

"It's okay." Ronnie got up. "I'll leave you alone now. But I'll be back tomorrow. Oh, do you want me to go with you to the precinct tomorrow?"

"Don't you have to work?"

"I can rearrange my schedule."

"Then sure. I'd love it if you went with me."

"Great. I'll be here around one thirty."

"Okay. See you then."

Lana closed the door after Ronnie left and collapsed against it. She wished she could take Ronnie back. She still loved her so much. It killed her inside. But she wouldn't trade the time she was spending with her for anything in the world.

She put the leftover pizza away and took a Vicodin. Then she changed into her pajamas and fell into a sound sleep. She awoke the next day feeling rested. It was the first time since she'd been home that she'd gotten a really good night's sleep. She showered, ate some pizza, and drank some coffee. She took a Vicodin and settled herself on the couch to wait for Ronnie to get there. She still had a couple of hours.

Lana dozed and woke to the ringing of her doorbell. Slightly disoriented, she answered the door to see Ronnie standing there.

"Is it one thirty already?" she said.

"Yep. You look like you just woke up."

"I must have fallen asleep on the couch."

"Well, are you ready to go?"

"Sure. Just let me grab my purse."

The closer they got to the station, the more nervous Lana got. She was grateful to have Ronnie there with her. She needed Ronnie's strength now more than ever.

They pulled into the parking lot.

"You doing okay?" Ronnie said.

"Not really."

"Do you need a minute?"

"No. I can do this. I have to, right?"

"Yep. You kinda do."

Lana took a deep breath.

"Okay. Let's do this."

They walked into the station and told the person at the desk what they were there for. She called Officer Winthrop to come get Lana.

"Can she go with me?" Lana said.

"No. I'm afraid not. She has to stay here."

Lana looked fearfully at Ronnie.

"You'll be fine, baby. Just identify her and we're out of here."

Lana nodded and followed Winthrop through a maze of corridors. They finally came to a dark room with a window in it.

"Now, remember, you can see them, but they can't see you. You're to identify your assailant by number. If you need a closer look, let me know and I can have them step forward. Do you understand?"

Lana merely nodded. She didn't want to see Whitney. She didn't know if she'd be able to hold it together. But she had to. This was important.

The light went on in the other room and several women walked in. She recognized Whitney immediately.

"It was number four," she said.

"Are you sure? Take your time."

"I know who it was. It was number four."

"Okay. Thank you for doing this. I'll walk you back out to the front."

Lana was on shaky legs as she followed Winthrop back to where Ronnie waited.

"Thank you again for your time," Winthrop said, then turned on her heel and left the area.

"How was it?" Ronnie asked.

"Pretty simple. I knew Whitney as soon as I saw her."

"That's great. What was it like seeing her?"

"I wanted to scream at her, to attack her, but I was cool. I just told them her number and that was that."

"Great. Let's get you back home. Unless you want to grab something to eat?"

"I don't go out in public, Ronnie. This was an exception."

"Oh, okay. Well then, we can order something for lunch, if that sounds okay."

"Yeah. That sounds good. Now that my nerves are settling, I think I'm getting hungry."

"How are you feeling, pain wise?"

"I'm starting to hurt. I'll take a Vicodin after lunch."

Lana was astonished, once again, how attentive Ronnie was being. She wasn't her girlfriend anymore. She didn't need to pretend to care. But Ronnie seemed sincere in her caring. It didn't feel like an act. Lana knew she didn't deserve Ronnie. She wondered if she should tell her to go away. But she so enjoyed her company. Selfishly, she chose not to push her away.

"Don't you have to go back to work?" Lana said.

"No. I took the whole afternoon off. Devon wasn't amused, but she got everyone rescheduled."

"Oh, good."

"Yep. So I'm free and clear."

They pulled into Lana's driveway. Lana was acutely aware of Ronnie's closeness behind her as she unlocked her door. She opened it and walked in, grateful to have Ronnie walking in after her.

"What do you want for lunch?" Ronnie said.

"Chinese."

Ronnie laughed.

"That's all you eat anymore."

"I love it."

"Okay. I'll order it."

"Will you please order lo mein and chicken fried rice?"

"Sure."

She called in the order while Lana got them sodas and sat on the couch. Ronnie soon joined her.

"I should bring some beer over just to have," Ronnie said. "I mean, if that's okay."

"That's fine." Lana smiled. "Though I doubt I'll be drinking any more wine while I'm on Vicodin. That wasn't smart."

"I understand. I'll pick up some beer before I come over tomorrow."

The food arrived, and they ate in quiet conversation.

"You seem to be loading up on carbs," Ronnie said. "That's good to see. I remember the nurse saying they would help you."

"Carbohydrates help burns heal faster."

"Right. I remember."

"Yep. And I should eat lots, too. I mean just in general. It's not easy sometimes because I'm in pain or weakened, but I try."

"Good. And now I'll be here to help you."

"You know, you don't have to come over every day, Ronnie."

"But I want to. I mean, unless it's too much."

"No. It's not too much. I enjoy the company. I won't leave the house, so it's nice having someone here to chat with. I get tired of talking to myself." She laughed.

"Good. Because I enjoy being here."

"Really? But surely you get disgusted by my face?"

"Not at all. I still think you're beautiful. You know that."

"You're so sweet, Ronnie."

"I'm only telling the truth."

After they'd eaten, Lana took a pain pill, and they settled in on the couch to watch a movie. Lana fell asleep soon into it and woke up disoriented. Ronnie was still there, though.

"What time is it?" Lana said.

"It's about seven. You've been asleep for a while. If you're okay, I'll take off now and let you get to bed. I didn't want to leave while you were sleeping."

"Seven o'clock is awfully early to go to bed."

"True. But you've had a big day."

"True. For me at least."

"I boxed up the leftover Chinese food so you can have it tomorrow, okay?"

"Thank you."

"No problem. I'll see you tomorrow, okay?"

"Sounds good."

She locked the door behind Ronnie, put on her pajamas, and climbed into bed.

Chapter Twenty-two

R onnie was in good spirits the next day at work.
"How'd everything go yesterday?" Devon said.

"It went great. She identified Whitney, and then we went back to her place."

"Are you any closer to getting her to take you back?"

"I don't know," Ronnie said. "I'm not pushing it, you know?"

"I guess that's a good thing?"

"It is. She has to get used to someone seeing her like that before she'll accept affection."

"Well, I hope you're not wasting your time."

"I'm not. She'll take me back. It's just a matter of when."

"Okay, Boss. I hope you're not setting yourself up for heartache."

"Thanks for all the support, Devon."

"I'm sorry. I just worry about you."

"Well, don't. I'll be fine."

The first model of the day was there, and Ronnie had to set up the shoot. She got it ready just as the model came out of the dressing room. Ronnie went to work shooting first one model, then another. She worked all day and managed four successful shoots. She got the last set packed up just as everyone was leaving for the day. She said good-bye to them all, locked the door, and got in her truck.

She called Lana.

"Hello?" Lana said.

"Hey. It's Ronnie. Do you need anything from the store?"

"No, thanks. Maybe some other time."

"Okay. I'll be over in a few."

She stopped by the store and bought a twelve-pack of beer. It took no time, so she arrived shortly at Lana's house.

Once inside, she put the beer in the fridge and grabbed one for herself then went into the living room to sit on the couch with her.

"How was your day?" Ronnie said.

"Not bad. My pain level was manageable."

"That's great."

"How was yours?" Lana said.

"It was great. Did four shoots and they all went well."

"That's great."

"Yep. I was happy with them." She took a sip from her beer. "What would you like for dinner tonight?"

"I don't know. I want something different."

"How about Mexican?"

"That sounds good."

Ronnie pulled up the menu and sat close to Lana on the couch so she could see it, too. The closeness made her dizzy with need, but she played it cool. She had to. She had to wait until Lana was ready, however long that took.

They decided on what they wanted to eat, and Ronnie placed the order. They settled back on the couch, and Lana suggested they watch a movie.

"Are you going to stay awake for it?" Ronnie teased her.

"Yes. I should be able to. I haven't taken a Vicodin for a while."

"Good. What shall we watch?"

They decided on a romantic comedy and Ronnie put the DVD in the player. They laughed together, and Ronnie melted every time she heard Lana's low laugh. They paused the movie halfway through when their dinner got there. They ate at the dining room table. Ronnie watched in amazement as Lana ate a burrito the size of her head, along with her rice and beans.

"You're doing a great job keeping up those carbs," Ronnie said.

"Are you making fun of me?" Lana smiled.

"No. I'm serious. I'm proud of you for keeping up the good work."

"Thanks. It's a good thing I love food, isn't it?"

"Yes, it is. Now go sit on the couch and I'll get the dishes washed. Then we can finish the movie."

"I'll come help with the dishes. We'll do them together."

Ronnie's heart soared. It would be just like old times. Why couldn't Lana see that? Surely she had to feel something for Ronnie, right?

They got the dishes in the dishwasher and the leftovers put away. Ronnie grabbed another beer and followed Lana to the living room. As was the norm, Ronnie sat at the far end of the couch to avoid any temptation.

They started the movie again, and Ronnie saw Lana's eyelids getting heavy.

"You want to rest your head in my lap?" she said.

"That would be great."

She laid her head in Ronnie's lap, and Ronnie stroked her hair, driving herself crazy in the process. Soon Lana's breathing evened out and she emitted the soft snores that told Ronnie she was asleep.

Ronnie tried to concentrate on the movie, but all she could think about was Lana's soft hair that she continued to stroke. It was like silk, and Ronnie stroked it carefully so as not to touch the bandages on Lana's face and neck.

She remembered the feel of her silky hair as Lana used to kiss down her body. She remembered how soft it was when it tickled her inner thighs. She adjusted herself on the couch. That line of thinking wasn't safe. She needed to get a grip on her thoughts that were running rampant in a very dangerous direction.

The movie ended and Lana was still asleep. Ronnie turned off the DVD player and switched the television over to regular viewing. She flipped through the channels until she found a baseball game. She settled back again to watch it.

Lana finally began to stir. She sat up and looked over at Ronnie, who looked so handsome sitting there.

"How long have I been asleep?"

"I don't know. A couple of hours maybe."

"I'm so sorry. You must think I'm a terrible hostess."

"No. I think you need your rest. Besides, it was kind of nice having you sleep on me."

"You say the sweetest things."

"I say the truth."

"Oh, Ronnie. I hope you're not still holding out hope we're going to get back together. That can't happen."

"Yes, if you must know, I am holding out hope. I don't understand why it can't happen."

"You deserve a complete woman, a beautiful woman. Not one with half her face burned off."

"That doesn't bother me. And if it bothers you so much, why don't you have plastic surgery?"

"I plan to. But that's down the road. Not in the near future. So I'll stay a freak for a while."

"Baby, you're not a freak. You're a beautiful woman."

She heard Ronnie's words and wanted to believe them. She loved her so much and wished beyond measure they could be together and things could be back to normal. Dare she hope?

"Don't do this, Ronnie."

"Why not? Tell me you don't still love me."

"That's just it," Lana said. "I do still love you. I love you too much to saddle you with a freak of nature."

"You're not a freak of nature." Ronnie spoke in a soft tone. "You're gorgeous, baby. Inside and out."

Lana's eyes teared up.

"Don't cry, baby."

"I wish I could see myself as you see me. But I can't. I'm deformed."

"No. You have some burns. They'll heal. You'll heal. And I want to be here with you through that process."

If only it were that simple.

"I can't ask that of you, Ronnie."

"You're not asking. I'm volunteering. Don't you see that?"

Ronnie moved closer to Lana on the couch. She reached out and wiped away an errant tear. Lana took Ronnie's hand and pressed it against her face. She turned ever so slightly and kissed Ronnie's palm.

She knew she was playing with fire, but she couldn't help it. Ronnie was making her feel things she shouldn't be feeling. Her resolve was weakening. She knew she needed to be strong, but she was faltering. She wanted so much to have a life with Ronnie.

"I should change my gauze," Lana said. "It got a little wet."

"Can I help?"

"No, but you can wait here for me."

"Okay. I'll do that."

Lana felt Ronnie's absence like the removal of a warm blanket. But she did what she had to do and took care of her gauze. It didn't take long, and soon she was sitting next to Ronnie on the couch.

"Feel better?" Ronnie said.

"I do."

"Good."

Ronnie must have felt emboldened as slipped her arm around Lana. Lana, rather than pulling away, leaned into her. Ronnie placed a tender, tentative kiss on the top of her head. Lana raised her head and looked into Ronnie's eyes. She saw love there. Love like she'd seen before. Ronnie dipped her head and tasted Lana's lips.

Lana surprised herself by kissing her back. It was soft, questioning, but it was a kiss nonetheless. Ronnie seemed to want to try for more but didn't. She pulled away, but Lana pressed into her and kissed her again.

The kiss was more powerful this time, and Lana ran her tongue along Ronnie's lips. Ronnie opened her mouth and welcomed her in. Their kiss intensified, as did Lana's need. She had denied herself for so long. Was it possible for them to be a couple? She hoped so. She hoped she wasn't making a grave mistake. She knew if she didn't break it off soon, she'd want more than she was ready to ask for. So, she broke off the kiss.

"That was nice," she said.

"Yes, it was. I want more. Why did you stop?" Ronnie said.

"Because it's making me want more. And I don't know that I can ask that of you."

"We'll figure that out. I've told you, I'll give you everything. For now, please kiss me again."

Lana couldn't have been happier. She kissed Ronnie again and eased back on the couch. Ronnie climbed on top of her and kissed her with everything she had. And Lana kissed her back in kind. Ronnie started grinding into Lana, and that's when she stopped kissing her.

Lana looked up at Ronnie's face just inches from hers and tried to remember why she'd wanted to block this loving woman from her life. None of the logic she'd been using stood up now. All that mattered was that she wanted Ronnie. In a big way.

"Don't get up," she said.

But Ronnie was already sitting a little way away from her on the couch. Lana sat up herself.

"What are you doing?" Lana said.

"I think I'd better get going."

"Ronnie, please don't. Please stay with me."

"I don't want to be a one-night stand, Lana. I need to know that if I stay, we're back together."

Lana looked at Ronnie, unable to believe her ears. How could they not be back together? Did Ronnie think Lana kissed just anybody like that?

"What?" Ronnie said. "Why are you looking at me like that?"

"I don't kiss random women like that," Lana said.

"I didn't think you did."

"I mean, please, Ronnie. Please, let's get back together."

"Are you sure? You're ready to accept me back?"

"I am. Please, Ronnie."

Ronnie closed the distance between them again and kissed Lana passionately. Lana grew lightheaded from the kiss. But she needed more. She had to have more. She pulled away from Ronnie and took her hand. She led her down the hall to her bedroom.

"God, I hope you're sure about this," Ronnie said.

"Please. No more doubting. Just make love to me."

Ronnie carefully took Lana's shirt over her head. She unhooked her bra and took her breasts in her hands. Lana groaned as Ronnie's thumbs played over her nipples. She was sending direct shockwaves to her nerve center, which Lana could feel swell by the second.

Ronnie undid Lana's shorts and pulled them down. Lana sat on the bed and allowed Ronnie to take them off. Next came her thong, which Ronnie peeled off with her teeth. Lana was on fire. Her need was all-consuming. She needed Ronnie to take her. And soon.

Lana sat on the edge of the bed and Ronnie knelt before her.

"My God, you're beautiful," she said.

She leaned in and ran her tongue over the length of Lana. She slid her fingers inside and ran her tongue over Lana's clit. It took no time for Lana to feel her world burst into a million tiny pieces. She lay back as she floated back to earth.

"You need to get undressed," Lana finally said.

Ronnie stripped out of her clothes and lay on the bed with Lana.

"Dear God, how I've missed you," Lana said.

"I've missed you, too, baby."

Lana skimmed her hand over Ronnie's body, allowing it to stop to caress one and then the other breast. She smiled to herself when she felt her nipples respond. Lana kissed Ronnie hard, and Ronnie allowed her tongue to make its way into Lana's mouth.

Lana's breath caught at the sensation. She loved the feel of Ronnie's tongue dancing with hers, but still she wanted, no craved, more.

She kissed down Ronnie's cheek to her neck. She sucked and nipped her way down to her chest and finally, stopped briefly to suck her nipples. She sucked them in as far as she could, then ran her tongue over them.

Ronnie moaned her pleasure. But Lana was just getting started. She continued to kiss down Ronnie's body until she came to where her legs met. She made herself comfortable as she kissed up each inner thigh in turn. Ronnie's legs quivered at the kisses. Lana licked the whole area between Ronnie's legs. She delved her tongue as deep as it would go inside of her and lapped at the juices flowing there.

Ronnie moved all over the bed, urging Lana on. Lana needed no encouragement. She licked her way to Ronnie's slick clit and took it between her lips. She flicked its tip with her tongue, and soon Ronnie was crying out as Lana took her to one orgasm after another.

Lana kissed her way back up Ronnie's body until she kissed her on her mouth.

"You are so wonderful," she said.

"So are you, baby. So are you."

They fell asleep, and when Lana woke up the next morning it was to Ronnie's hand playing between her legs.

"Good morning," Lana said.

"Good morning, my love."

Ronnie's talented fingers coaxed Lana to climax again and again. When she protested she didn't have any more inside her, they decided to shower together since Ronnie had to get ready for work.

"Are you sure I won't be a distraction?" Lana said.

"I'm counting on it."

Lana laughed. Her shower was much smaller than Ronnie's, but they both fit, and Lana was soon running lathered hands all over Ronnie's body. She slid them between her legs and stroked deep inside her. Ronnie leaned against the wall to maintain balance. Lana slid her fingers over her clit and Ronnie cried out.

Ronnie dropped to her knees and buried her tongue inside Lana. Lana closed her eyes and reveled in the sensations she was creating. When she felt Ronnie's tongue on her clit, she grabbed Ronnie by the shoulders and arched into her, riding wave after wave of orgasm.

They got out of the shower and dried each other off. Ronnie was careful and tender when drying Lana's burns.

"I can't believe they don't disgust you," Lana said.

"Would you stop saying that? You have an injury. It'll heal. I love you, baby. No part of you is going to disgust me."

"You really do love me, don't you?" Lana said.

"I do."

"I love you, too."

"That's a good thing, because you're never getting rid of me."

"Good. Because I never want to."

They made coffee and sat together drinking it.

"So, what do you plan to do today?" Ronnie said.

"Well, if you don't mind, I'd like to take some things over to your house. I prefer staying there than here."

"That sounds great."

Ronnie took her house key off her ring and handed it to Lana.

"You know," Ronnie said. "We should consider consolidating houses for real."

"What do you mean?"

"I'd like you to move in with me. Not just temporarily, but permanently."

"Do you mean that?"

"I do."

"Oh, Ronnie, let's do that. I'd love to move in with you for real."

"Great. Today, at least move some of your stuff, and then tonight we'll decide how to consolidate our households."

Lana moved into her arms and kissed her firmly on the mouth. Ronnie wrapped her arms around her and pressed her against her. Lana was breathing heavily when the kiss ended.

"Are you sure you have to go to work?" Lana said.

"Unfortunately. But don't worry. I'll be home tonight and we'll talk about our future."

"I love knowing my future includes you, Ronnie."

"So do I, baby. So do I."

About the Author

MJ Williamz was raised on California's central coast, which she left at age seventeen to pursue an education. She graduated from Chico State, and it was in Chico that she rediscovered her love of writing. It wasn't until she moved to Portland, however, that her writing really took off, with the publication of her first short story in 2003.

MJ is the author of seventeen books, including three Goldie Award winners. She has also had over thirty short stories published, most of them erotica with a few romances and a few horrors thrown in for good measure. She lives in Houston with her wife, fellow author Laydin Michaels, and their fur babies. You can find her on Facebook or reach her at mjwilliamz@aol.com

Books Available from Bold Strokes Books

Dangerous Curves by Larkin Rose. When love waits at the finish line, dangerous curves are a risk worth taking. (978-1-63555-353-6)

Love to the Rescue by Radclyffe. Can two people who share a past really be strangers? (978-1-62639-973-0)

Love's Portrait by Anna Larner. When museum curator Molly Goode and benefactor Georgina Wright uncover a portrait's secret, public and private truths are exposed, and their deepening love hangs in the balance. (978-1-63555-057-3)

Model Behavior by MJ Williamz. Can one woman's instability shatter a new couple's dreams of happiness? (978-1-63555-379-6)

Pretending in Paradise by M. Ullrich. When travelwisdom.com assigns PR specialist Caroline Beckett and travel blogger Emma Morgan to cover a hot new couples retreat, they're forced to fake a relationship to secure a reservation. (978-1-63555-399-4)

Recipe for Love by Aurora Rey. Hannah Little doesn't have much use for fancy chefs or fancy restaurants, but when New York City chef Drew Davis comes to town, their attraction just might be a recipe for love. (978-1-63555-367-3)

Survivor's Guilt and Other Stories by Greg Herren. Award-winning author Greg Herren's short stories are finally pulled together into a single collection, including the Macavity Award nominated title story and the first-ever Chanse MacLeod short story. (978-1-63555-413-7)

The House by Eden Darry. After a vicious assault, Sadie, Fin, and their family retreat to a house they think is the perfect place to start over, until they realize not all is as it seems. (978-1-63555-395-6)

Uninvited by Jane C. Esther. When Aerin McLeary's body becomes host for an alien intent on invading Earth, she must work with researcher Olivia Ando to uncover the truth and save humankind. (978-1-63555-282-9)

Comrade Cowgirl by Yolanda Wallace. When cattle rancher Laramie Bowman accepts a lucrative job offer far from home, will her heart end up getting lost in translation? (978-1-63555-375-8)

Double Vision by Ellie Hart. When her cell phone rings, Giselle Cutler answers it—and finds herself speaking to a dead woman. (978-1-63555-385-7)

Inheritors of Chaos by Barbara Ann Wright. As factions splinter and reunite, will anyone survive the final showdown between gods and mortals on an alien world? (978-1-63555-294-2)

Love on Lavender Lane by Karis Walsh. Accompanied by the buzz of honeybees and the scent of lavender, Paige and Kassidy must find a way to compromise on their approach to business if they want to save Lavender Lane Farm—and find a way to make room for love along the way. (978-1-63555-286-7)

Spinning Tales by Brey Willows. When the fairy tale begins to unravel and villains are on the loose, will Maggie and Kody be able to spin a new tale? (978-1-63555-314-7)

The Do-Over by Georgia Beers. Bella Hunt has made a good life for herself and put the past behind her. But when the bane of her high school existence shows up for Bella's class on conflict resolution, the last thing they expect is to fall in love. (978-1-63555-393-2)

What Happens When by Samantha Boyette. For Molly Kennan, senior year is already an epic disaster, and falling for mysterious waitress Zia is about to make life a whole lot worse. (978-1-63555-408-3)

Wooing the Farmer by Jenny Frame. When fiercely independent modern socialite Penelope Huntingdon-Stewart and traditional country farmer Sam McQuade meet, trusting their hearts is harder than it looks. (978-1-63555-381-9)

A Chapter on Love by Laney Webber. When Jannika and Lee reunite, their instant connection feels like a gift, but neither is ready for a second chance at love. Will they finally get on the same page when it comes to love? (978-1-63555-366-6)

Drawing Down the Mist by Sheri Lewis Wohl. Everyone thinks Grand Duchess Maria Romanova died in 1918. They were almost right. (978-1-63555-341-3)

Listen by Kris Bryant. Lily Croft is inexplicably drawn to Hope D'Marco but will she have the courage to confront the consequences of her past and present colliding? (978-1-63555-318-5)

Perfect Partners by Maggie Cummings. Elite police dog trainer Sara Wright has no intention of falling in love with a coworker, until Isabel Marquez arrives at Homeland Security's Northeast Regional Training facility and Sara's good intentions start to falter. (978-1-63555-363-5)

Shut Up and Kiss Me by Julie Cannon. What better way to spend two weeks of hell in paradise than in the company of a hot, sexy woman? (978-1-63555-343-7)

Spencer's Cove by Missouri Vaun. When Foster Owen and Abigail Spencer meet they uncover a story of lives adrift, loves lost, and true love found. (978-1-63555-171-6)

Without Pretense by TJ Thomas. After living for decades hiding from the truth, can Ava learn to trust Bianca with her secrets and her heart? (978-1-63555-173-0)

Unexpected Lightning by Cass Sellars. Lightning strikes once more when Sydney and Parker fight a dangerous stranger who threatens the peace they both desperately want. (978-1-163555-276-8)

Emily's Art and Soul by Joy Argento. When Emily meets Andi Marino she thinks she's found a new best friend but Emily doesn't know that Andi is fast falling in love with her. Caught up in exploring her sexuality, will Emily see the only woman she needs is right in front of her? (978-1-63555-355-0)

Escape to Pleasure: Lesbian Travel Erotica edited by Sandy Lowe and Victoria Villasenor. Join these award-winning authors as they explore the sensual side of erotic lesbian travel. (978-1-63555-339-0)

Music City Dreamers by Robyn Nyx. Music can bring lovers together. In Music City, it can tear them apart. (978-1-63555-207-2)

Ordinary is Perfect by D. Jackson Leigh. Atlanta marketing superstar Autumn Swan's life derails when she inherits a country home, a child, and a very interesting neighbor. (978-1-63555-280-5)

Royal Court by Jenny Frame. When royal dresser Holly Weaver's passionate personality begins to melt Royal Marine Captain Quincy's icy heart, will Holly be ready for what she exposes beneath? (978-1-63555-290-4)

Strings Attached by Holly Stratimore. Success. Riches. Music. Passion. It's a life most can only dream of, but stardom comes at a cost. (978-1-63555-347-5)

The Ashford Place by Jean Copeland. When Isabelle Ashford inherits an old house in small-town Connecticut, family secrets, a shocking discovery, and an unexpected romance complicate her plan for a fast profit and a temporary stay. (978-1-63555-316-1)

Treason by Gun Brooke. Zoem Malderyn's existence is a deadly threat to everyone on Gemocon and Commander Neenja KahSandra must find a way to save the woman she loves from having to commit the ultimate sacrifice. (978-1-63555-244-7)

A Wish Upon a Star by Jeannie Levig. Erica Cooper has learned to depend on only herself, but when her new neighbor, Leslie Raymond, befriends Erica's special needs daughter, the walls protecting her heart threaten to crumble. (978-1-63555-274-4)

Answering the Call by Ali Vali. Detective Sept Savoie returns to the streets of New Orleans, as do the dead bodies from ritualistic killings, and she does everything in her power to bring them to justice while trying to keep her partner, Keegan Blanchard, safe. (978-1-63555-050-4)

Breaking Down Her Walls by Erin Zak. Could a love worth staying for be the key to breaking down Julia Finch's walls? (978-1-63555-369-7)

Exit Plans for Teenage Freaks by 'Nathan Burgoine. Cole always has a plan—especially for escaping his small-town reputation as "that kid who was kidnapped when he was four"—but when he teleports to a museum, it's time to face facts: it's possible he's a total freak after all. (978-1-63555-098-6)

Friends Without Benefits by Dena Blake. When Dex Putman gets the woman she thought she always wanted, she soon wonders if it's really love after all. (978-1-63555-349-9)

Invalid Evidence by Stevie Mikayne. Private Investigator Jil Kidd is called away to investigate a possible killer whale, just when her partner Jess needs her most. (978-1-63555-307-9)

Pursuit of Happiness by Carsen Taite. When attorney Stevie Palmer's client reveals a scandal that could derail Senator Meredith Mitchell's presidential bid, their chance at love may be collateral damage. (978-1-63555-044-3)

Seascape by Karis Walsh. Marine biologist Tess Hansen returns to Washington's isolated northern coast where she struggles to adjust to small-town living while courting an endowment for her orca research center from Brittany James. (978-1-63555-079-5)

Second in Command by VK Powell. Jazz Perry's life is disrupted and her career jeopardized when she becomes personally involved with the case of an abandoned child and the child's competent but strict social worker, Emory Blake. (978-1-63555-185-3)

Taking Chances by Erin McKenzie. When Valerie Cruz and Paige Wellington clash over what's in the best interest of the children in Valerie's care, the children may be the ones who teach them it's worth taking chances for love. (978-1-63555-209-6)